Deadweight

Paul Forster

Copyright © 2020 Paul Forster

Book Cover Design by ebooklaunch.com

All rights reserved.

1

Peter had spent four lonely weeks in his house. He'd seen neighbours and strangers try to flee and then be murdered in front of him. These things weren't particularly fast, and they didn't even appear to be that strong. Sometimes it'd be just one or two, he'd even gone a day seeing none of the monsters. But it's when they came in numbers, that's when you could see their power. Mobs, dozens strong in numbers stumbling past his house, looking to taste the flesh of anyone or anything stupid or desperate enough to be on the streets.

John and Anna had lived opposite Peter for nearly three years. They were in their early thirties and recently started trying for a baby. They were in great shape. John was a brick outhouse of a man. At 6-feet 4-inches, he was intimidating, that is until you spoke to him, then you saw the gentle giant for what he was. Anna was nearly 6-feet tall herself, attractive and athletic. She had run the London marathon last year and achieved a personal best. Compared to Peter, these people were Olympians. Peter was a slightly overweight 33-year-old standing at 5-feet 9-inches tall, he wasn't impressive. Years of sitting behind a desk as an IT Security consultant hadn't prepared him for the world as it was on this day.

Peter saw John and Anna as they made the move he was too much of a coward to contemplate. Their front door quietly edged open and John nervously stepped out. John wasn't a foolish man and had built himself some personal armour. A thick leather jacket and a cricket batsman's helmet would hopefully offer some protection and no doubt it'd protect against a single bite or scratch, but that isn't how these creatures operated.

John held a cricket bat firmly, a hatchet and a large kitchen knife dangled from his waist. He gave a quick glance to check everything was clear before signalling Anna to join him. Anna didn't have the luxury of a helmet or thick jacket; agility and speed would be her protection. Her weapon of choice was a spear created with a broom handle and a kitchen knife.

Peter admired them. They were making a break for it. They had a small backpack each with the last of their supplies and they were going. Peter hoped they'd see him and take him with them. He waved but they didn't look up. John and Anna didn't care who or what lurked in the houses. They only gave their attention to the things outside. Peter didn't dare bang on the windows or shout. He was a coward. He was scared, but he knew that was a bad idea for himself and his neighbours.

The first of the creatures slowly ambled out from a collection of shrubs at the end of the road. It was a good 50 yards away and Peter was confident it wouldn't pose a problem for his brave heroes. The monster was grotesquely swollen; its flesh discoloured and what remained of its clothing stained with blood and other bodily fluids. This was an old one. It wasn't recently turned; it must have been right at the beginning of the outbreak. Its face had several large boils; that wasn't normal even for these things. Peter squinted to see if he could recognise it as a former neighbour. He was concentrating so hard he'd taken his attention away from John and Anna. It startled all three when it let out a loud deep groan. Jesus, Peter had never seen one do that before.

As fit and brave as they were, just like Peter, they were unlikely to have fought one before. How should they do it? Should they do it at all? Their car was clear, and they could drive off and just ignore it. It was a big bastard, but it wouldn't be a match for the silver Honda CRV. That was when the second one appeared behind them a little distance off. This was a fresh one. Its body still kept much of its colour. Give it a shower and a change of clothes it could almost pass as human. John appeared to decide - they'd run, get in that car and drive. Somewhere. Anywhere.

Still none of them had noticed number two, and it was getting closer.

It was nearly in reach of Anna when Peter saw it. He wanted to scream, bang on the glass. But he couldn't. Its hand reached out towards Anna's neck. As it was about to grab her, she spun around and stabbed it in the eye with her spear. The force knocked it to the floor and Anna used the blade to scramble its brains through the eye socket. It thrashed but didn't scream out. John had now joined the attack and bashed it firmly on top of the head with the cricket bat. The crack it produced was sickening. It stopped moving nearly instantly. Time to go.

John grabbed Anna and pushed her towards the car. Now the original creature was upon them. John swung out with the bat and connected firmly with its face, separating the flesh on its cheek from its jaw. It stayed on its feet and let out another loud groan; this time whistling through the extended hole freshly created in its face. In the distance, another groan sounded out. John stumbled back, stunned by the sight of the damage to this creature in front of him. He dropped the bat and went for his hatchet. Raising it above his own head he swung it down with all his might landing it on top of the creatures' skull. It howled out once more. This time two distant responses answered.

It stepped back but remained standing, the hatchet still firmly embedded in its cranium. It swung out and grabbed John's wrist, digging nails deep into the leather sleeve and into his flesh. It was John's turn to scream out. Peter was nearly crying.

The engine started on the car and Anna put her foot down before ploughing the car into the creature, sending it on its arse and 10 feet away as she slammed down the brake pedal.

John threw open the door and jumped inside, blood dripping down his arm.

The creature looked up to them and again made a terrifying cry.

Anna didn't wait for John to shut the door, the car sped off, dealing a glancing blow to the monster on its way through. The car had gone. They'd made it with only a minor injury.

The creature got back to its feet, looked at the direction the car had gone and gave a slow, determined pursuit. This wasn't good. He'd seen these things take punishment before, but never this much. Never had he heard one make that noise; now they appeared to be communicating.

For the first time, he knew his future would be in his own hands. Any hope Peter had of this all blowing over and being rescued had gone with the realisation that things could get worse. They just did.

His options seemed limited to how he'd die. Starving to death alone and afraid or being eaten alive by one of these things? Neither option was attractive. Maybe he should just kill himself - take back control and not become a meal for one of those stinking bastards. Peter didn't have any pills. He didn't have a gun. He'd have to cut his wrists. He had just the knife. It was the sharpest in his kitchen and had tasted his blood frequently when he proved his clumsiness.

So, he'd kill himself; slit his wrists but when? His house had proved safe, but food was running low. He had maybe three days left of his meagre supplies. It'd be a shame to kill himself now, however unlikely it was that help may be around the corner. But Peter knew it wasn't, so why prolong this suffering? The food supplies he had left comprised of a tin of tuna, one of corned beef, two jars of pasta sauce, a pack of ready-mixed porridge oats and five tins of sweetcorn. He didn't even like sweetcorn, he hated it, and the tins had been in the cupboard since he moved in, courtesy of a care package from Peter's mother who was unaware of his sweetcorn aversion.

Fuck it. He'd have that bottle of Merlot he'd been saving

then end this miserable existence. He'd rather that than eat the fucking sweetcorn.

2

Josef Rasiak hadn't had a difficult upbringing, but he was raised by those that did. Jo's grandfather, who they named him after, was a Polish merchant seaman during the second world war. Josef was a young man who wanted to fight the Nazis but with the invasion of Poland successfully completed so quickly, he didn't even get the chance to raise a rifle toward a German soldier. Before the Nazis had triumphantly announced their victory, he was already boarding the ship he'd serve on for two years before a German U-boat sank it. He'd survive and serve on another ship until the end of the war.

By that time, Josef had met a young English girl, and shortly after the war they were married and expecting the one and only child they would have. Settling in Kent, Josef raised his son whilst working out of the old Dockyard in Chatham. He only wanted to give his son more than he'd had and worked tirelessly for this. His son Robert would follow in Josef's footsteps working hard in the Dockyard, marrying and having a solitary son, whom he gave his father's name. He'd also work every hour he'd have to give his son a start in life; this was what his father had tried but failed to give him.

The younger Josef lived up to the hopes of his father and grandfather, excelling through his education. The only piece of the puzzle missing was where he'd apply his brilliance. Fate would provide the answer.

First, the elder Josef, now retired and enjoying a meagre but loving existence with his wife, fell ill, and within weeks Robert also had the same symptoms. Like many who worked in the dockyard, they'd both been exposed to Asbestos. Since the dockyard's closure in 1984, many cases had come to light and Josef and Robert had both lost friends to various diseases caused by Asbestos exposure. Whist they hoped they wouldn't succumb to the same fate, they acknowledged they had no more right to evade it than the men they worked with. The younger Josef now had a purpose, medicine.

His studies would take too long for him to save his father and grandfather, but young Josef was determined that their deaths wouldn't be in vain and their legacy would be his work. Biology, Chemistry, and even Mathematics, Josef mastered them all. By the time he'd reached 34 years old, he was a respected scientist who'd worked on breakthrough malaria drugs that had helped to save thousands of lives and had been working with a large team in Switzerland creating a treatment for prostate cancer. None of this work brought his loved ones back, but he liked to think his work was a dedication to the great men they were.

Everything changed for Josef when he was approached by James Cahill who had created a new company called NewU Pharmaceuticals. Cahill was a good businessman who had flirted in the pharmaceutical industry for several years, picking up the patents for several innocuous but profitable drugs along the way. NewU Pharma would be funded by the patents for the existing drugs to develop something new for the market. Cahill didn't care for curing cancer or easing suffering. He desired wealth. He wanted to create a cure for fat. People would pay for a weight loss pill that worked. If they could crack it, they could charge whatever they wanted, and people would pay. Cahill had brought together a fine team to develop his weight loss drug, but after two years, they were no closer to a breakthrough. He'd never developed a drug himself; he always swooped in and picked up the finished article. He knew these things took time, but he didn't want to wait a day longer than needed. Josef had a fine reputation, but this wasn't his field. He'd only ever shown a desire to help the sick and cure disease. To him, a fat loss drug would be in the same arena as breast augmentation or a facelift. He had nothing against such things, but he wasn't about to spend his considerable expertise in a field that would benefit the vain and the lazy.

Cahill had done his research. He knew wooing Josef would not be an exercise in throwing money at him, taking him to fancy restaurants or plying him with expensive prostitutes. He had to appeal to his humanitarian side and not sell a money-making fat drug, but one which would improve the lives of millions of people, stop fatal diseases and cancers from occurring in the first place. Obesity caused many issues, and Cahill would thoroughly discuss every one of them. By the end of the three-hour meeting, even Cahill was believing this drug could save the world. With the promise of a large team, the best resources and equipment, Josef was interested. The clincher was the promise of Josef choosing his next project. Cahill figured that as long as the weight loss drug was completed, he'd be just as happy to fund Josef playing ping pong on the International Space Station as he would fund a cure for cancer.

Jo returned to his empty, rather small home. The house was an adequate size but put function over form - no artwork, pictures or plants. The television was small, the furniture purchased from a catalogue, each wall painted magnolia and carpets a hard-wearing beige. Time or money hadn't been wasted on luxuries or even anything over basic necessity. Jo boiled the kettle and began writing on a large notepad. Ideas flowed, random words, partial thoughts. It could have been the ramblings of a madman, but this is how Jo found he did his best work -get everything down on paper no matter how ridiculous, basic, complicated or incoherent. Jo would join the dots later and refine the good ideas. He had filled seven pages of notes before realising he'd boiled the kettle some time ago but hadn't made the beverage. Finding the kettle now lukewarm, Jo flicked the switch and waited by the boiling kettle determined not to let a little thing such as curing global obesity impede his cup of green tea.

3

For so long, he'd saved that bottle of wine for a special occasion that never came. It seemed nearly inevitable that the bottle was corked. The one thing that Peter had left to look forward to was a half-decent bottle of red wine, courtesy of his boss for a job well done on a project that no longer mattered. But it was corked. Peter couldn't decide whether to laugh or cry, so he ended up doing both. If this was to be his last day on earth, it had taken a last, well-aimed kick to his balls.

Peter ran himself a bath. Remarkably, although electricity had long since gone off, the gas supply hadn't. He had enjoyed central heating and hot water. He could even heat food on the hob. But now the task was grimmer, and a hot bath no longer a luxurious thing, instead a tool to help end his suffering. He didn't know why he should slit his wrists in a warm bath, but he'd seen this several times on TV and in film so there must be something to it. As the bath ran, he thought out some details. He decided he'd get in fully clothed. He didn't think anyone would ever find him, but if they did, he'd rather not think the first thing they'd do when discovering his corpse, would be to laugh at his very average penis and chunky physique. He'd climb in fully clothed and slit his wrists, right? What about a note? Again, he couldn't imagine someone would ever read it but surely his life deserved some brief words. There wouldn't be a funeral; so no friends or family would perform a eulogy.

Peter would need to write something. He felt like telling the world to go fuck itself, but it already had. Maybe he should explain why he decided to kill himself, but as he started writing the words, he felt ashamed. He couldn't admit he was a coward. He didn't want to be a coward. No. Maybe he should say what he loved about life and why with that gone, there wasn't a place for him in the world. He loved nothing about the world as it was. People were arseholes, work was a grind, and he lived alone with no real friends to share his life with. At least the world today was more honest. People either wanted to eat you or avoid you. There was no bullshit anymore. Well, Peter imagined there were still pricks out there, but at least now society didn't make you feel you had to take their shit with a smile. He hated the old world, feared the new one and still, he was procrastinating over a stupid note that no one would ever read. The bath was full and ready for him, but Peter wasn't ready to take his own life. He stripped off and had a bath. The knife remained unused and he remained very much amongst the living, just cleaner.

Peter needed the bravery the bottle of alcohol would give him to do what he wanted to do. With suicide off the table, it was starvation or make a run for it.

Peter had never been one to take a risk and his life showed that. Maybe now he should take that chance.

4

It had been nearly three months since Josef had accepted the role at NewU Pharma, but this had been his first week in his new lab. He'd met the nine members of the team who were already onboard and re-acquainted himself with the three colleagues he'd requested. As promised, the laboratory was state-of-the art with no expense spared. Jo had been careful to keep his demands realistic, but he had the experience to know that if you don't ask, you don't get. He chose a few luxury pieces of equipment to give up when told the budget wasn't enough to cover every demand. However, Cahill had been a man of his word and Jo had everything he asked for. In fact, Cahill had even welcomed him with a blank cheque. The cheque, Cahill explained was for whatever Josef wanted, people, equipment or a fast Italian sports car. It was his to do with as he pleased. The gesture didn't impress Josef. He knew that all this bravado would mean nothing two years down the line when costs were mounting and the product was yet to yield marketable results.

Welcomes aside, Josef got to work with his team. Ever since he had accepted the role, he had spent every free moment developing ideas and researching. He knew he would have to hit the ground running and push his team to the breakthrough that had evaded them. Cahill had in the last two weeks forwarded limited data packs summarising the work so far. It was all fucking worthless. Josef, on reading the first data pack, felt immense rage, not with Cahill, not with the team but with himself. He'd allowed himself to be tricked into working on another man's vanity project and it was nonsense. He had calmed himself at least seeing that if nothing else, the team had proved many ways of not creating a weight-loss drug.

He had made the team aware that he was drawing a line through their work and they would salvage nothing useful from it. He savaged their work, but then offered them a glimpse into his vision. He knew he had to knock them down and build them back up and quickly. His idea was simple, look to nature. His research led him to a microbe, a discovery from the 1960s in the jungles of Vietnam. French scientists had discovered it then promptly ignored it, but they named it, "Gros Mangeur" - or Fat Eater. They had found this microbe was rife within a closed-off source of water deep in the jungle where the locals wouldn't eat the fish or animals close to the pond. Being fat is a western problem, if you live in a small village in South East Asia, losing a few pounds could mean the difference between life and death. The French scientists had found that the microbe had been resilient, even fish that had been caught and dried still had the microbe infesting them in a preserved dormant state. When examining the microbe, they discovered they could tease it back to life with water and the salt from the preserved fish. When the war broke out, the French had other issues to occupy themselves, so the discovery became little more than a few pages of an academic paper and some freely published notes.

Josef had already started to source samples. It wouldn't be cheap, and he had no guarantees that the microbe still existed after all this time. If it did, he was certain they could use it. He'd made sure his additions to the team had the expertise he'd require to manipulate the microbe and develop it into a usable treatment. Resilience could be an issue, two-fold. First, if the microbe remained constantly present, it would infect the patient for life, this may lead to complications. If the patient suffered from another condition, the inability to gain weight may cause problems. Second, Cahill would want repeat customers. Whilst Josef was sure if it was a one-off treatment, Cahill would just charge accordingly, a regular dose would raise more money for Cahill and importantly result in some clinical control. Josef also knew that providing a 21st Century tapeworm would be a tough sell for the marketing team. He wanted to take the microbe and change it to a point it would be barely recognisable; it would have a very short life before being digested. Ideally it would be cleared from the patient's system within 12 hours. They would need to grow it in their lab in its changed form. Josef had a path to follow, and he was content but keen to start. The samples couldn't arrive soon enough.

5

Gareth had only recently started at NewU Pharmaceuticals. In fact, he was new to the whole industry. But he wasn't new to making money for his employers and lots of it. NewU Pharma's CEO, James Cahill, didn't bring Gareth on board for his charm, despite this oozing from him. He was a man people wanted to be around. Just over 40-years old, he turned heads when he entered a room, and not just those of women. He was tall, good looking and engaging. Gareth was a man going places, but he wasn't going there quick enough for his own liking. So, when Cahill and the NewU Pharma board hired him, they knew what they were doing. They were bringing a man in who'd turn their penny share company into a major player. They weren't in this for the long game. They wanted a buyout from one of the big boys; none of them cared who. They wanted their millions of self-issued shares to soar from less than a penny each to 20 or 30 pounds. In private they'd joke about the islands they'd buy and the women they'd sleep with. They were a group of repugnant men too old to act the way they did, too young to know any better.

Gareth knew exactly how to play them. They were greedy. He'd promised them wealth at a level they had never dared to imagine, so he just needed a level of autonomy they weren't used to granting. But they were keen. Hell, if he did something wrong, they'd hang him out to dry, and they'd continue with only the slightest delay. You don't develop a weight loss drug to make the world thin. You do it to make yourself filthy rich. Gareth knew that as unlikely as it was, Cahill would snuff any dissenting voices on the board.

The board meeting didn't take long. Gareth had used his brief time at NewU Pharma to familiarise himself with their product and its people. They had some brilliant minds developing their breakout fat-busting product, no doubt stolen away from curing cancer or developing Parkinson's treatments by the promise of wealth and power. The development team comprised of four key personnel and half a dozen assistants who seemed aware their job was merely to do whatever the main four told them. Gareth didn't have to worry about the assistants, just the four key scientists. Just like Gareth and the board, the scientists were up and comers in their field. Dr. Josef Rasiak was the main drive, but he was a good, honest man. There would take no shortcuts on his watch. The same went for Dr. Christina Morelli; she wanted wealth and power, but she would only do it by playing by the rules. They knew they were developing something special and had no problem waiting until they had dotted every "I" and crossed every "t".

No, Gareth knew he wouldn't be able to sway them. Dr. Roger Smith and William Johnson presented Gareth with an option. Like himself, they were rising stars in their fields and like Gareth, neither of them felt they were getting to where they wanted to be as fast as they hoped. They were known behind their backs as Laurel and Hardy because of their physical appearance more than their sense of humour. Smith was in his forties, slim and stern, whereas Johnson was in his late twenties and morbidly obese. For Gareth, it was simple. Smith and Johnson would help get the product over the line quickly, they'd fudge a result here, lie there and even perjure themselves if it meant getting the product out there and themselves disgustingly wealthy.

6

His small man-bag was adequate for his iPad, a notepad, and a sandwich when he'd go to the office. Now it seemed ridiculous for his present requirement. It was the small satchel or a full-on suitcase. He was ruing his decision to leave his laptop bag at work when they had been evacuated from the office. That backpack would have carried all the stock of food he had, several bottles of water and some spare clothes. No. Now Peter had to decide what he'd leave behind and hope he could scavenge something more suitable. He'd feast on several tins of corn mixed with pasta sauce and the rest would squeeze into the bag and about his person. Water was a problem. He'd carry a day's supply and hope he could find more. For a weapon, he had a small blade attached to the end of a mop handle and he had plans on picking up the cricket bat John had previously dropped.

His plan was simple - get some good sleep, perhaps his last, get up before dawn, eat what he couldn't carry, drink as much water as possible and enjoy one last good shit in security and comfort. When the sun was up, he'd observe outside for any sign of the creatures and when he was sure it was clear, he'd make his move. There was only one destination, Southampton. The last broadcasts Peter had picked up on his old radio before he'd run out of D Cell batteries called on survivors to make their way to the University of Southampton. Here the military had put together their main southern base. There were several camps and outposts but the list of these repeated on the broadcast had grown shorter every day. It didn't inspire confidence in the facilities away from the main base. For all Peter knew this had gone the way of the smaller outposts, overrun and full of nothing but these hungry bastards waiting for a freshly delivered meal. The broadcasts would advise of the local camps open to survivors and those that were no longer safe. Several nearer camps had opened and had been lost since he'd been listening. After his radio died, they could have opened another in the local park, and he'd have no idea. He had to assume if anything near had opened, it would have been small and suffered a familiar fate.

The camp in Southampton stayed constant throughout. The broadcasts told of thousands of soldiers with tanks, helicopters, and even air support from an aircraft carrier patrolling the English Channel. The messages were automated, but if they had power to maintain a signal, they must still have something going for them. This was Peter's best hope. He just had to fucking get there.

7

Progress had been better than Josef could ever have dared dream. In the six months since the microbe samples had been delivered, they had a working drug that in tests worked nearly entirely as planned. Animal testing wasn't something Josef was comfortable with, but he still used it. With mice, the drug was 100% effective at consuming fat. It succeeded in this quickly. They had fed the test subjects a particularly weight inducing diet in the run-up to receiving their doses. They would continue with a weight gain meal plan whilst taking the experimental medication.

All lost weight. Before they applied the doses, all the mice were an obscene 35g weight, near double the normal mass. After day one, they had lost 5g. By day two, they were down to a more normal weight of around 20g. By day three, they had to be given extra rations and by day five all had died. It was too effective, and they hadn't yet limited the microbe's life expectancy. They didn't know how. The doses applied were varied, but the results were exactly the same. Even the mouse with the smallest dose was riddled with the microbe when it had expired.

They took samples, examined the subjects and then destroyed them. Josef didn't find cause for concern. They were so far ahead they had the time to get it right. Cahill and his new man Gareth weren't as patient. Early promising results were great, but they raised expectations unrealistically high with the money men, and with the latest results, Josef was being called to discuss the exciting new developments. He was already late and grabbed some notes before making his way to the boardroom. He'd expected to be met by all the board, but just Cahill and Gareth waited for him by the grand table. A dozen empty seats made the room appear grander than it was.

"Jo, please come and take a seat," Gareth warmly greeted Josef who sat down and readied his notes.

"We're all very excited by the latest sets of results. Gareth thinks we should look at stepping up testing," Cahill beamed with confidence and readied to hear exactly what he wanted to hear. It was as Josef had feared, the marketing man giving clinical observations and the money man expecting his payday sooner.

"With all due respect, Mr. Cahill, we're a long way from stepping anything up at the moment. The treatment is 100% effective at destroying fat hosted in the subject, but it's also 100% effective of curing the subject of life." Josef thought he'd take a sip of water and let that sink in with his audience but Gareth had other ideas.

"Jo, you have made tremendous strides and we all think you're amazing. You're a genius, but we just wish you had the confidence in yourself that we have in you. We're not pushing you; we're just eager to share your miraculous work with the world. It's amazing and you will save millions of lives." Gareth thought maybe he'd overdone the bullshit but found most intelligent people's weakness was flattery.

Josef couldn't believe this marketing prick was trying to push him into unsafe practice with a handful of comments appealing to his vanity.

"Mr. Cahill, we're progressing faster than we'd ever hoped. My team is working around the clock to find a solution. I can't promise that it'll present itself in the next few weeks or even months but we need to do this right. The treatment is effective. Once we can crack the microbes' lifespan problem, we'll step up testing but not before. You knew going in that we'd be years away from having a working drug."

Cahill looked disappointed but offered Josef half a smile, "I understand, I do. We're excited but you're in charge. You carry on and if you need anything at all, people, equipment, whatever, let me know. Thanks for your time." They invited Josef to leave. The interruption frustrated him' trying to push him towards a bad course of action. He left the room and closed the door behind him.

Gareth sat back in his chair, "I told you. We won't be able to shift him."

Cahill nodded, "You've felt his team out?".

Gareth sat back up, "I have some people down there I can work with. I think 2 million ought to do it. I'm taking them out tomorrow. I'll expense it. Just don't look too closely at the receipts. We need this whole death thing resolved though."

"Agreed. Get everything lined up so when we need to move, we can do so quickly."

8

The toilet flushed and Peter was nearly ready. He just had to wait for his moment. Everything had changed in the last month, but Peter had woken in the same bed every morning he had for the last six years. He ate in the same kitchen. Wore the same clothes. Pissed in the same toilet. Stared at his rotund face in the same mirror. His life had only changed because he didn't go to work and hadn't got online for weeks. Many other details remained unchanged. The crisis may be a month old, but Peter would today for the first-time witness first-hand what the world had become beyond the street he lived on. He stood by his front door for what seemed like hours. In fact, just minutes had passed since he'd looked out the door and listened before gently closing it again. Peter knew he couldn't put this off any longer. He tentatively placed his foot on his doorstep and took his first step into the new world. He decided against closing the door in case he needed to beat a hasty retreat.

Quietly, he tentatively made his move to claim the cricket bat. The blood on the bat had turned nearly grey and shimmered in the light. A tooth lodged in the willow turned Peter's stomach, but it was a weapon. A quick rub on one of his neighbour's overgrown lawns removed most of the gore.

Peter walked to the end of the road and saw the first creature. This time their roles were reversed. It was in the house at the end of the street, looking out at him standing in the road. This one was thin; so thin it looked like a skeleton wrapped in skin. It banged on the window, trying in vain to break through the double-glazed glass. Peter didn't dare to stop to ponder how the poor soul had transitioned from regular woman to trapped ghoul. It worried him that the noise it was making would attract more so he pressed on.

He was on foot and his destination wasn't close. By his reckoning, from Redhill to Southampton could be 100 miles. He didn't have a map and without the internet, he couldn't plan a journey. All he knew was that it was southwest of Surrey; so that's how he'd start. Without a compass or map, he would head in the rough direction and hope he might get lucky and add the missing items to his growing shopping list of food, water, a bigger backpack and a better weapon.

As he headed off cautiously, he heard the now familiar, but still terrifying groan of one of the bigger creatures. It didn't sound too close, but that didn't give Peter much in the way of comfort.

9

Josef allowed himself a beaming smile. It was a rarity that he'd allow emotion to enter his work life. He had taken a backseat during the presentation, allowing each of his team a chance to show off their efforts. He knew the board didn't care who had done what, but they'd allow this indulgence as they knew what was coming. It had gone very well. Tell a room of people that you just made them rich, and they'll clap, cheer, and give you a very hearty handshake. It had been a whirlwind success. After 17 months, they had it. He still couldn't believe it. The amount of progress in the last two months had been nothing short of miraculous. What Josef was mainly happy about was his next project. He'd already started brainstorming his next great contribution to the health and wellbeing of humanity. He could wind down his day-to-day involvement with the moronically named "FatBGone" and start on something meaningful.

Roger and William had performed admirably, way above expectations. Josef knew they were competent but had only given them that much credit, but now they proved much more able. It was Roger and William who had come up with the solution to the microbe's lifespan. Whereas it seemed like it was uncontainable, they introduced a change into its genetic makeup that limited its life post "reanimation" to between four and seven hours. It gave it plenty of time to get to work before becoming dormant after entering the bloodstream, and then it was sweated out. Every test they had performed since that revelation had been successful. Just three months ago, this too appeared to be, yet another dead end and Josef wasn't confident this hell would ever be over. But his team rose to the occasion and here they were, in the home straight. There was still a lot of work to do, but Cahill would pump in the required funds to get the approvals in place and get the drug signed off and cleared for clinical use. Josef was confident he could start making use of part of his team to work on his new project and was happy Roger and William could lead the completion team.

With the presentation over, Josef's team was again congratulated, thanked and then invited to get back to their day jobs. Josef remained, eager to put across his desire to switch focus and handover the project to some of his team members. He wasn't naïve to the fact that until the treatment was on the market, they would try to keep him working. He was ready to put his case forward, argue and make threats he knew were idle.

"I think we're in a great place, the team has been amazing, and I think it's time I switch to our next big venture." Josef knew he could have made a stronger opening.

"We've discussed it Josef, and we agree. Roger and William are fine men and we think they can do the remaining grunt work allowing your considerable expertise to shine on something new," Gareth grinned wildly as he spoke and Cahill nodded enthusiastically. Josef had run through several scenarios in his head, but getting what he wanted with minimal effort wasn't one of them. For a second he genuinely thought maybe they were making fun of him. But that wasn't how they conducted themselves.

"Can I get to work straight away?" Strike whilst the iron was hot. Josef was already ahead but keen to push his luck further.

"No, I don't think so," Cahill responded.

"We think you need some time to reset. You've been

amazing but you need a break."

"I really don't. I'm ready to get to work, right now. I already have a plethora of ideas." Josef wasn't about to beg. He was already doing better than he thought and didn't wish to push it too far.

"Still, we insist. We're talking two, maybe three weeks." Cahill was being stubborn if only to keep Josef out of the lab whilst his people did what they needed.

"How about one week? I can take a break, getaway, then get back to work," Josef lied, they might not want him working in his lab, but they couldn't stop him starting at home. That's all he needed anyway; himself, his books, good coffee the odd green tea and some quiet. In fact, he was falling in love with the idea.

"One week, but you need to rest," Cahill relented.

"Of course," Josef happily lied. With that, more hands were shaken and Josef left the room a happy man. Those left in the room were equally happy.

10

Everything was falling into place. Whilst Josef had been working hard in the lab creating FatBGone, Gareth had been working hard forging relationships, gaining leverage and making the path to market as smooth as possible. He sat in his grand office casually flicking through the report he'd unofficially helped to co-author. Gareth loved the name FatBGone. He knew it was naff, but he also knew that it was on the nose and sometimes that's what you wanted. This was the market he was catering to. Also, the lowbrow nature of the name was a fuck you to Josef. There was little doubt Josef was a genius, but when he got going, he'd let you know it. A genius yes, but also so very naïve. So desperate was Josef to save the world, he was ready to drop his involvement in FatBGone before they completed it. Josef didn't realise this was what Gareth and Cahill wanted. FatBGone worked, but it wasn't perfect. The side effect of death had been resolved, but FatBGone stayed present in the human body, although in a dormant state. Roger and William had done their best to sway the results and made sure that it would pass scrutiny. They'd done a good job, but Josef's observant eye would have spotted the issue if he wasn't so eager to move on. Where they hadn't been able to fudge the outcome, Cahill's money had. Most of the board knew nothing, mainly through choice, but they had spent money to ensure that the dormant microbe was ignored.

What harm could it do?

If Josef hadn't allowed his new ego project to distract him, he'd have not allowed the drug to progress further until the microbe was completely eradicated from the body. 50 to 70 percent of the microbe was passed in the patient's sweat. The remaining microbe would be dormant, and through all their testing, remained that way. Cahill, Gareth, Roger and William were content this was enough and not a stopper on becoming filthy, stinking rich. A couple more weeks and they'd be clear, having thrown money at every legal method to speed up getting the treatment approved and pursuing every illegal one too. Then came the knock at the door.

It was Josef. He should have been enjoying his break from the lab before starting his new project. He looked apprehensive, standing in the doorway with a heavy bag slung over his shoulder.

"Gareth, I was looking for Cahill but apparently he's in New York?"

Gareth gestured for his guest to take a seat, "Josef, you're supposed to be sunning yourself in the Maldives, reading your science books or anything but being here."

"I was going through the test reports. I think there's an issue." Josef was concerned, with a near hint of panic.

Gareth gave his best-concerned face, "What is the issue?" He needed to put this to bed.

"I really need to speak to Cahill," Josef adamantly said.

"I have full authority, you know that. I want this drug out there. So, if there's an issue, I need to know. I need to get it resolved so we can get it on the market. What is the issue Josef?" Gareth was making it clear, he was the boss.

Josef sighed, "I think there's been a mistake in the testing, I've checked and double-checked and there is an inconsistency. No, it's not an inconsistency; it's an outright error."

Gareth held up the report he'd taken great pride in, "This doesn't mention any errors, it doesn't mention anything other than a working drug, the drug you created."

"It works, but the microbe... I don't think it's clearing from the system. I don't know what William and Roger were thinking, but between them they've missed it."

Josef produced a folder from his bag. "Here, the number, it's wrong," Josef pointed at a section in the folder. "And here, that's just not right, in any possible way."

Gareth looked at the documents and shrugged his shoulders.

"Jo, I don't know what I'm looking at. But if you say there's a problem, there's a problem. Have you spoken to anyone?"

Josef felt a slight relief. He was being listened to. Now he just had to get action. "No, I wanted to talk to Cahill. Get this looked into quietly. I think this might be deliberate."

Fuck, why couldn't he just leave it alone? "Do you suspect Roger and William?"

He believed him; this would get resolved. The relief grew. "That's my thinking, they had the access and opportunity. I just can't work out why."

"Okay, I'll deal with this. Just give me two days. I'll put the brakes on, and we'll get this sorted. Trust me and don't talk to anyone. We don't know who's involved." Gareth knew his options were limited. Whatever happened, Josef was now suspicious and getting anything past him would prove nearly impossible.

Josef nodded sombrely. He had feared that they would ignore him. He felt some relief from Gareth, but not enough. Gareth walked from around his desk and patted Josef on the shoulder

"We'll get this sorted, I promise. Go home. I'll contact you once I've done some digging."

Josef gathered himself, nodded, and calmly walked out. Gareth placed himself back in his chair and stared at the report deep in thought. Damn it, some people were just too smart for their own good.

11

Peter had been on the move for nearly three hours and had found the journey slow going. Every rustle of a bush, tweet of a bird or bark of a hungry dog caused him to freeze and his heart to skip a beat. He had opted to avoid going anywhere near the town centre; surely, that would be trouble. Sticking to the residential areas, he knew he'd face trouble at some point, but nothing compared to the town. In fact, he was sure he'd have had the chance to test the bat or his spear before now, but every one of the infected he'd seen had been locked inside of a house, desperate but unable to taste his flesh. He was expecting to see hundreds of them, but they had been conspicuous by their absence. It nearly made the tension worse. Then he saw her.

She would have been in her mid-twenties. She wasn't much to look at now, but a month ago Peter imagined she would have been stunning. The kind of girl that would have shown no interest in a boring overweight man like him. Now though things had changed, she was very interested in Peter. Just not in the way he'd have liked. He'd seen her and froze, hoping she'd shuffle onwards and not notice him. She turned and saw a substantial fresh meal, the first her greying eyes had seen since she transitioned. Dogs, cats, foxes and pigeons had been the poor excuse for food until this point. Now, this fat man was in front of her and her instincts took over. She wasn't fast, but she was determined. She moved with a grace that her decaying flesh would have you believe is impossible. This caught Peter off-guard. She closed the distance in an unfeasibly quick time. Peter, spear still planted firmly in the ground and cricket bat limply held in his left hand, stumbled back as she pounced.

The spear found its way firmly in her throat, popped up through her jaw and found its way through the skull and straight into her brain. Peter achieved this by doing nothing more than stumbling back and her fluid movement and momentum did the rest. He stood firm, holding the spear balancing her lifeless rotting body inches from his own. Her grey dead eyes still full of anger, full of lust as they stared back at him, but her body now lifeless. Peter snapped out of his daze and pushed the spear to the side, sending her tumbling to the floor along with it. She hit the ground with a dull thud. He wrestled with the spear to free it from its new home; eventually, it popped free. The spear now reverted to its previous incarnation of a mop handle. The small but sharp knife was somewhere in the girl's head. Peter wasn't even going to try to retrieve it. It was lost. Peter cursed his luck, the cheap gaffer tape and the girl. The poor girl.

12

The street Josef lived on was quiet and rundown. For a man of his intellect, he sure didn't waste time or money on the niceties that life could offer. It was a small mid-terrace house hidden amongst the dozens of similar ones. Gareth approached the dark and unloved porch. The light was broken, and a large crack in a step made Gareth stumble as he approached the door. Unable to see a doorbell he knocked lightly. A light turned on inside the house and the door opened.

Josef looked dishevelled, worried and hadn't slept since their last meeting and allowed himself to get worked up. A characteristic he didn't recognise in himself, but he had never been conspired against before. Whether it was just Roger and William, or it involved more, he had witnessed nothing like it. The money had dirtied everything. Seeing Gareth offered him no further comfort.

"I spoke with Cahill. Can I come in?" Josef stepped aside and Gareth entered.

The door had just clicked shut when Gareth pounced. He whipped out a small kitchen knife he'd stashed up his sleeve and plunged it into Josef's stomach. Josef reeled backwards in shock and pain, staring at Gareth but unable to find the words to ask why.

"I'm sorry. I'm sorry!" Gareth didn't want this, but he needed to do it. Josef regained some sense and survival kicked in. He clutched his stomach and stumbled through the hallway to the kitchen.

"Please, no," he begged. It wasn't his time. He had so much more to achieve. Gareth followed, the bloody blade dripping blood onto the wooden floor.

"You should have left it alone. Why couldn't you just fucking let it go? You could have moved on!"

Josef looked for something to defend himself with and he picked up a solid wooden chopping board. Again Gareth lunged with the knife. Josef partially fended off the blow, the blade slipping off the board slicing open several of Josef's fingers. Josef struck out at his attacker landing a blow to Gareth's head with the chopping board, but victory was short-lived. Injured, off-balance and using his shield as a weapon he left himself open and Gareth took his opportunity. He grabbed Josef by the throat and planted the knife just under Josef's ear. Josef fell back and pulled Gareth with him to the floor. The knife eased out, bringing with it a thick slew of dark red blood.

"Die, just die," Gareth repeatedly stabbed Josef in the throat until the doctor's eyes drained of their horror, replaced with a sad stare fixed on him.

Gareth felt exhausted and rolled himself off of Josef. The blood leaking onto the floor slowing as Josef's heart made its final beats. It was a bloodbath, and this wasn't the plan. Gareth looked at the corpse beside him.

"You stupid fuck," he said simultaneously to Josef and himself. He knew he hadn't finished his work. He had a robbery to stage, prints to wipe and DNA to purge. He got to his feet and started to search the kitchen cupboards and found what he was looking for, several cleaning products, bleach, a bottle of Vodka and matches.

He started throwing the cleaning products all over the bloody scene, taking little care to be effective. The chemicals washed through the blood, spreading it further around the body, doing little to clean the scene. Next, Gareth started looking for anything combustible. Josef's large collection of books fitted this bill. He threw them on and around the lifeless body, only stopping to rip out fistfuls of pages to scatter amongst the books. The volume of books took longer to move than he'd envisaged, and he was aching to get away. He hastened his pace and then as soon as he was reasonably happy, he poured on the Vodka and started on lighting the matches. The first three matches fizzled out without even singeing the paper he gripped firmly in his hand. Striking several matches at once and holding it to the paper, success. He dabbed this around the pile of books and alcohol. First with smoke, then with small flames, the fire began to take hold.

He waited a moment, just to make sure the fire continued to grow. Within moments Gareth felt satisfied and edged towards the front door, spilling shelves of their contents as he walked. He stopped briefly to compose himself then confidently exited the house, the growing glow illuminating his silhouette.

13

Peter edged out from the last row of houses and could see the yellow fields of rapeseed the road led to. It had been slow going through the residential areas, but finally, he was close to the expanse of the countryside. A police checkpoint was visible 100 meters further down the road. He'd become used to abandoned cars, but there were more here. The checkpoint had maybe 20 or 30 cars, some turned over, a few more burnt out, and there was movement. It was hard to tell, but at least 100 figures were milling around the scene. Peter hoped they were people, but he knew they weren't. He heard the now-familiar loud groan from the group ahead. This road was not the way out of town. He could go back, but that didn't appeal, so he decided he would press forward. The crops in the fields were maybe a meter tall. He may sneak through unnoticed by the mob. It would be slow going but he could do it. It might take an hour of crawling, but once clear of the checkpoint, he could pick up the speed.

    He jogged across to a gap in the low hedgerow opening on to the field, careful to stay low and not attract attention. He paused and fixed a point in the distance to follow, hoping it'd keep him from veering back towards the road. The smell of the rapeseed struck him. It was a change to the scent of death and rotting flesh he'd grown used to and a welcome distraction. He got on his hands and knees and began the slow and deliberate crawl, mop handle in one hand, cricket bat in the other. Within a few feet, it already felt like hard work; pushing through the crops wasn't as easy as he thought it would be; the uneven hard ground scraped on his clenched fists. Visibility was only a few feet ahead, and it didn't take long before Peter climbed to his knees to look at the path ahead and towards the checkpoint. All was well.

He continued, aware that he had to stay at a slow pace to minimise the movement of the yellow flowers above or the noise that they made, aware of every crunch of dirt, snap of a stem and every distant groan. Within 20 minutes he was halfway across the first field, the slight rustle as he moved kept him on constant edge. He again rested and listened. The rustling continued. He got to his knees and glanced over to the road. He was closer now and could see the figures. There was a big one like he had seen before. The rest were a mix of the creatures. Fresh ones, old ones, damaged ones, young and old. Peter guessed there was probably every variety of the infected all bouncing off of cars at this one failed checkpoint.

More rustling. Peter looked around and stopped dead. About 10 feet ahead he could see something moving through the crops. He clenched his cricket bat and waited, praying to himself it would somehow change course and go in the other direction. His breathing gained pace as his heart pounded in his chest. It drew closer and Peter tensed, ready to strike. It picked up pace and lunged towards him. A West Highland terrier. Its coat was matted with dirt and blood and it was thin and hungry. The Westie let out a low growl as it spotted Peter.

Should he bash it? Was it infected? It was just a fucking dog, trying to survive like him.

"Shoo, skedaddle, scarper," he whispered hard. The little white dog continued to growl. Then it happened. It barked. Peter's heart could have stopped. It barked again and again. Peter slammed the bat down on the dog's head. It yelped and limply fell onto its side. He looked over at the checkpoint and could see the first of the things trying to climb over the small fence to get to him and this tiny mutt. One made it, then another. As they threw themselves over the fence they got back onto their feet and started staggering towards Peter. He looked down at the small dog full of remorse as its leg twitched and it struggled for life.

He glanced once more at the creatures and decided he would have to run. He got to his feet and moved as fast as he could through the field, struggling for footing as he glanced behind him. More of the infected were now giving pursuit, one of the big ones let out a groan. The first two reached the downed dog. It let out one last sound, a sickening scream as they pulled it apart greedily feasting on its small carcass. Peter continued as fast as he could, but he wasn't built for running. He still had a healthy lead but needed to slow his pace for a moment to catch his breath. Maybe 30 of them were following, a few joined in the fight to feed on the dog, but the others remained focused on the bigger meal.

Peter started a light jog, regaining some of the lead he'd forfeited through his lack of fitness. He reached the edge of the field and flopped over the fence. The next field was grass, only a foot or so high but a gentle slope downwards. It was already easier going but he knew now that he couldn't stop. A small wooded area was the next goal at the end of this field. Maybe he could lose his pursuers there.

Halfway through the field he looked back. The first of them were just reaching the fence line and trying to negotiate it. His lead had increased, but his breathing had become more strained and legs now felt like molten jelly. The mop handle became a walking stick as he again slowed down, desperate not to stop, unable to continue running. One of them flopped over the fence but now Peter was at the edge of the woods and could quicken his pace slightly.

The woods didn't look too deep and he couldn't be sure what was inside as the foliage thickened, but he knew what was behind him and that was good enough to proceed. He carefully entered, all too aware that a creature could emerge from behind any tree or bush. His heart raced and he could barely hear the world around him above the sound of his own heartbeat. He looked behind to confirm his pursuers hadn't gained on him.

Peter didn't hear the low groan. He didn't see the figure step from behind the tree he was approaching. A loud thud as Peter ran straight into the slobbering mess of a former man. Both hit the ground, momentum separating them on the floor by a few feet. The mop handle was further out of Peter's grasp. The cricket bat was much closer. In an instinctive motion, he picked it up and swung it down with the little power he could muster onto the creature's head. He stunned it only for a fraction of a second before he rained down the next blow, again with disappointing power. Peter scrambled to his knees and struck down a further two times with the bat before it hissed as its face was being planted into the ground by the impacts. Its body still writhed, and Peter gave it one more pathetic whack as he got to his feet.

The creature stirred slowly, but Peter was content it was incapacitated long enough for him to escape, saving the little energy he had for the next confrontation. He picked up the mop handle and scurried off ahead to the edge of the woods. Beyond him, more fields and to his right the road picked back up after the checkpoint.

Peter stayed in the fields and moved parallel to the road but not venturing too close. He slowed his pace to a fast walk, keeping a careful eye in front and the regular glance behind. He got to the end of the next field and saw no monster giving chase. He fell onto his knees and vomited. Then he rolled himself to sit down next to his creation and treated himself to a moment of rest before regaining his composure and carrying on.

14

Gareth entered his apartment; his dark clothes hiding obvious signs of the struggle with Josef. The apartment was big, flash and expensively decorated. It was every bit the extension of him. The building was exclusive and enjoyed a spectacular view of the Thames. He turned on a light and made his way to a mirror. He checked himself for any marks, injuries or blood, anything that might give him away. Looking down, he saw a small patch of blood on his jacket and a small tear to a pocket but nothing too bad. The jacket was black and the blood hard to see, but it was there, still tacky to the touch. It would be a good excuse to refresh his wardrobe.

He slung the jacket straight into the washing machine. He had no intention of keeping it but didn't want to risk it being found soaked in blood, so a visit to the dry cleaners wouldn't be required. He checked the rest of his clothes; they were fine. He'd clean those separately. His left shoe had a solitary speck of blood, dried and small. Gareth made his way to the bathroom, ripped a piece of toilet tissue from the roll, ran it under the tap, gave his shoe a good wipe then popped the paper into the toilet and flushed. He stripped off the rest of his clothes and hopped in the shower without a care in the world.

He didn't worry too much about whether he had gotten away with it. He had. Any guilt he had experienced whilst murdering Josef had drifted away with every passing minute.

He expected the body would be discovered shortly, depending on how strongly the fire had taken hold. They would take some time to confirm the identity of the body. Maybe the next day the police might get in touch with the office, but even then, why would he be a suspect? His star scientist, who was about to make them billions, has been killed. On the face of it, he should be their last suspect, and that's how he'd sell it if he needed to.

He was careful to wash thoroughly, scrubbing a little harder than normal, the water a little hotter, and spending more time and attention. When he emerged, he was clean and fresh. He felt good. He dried himself with a towel and wandered through the apartment to the kitchen and poured himself a gin and tonic before sitting in the living room and closing his eyes. He fell asleep within minutes, glass still in hand.

15

Darkness was fast approaching, and Peter began to wonder what he had done by leaving the safety of his own home. He wasn't sure how far he'd walked and wasn't confident he was going in the right direction. He felt exhausted and hungry; he'd kill for a burger. Lately, that had become the problem, everyone was ravenous.

The street he found himself on was much like the ones he'd been walking through for various parts of the day. The main signs of life were the odd infected soul trapped in a house or a scared animal breaking cover. Occasionally, he'd hear or see one in the distance and he'd change course. They were definitely around but not in the numbers he'd expected. He missed the openness and tranquillity of the countryside. After the initial confrontation near the checkpoint, it had been uneventful bliss. The few creatures he saw were a distance enough away that he could give them a wide berth. The visibility made it so easy. The towns were a risk, but he preferred sleeping in a bed to sleeping under the stars with no protection. The risk was worth the reward. All he had to do now was to find somewhere to sleep.

He had been on the lookout for an open door, figuring that anything inside would have escaped which meant that he wouldn't need to make any unnecessary noise. He'd seen a few houses that fit the bill, but he had found various reasons to not enter. The first was too big, too much space to clear and defend. His needs were meagre. The second had blood on the doorstep. Trouble had visited this place. He wouldn't. The third had a beware of the dog sign. That stupid poor fucking dog. Society had fallen, monsters roamed the streets, and he was remorseful of a dog that could have gotten him killed. That stupid, scared mutt.

Then there it was. Small, detached and the last house but one at the end of the street. The front door was open, some clothes and belongings were trailing from the porch onto the driveway. A tin of stewed steak caught his eye and sealed the deal. Peter scooped it up and slid it into his pocket, clenched the cricket bat, and approached the door. He stopped and listened intently, sure he'd hear a creature bumping around the house. Silence. The house was modest, a two up, two down, but looked to have been turned over. Maybe the owners left in a hurry. Maybe it had been looted. Probably both.

Peter slowly crept through the downstairs of the house, being small it was easy to search for ravenous fiends. Upstairs proved equally vacant. Satisfied it was empty he made his way downstairs. One last glance outside and he closed the door. It was home for a night.

He searched the kitchen. The cupboards were bare, the fridge long since disconnected and a biohazard in its own right. At least he had the tinned steak, and the gas was on. The taps were working so Peter gulped down several mouthfuls of water whilst the stew slowly warmed on the hob. He examined the knife rack and admired a replacement spearhead for his mop handle. It was another small sharp blade. He placed it on the work surface for later and pulled out a much larger knife.

He carried this with him as he gave his accommodation a more thorough investigation. Several family pictures; a young couple with a baby. There were a lot of pictures of that child. At its oldest, it was maybe two years old, toddling around enjoying its short life. Peter felt bad thinking about that family and narrowed down his search. Looking at family memories was a waste of energy, and he had none to spare.

He began to look for anything he might put to use, but he'd been beaten to it; besides a few throws and the kitchen knives, there wasn't anything of use downstairs. Peter carefully climbed the stairs and searched the first bedroom, a nursery. There was a chest of draws that had been emptied in a hurry, a few toys, a selection of children's books and a cot bed, undisturbed since its last use. Peter didn't dwell and moved to the next room. The bathroom was small, the medicine cabinet empty but there was a toilet. Peter smiled; not a total bust.

The bedroom was in tatters, but the bed was still present and partially made up. He examined the door and looked to see what he could use to barricade it. A chest of drawers would fit the bill. Peter drew the curtains and then made his way back to his stewed steak. He emptied the steaming food into a bowl and tucked in as he made his way to the bedroom. This would be home for tonight. Tomorrow would be harder, but tonight he could sleep in some comfort, use a real toilet, enjoy safety and have some hot food in his belly. His worries took a backseat to his exhaustion. His eyes closed, and he was instantly asleep.

16

When the police arrived in the office and broke the heartbreaking news of the fire, the burglary and murder of their beloved colleague, Josef, it was hard to take. Josef was not just a genius, he was well respected and liked. He had it in him to be an arsehole, but there was always a justification for it. He wouldn't turn on a member of staff because they got his coffee order wrong or if they were a few minutes late to a meeting. Dangerous or stupid were his red lines, and those who disagreed didn't last long. Those who remained liked him and could see the benefits into falling into line and riding on his coattails. None appeared more upset than Gareth when he spoke with the detective.

"He had just made an incredible breakthrough on our new drug. He was already starting to sketch out his next genius project and James Cahill would throw everything NewU Pharma had at him." Gareth was at his desk and slumped down in disbelief.

The detective was a man in his early forties, a little overweight and was wearing a cheap suit. "Did he have any problems with anyone here? Any problems you know of?"

"None. He was a genius and hugely respected in his field. His work has cured so many people and made the world a better place. Our new drug is completing certification. He cured obesity and it will be huge. A man of his intellect could cure cancer or dementia given the right resources, and we would give him everything he wanted." Gareth had to play up how important and special Josef was. There would always be some suspicion, but he had to reduce the plausibility. Why burn your winning lottery ticket?

"So you were okay with Josef being the star here?" The detective didn't seem interested in his own question, the accusatory tone felt forced as if he'd watched too much Columbo.

"I've got stock options, a great salary and looking at an amazing bonus. Everyone here has a great package, one that is massively enhanced with success. And Josef gave us our first great product. I don't know where the next one might come from." What a load of bullshit. The fat drug was the payday they all wanted. No one gave a shit about a long slog of an unprofitable dementia drug.

The detective had heard enough. Probably it was just a random burglary gone wrong. Forensics weren't hopeful of finding anything useful and the chances of finding a random junkie willing to confess were remote.

"Thanks for your time, if you think of anything please let us know." Both stood up and Gareth was handed a card as he showed his guest the door.

When the door clicked shut, Gareth sat back down, turned to the window behind and gave a small smile. He hadn't gotten away with anything yet, but he hadn't fucked it up either. Cahill didn't need to know the facts, he didn't need to know the problems, all he needed to know was that Gareth was dealing with it. That's what he paid him for. Amongst his responsibilities, he'd have to talk to the staff, and that was his next duty. He popped open his desk draw and eyed a bottle of Scotch. "Maybe, later." He left the office and made his way to the lab.

The mood was downbeat, for most. Roger and William seemed relieved more than sad. Their job had just become easier. With Josef gone there was no need to worry about their fraud being discovered. He was the only one with the expertise, knowledge and experience to spot their crimes. They were intelligent men, but not smart enough to realise that luck didn't really exist and that the death of Josef wasn't by chance. Maybe they suspected, but they didn't want to believe it and rock the boat. So why even allow themselves to question their good fortune?

Gareth entered with confidence, ready to talk to the staff in the lab, make a short boilerplate speech and show his face. He stood at the front and observed the eggheads going about their work. One or two of the junior ones noticed and stopped, waiting for him to begin.

"Excuse me guys, I'd like to say a few words. James is unfortunately tied up in New York, but he asked me to come and see you. Obviously, you've all heard the devastating news about Josef and we're here to support you. If you need anything, talk to Jane in HR and she will assist you." *Don't bother me, I don't care.*

"We all know the fantastic work that Josef did here." *The work that will make us upstairs rich beyond our wildest dreams, and will be a nice line on your CVs.*

"Let's get it over the line. Let this be Josef's legacy, a lasting testament to his genius and ability to help his fellow man." *Don't slack off now, my bonus hasn't been calculated yet.*

"My door is always open, and Jane has some great resources to help." *Just leave me alone.* Short and not particularly sweet.

Gareth stopped for a moment, leaving enough time as if to invite questions but not enough time to allow them. "That's great guys, thanks for listening."

Roger and William were at the back of the lab. They'd listened like the rest but didn't care. They knew they were being looked after. "Roger, William, how's it looking?" This was the most interested Gareth had been in any conversation he'd had in the lab. They were so close.

"Great, we've worked out the issue with testing and getting the rights results, every time. We're ready to progress and submit for full validation," Roger stated this matter-of-factly, he knew the road was long and tedious and it was still years away from getting approved.

"Fantastic, whatever you need let me or Cahill know; we'll get it for you."

Either Gareth didn't appreciate they were at the start of a marathon or felt he could cheat the system, William felt the need to temper expectations. "This still won't be a quick process. It could take another 10 years for approval. In fact, I can't see us being on the shelves for at least 10 years, maybe even 15."

Gareth knew this was a slow process, but 15 years? No, that wouldn't do. "Look, it'll take as long as it takes, but we can always shave some time off. There's nothing in this world that can't be shuffled along with a smile and a few more pound notes waved in the right direction."

Gareth wouldn't be able to grease any palms until he knew which ones to target. He already had a professional gathering information on various government officials, ministers, and shadow ministers - anyone with influence. Fat can't be a lifestyle choice. It has to be an epidemic; one that demanded a cure. He would stress the strain on the NHS, chubby children struggling to breathe shoving chocolate down their own throats, middle-aged men knocking back pints on a Saturday afternoon before keeling over clutching their chests. Getting those in authority behind a push to defeat obesity wouldn't be hard, with the right backing. He'd fund, bribe, blackmail. Whatever it took. Like hell he would wait around for ten years to get his money. He could do it in three.

17

His alarm wouldn't stop. Peter fumbled with his eyes closed to turn it off but failed. He sat up and then remembered that this wasn't his bed, this wasn't his house, and he didn't have an alarm. A car outside was causing the racket. Peter soon woke himself and peeked out of the curtains. One of the older ones from the beginning was pushing against a car, trying to get at something inside. The noise had attracted others, just two or three that Peter could see, but others were no doubt closing in.

He grabbed his things and moved the barricade as he quickly briskly made his way downstairs. He could see shadows moving in front of the house through the glass and turned to the back, to the kitchen. He picked up a knife and looked into the back garden. It was clear.

Peter silently unbolted the door and walked to the end of the garden. There was no gate and the fence was maybe 7 feet tall. He looked for something to stand on and found a bucket, he turned it upside down, stood on it and stretched to look over. Another garden, it had a side passage and he could see a gate at the end. He could see one creature in the house, but the glass patio door was closed. It swayed gently as it stood staring into the garden. This was still a better option than the street in front of the house, one trapped one or maybe half a dozen gnashing, clawing ones.

Some people would be able to scale the fence without issue.

Most would get over it at maybe the second or third attempt. Peter's heavy breathing rivalled that of the car alarm out front. In two minutes, he'd not got close. It would have been embarrassing if it wasn't so exhausting. Peter flopped down on the ground to rest. He looked around for something else to stand on. The small well-kept garden yielded nothing useful, a tasteful garden gnome was neither steady nor strong enough. Then he noticed the fence panel. He lifted the panel, and it slowly slid upwards between the posts. It was heavy, but he could do it. Peter sat on the floor and eased the panel back up and above his head as he began to drag his body through and propped the fence panel up on his shoulder. He reached back across and blindly fumbled for his bag, bat and bladeless spear unable to see with the panel resting on his shoulder.

It had been in the neighbouring house and heard the panting, sweaty mess of a man in the garden next door. The outside door was open. The fence was short. It needed to do nothing more than reach out as it walked to flop over on to the unkempt lawn. It stood itself back up and eyed up its prey under the fence. Peter hadn't noticed the thing bearing down on him. He swung his legs clear and gave the panel one last heave to get it off his shoulder and rolled onto the floor just as it struck.

The first Peter knew of how close he came was the greying arm thrashing around under the panel inches away from him. He rolled further clear and grabbed his mop handle. He hadn't attached the new blade so opted against lashing out. He stood up and checked his surroundings. The creature in the house had taken notice of this potential meal and it pressed itself against the double-glazed pane of glass. Peter composed himself ready to face what may lie beyond the gate. He just prayed the fucking thing wasn't locked.

He moved through the garden glancing for anything useful. The people in this area didn't believe in gardening. The hope for a shovel or hatchet to arm himself further with were woefully blown. The gate was unlocked and Peter carefully opened it to look out at the street beyond nothing. Not a monster, pigeon or even a stray piece of litter blowing in the wind. Peter cautiously entered the street, cricket bat and mop handle ready for action, even if he wasn't.

A loud cry erupted from the direction of the car alarm. Peter shuddered. They had got whatever they were hunting. He didn't quite have his bearings but didn't want to stop moving. It was early, he'd slept, taken on some calories and had a full water bottle. He wished he'd had time for good crap, but he'd have to wait until his next digs. He headed out of the cul-de-sac at a steady pace, no point running when he wasn't sure where he was or where was safe. He would keep moving in the direction that should take him back out of the built-up area, avoiding any great risks. Despite his rest, he wasn't built for this much activity and he ached. He knew he probably would have to slow down or stop within the next half an hour, by then he hoped to have skirted around the town and be back in the countryside where his visibility would be better.

18

Natasha had feared she'd always be fat. She hated herself and thought others hated her too. At 23 years old, she had a lot of life to live but shied away from the crowd. Her friends were few, and she dared not socialise with the girls at work. She was embarrassed to stand next to those stick insects. No, Natasha knew it was best to keep herself to herself. Her modest ground-floor flat was home to her and Renton, her British Blue cat. She had tried every fad diet, every slimming club, and even one of those army based park fitness groups. Tried and failed. Some had a small short-term benefit, but Natasha just couldn't stick to any of them. At any bump in the road, she found comfort in chocolate and crisps, and she had a lot of bumps in the road.

It was an average Friday night. Natasha was home watching her reality shows whilst browsing the internet on her laptop. This is how she would spend most nights. One celebrity she followed, a hugely talented but damaged singer/songwriter from Australia known as "Shaz," was one of Natasha's favourite influencers. Normally, it'd be some shocking celebrity story or a link to some overpriced, under quality clothing. Tonight didn't seem any different. Shaz, like Natasha had fought her own battle with weight all her life, but she was now tweeting about a stone loss in just one week. Natasha was excited. In a series of tweets, Shaz shared how easy her solution was, no exercise and no rabbit food. Shaz could eat whatever she wanted, and the weight would still come off. As if to prove this, Shaz shared a series of pictures of her meals that week. They were less a collection of evening meals and more examples of what a prisoner on death row may request for their last meal.

This was what Natasha had been dreaming of. Hell, this is what the world had been dreaming of. Shaz finally shared a link to a website offering FatBGone - a one a day diet pill that offered unbelievable results. The site didn't look impressive or official and this brand-new treatment was only available in limited quantities. The link was live for all of five minutes before it went offline and Shaz deleted all the related tweets. That five minutes was enough for Natasha to have gone to the site, put an order for a month's supply in her shopping basket for the bargain price of £600 delivered. Card details punched in, she hovered over the order submit button. This was nonsense, surely? Nothing could be this easy and effective? Was it a scam? Had Shaz's Twitter account been hacked?

Natasha decided she didn't care. Her credit card company would surely reimburse her if it was some nerd at his computer stealing card details, and if it was legitimate but didn't work, it would just join the extensive list of failed weight-loss attempts. With the submit button hit, Natasha smiled, imagining the possibilities of how she might look in just a few months.

19

Natasha returned home from work as if it was any other day, but it wasn't. She'd received a text from the courier confirming they had delivered her parcel to a neighbour at Flat 3. Thank goodness for that. Mabel, who lived at Flat 3, was a kindly widow in her early eighties who Natasha would run the odd errand for and sometimes just pop round for a chat. Had they delivered the parcel to Flat 1, Natasha may not even have bothered to retrieve it despite the value. At Flat 1, Kerry lived with her boyfriend Mark. They both cruelly referred to Natasha as "Fatasha" and did just enough to make her life miserable, without stepping over the line to risk eviction by the council or having their housing benefits taken away. Natasha knocked on the door and Mabel gleefully opened it.

"Would you like a cup of tea?" Mabel was always delighted to see Natasha and the feeling was mutual.

"That would be lovely, Mabel."

Natasha entered the flat which would have been dated 20 years ago but was immaculately tidy and everything inside was in pristine condition. They both made their way to the kitchen as the kettle on the stove began whistling away.

"So, you've been buying off the internets again?" Mabel handed over the unassuming box. It was the size of a house brick and had no weight. It didn't feel like it should have cost £600. It didn't feel like it should have cost £6, but it was too late now.

"It's a new diet pill." Natasha felt embarrassed but knew Mabel wouldn't judge her too harshly.

"Another one?"

"This one is supposed to be amazing, Shaz, the singer, lost loads of weight using it." Natasha could hear the desperation in her own voice, but didn't care to hide it. Mabel reached out and touched Natasha's shoulder.

"You shouldn't worry about being bigger. You're a lovely young, beautiful girl." She was sincere. But little old ladies weren't the problem. They all loved Natasha. People her own age, they judged her far more harshly.

"I know, but I'd really be happier if I just lost a little."

Mabel poured the hot water into the teapot on a tray, ready with two cups, a small milk jug and a plate of biscuits. She led Natasha through to the living room with the tray and they both sat down.

"So, you won't be wanting any of these custard creams then dear?"

"That's the beauty of these pills, I can eat whatever I want, whenever I want." As Mabel poured the tea, Natasha took a biscuit. Then a second and a third biscuit, offering a cheeky embarrassed smile.

"You have as many as you like dear."

20

Natasha sat on her sofa with Renton majestically standing by her side. It'd been three hours since she had returned from Mabel's flat and she couldn't bring herself to open the box. What if inside there weren't 30 pills, what if it was empty? Or worse, the pills weren't genuine and were toxic? She could have 30 doses of cyanide wrapped in a nice little bundle for all she knew.

She opened the plain brown exterior box, and inside was a very colourful, well-designed smaller box with "NewU Pharma" proudly above the FatBGone product name. This somehow gave Natasha some confidence; the name was naff, but it looked genuine. They had put enough effort into the design and finish that even if the pill was a fake, it probably wouldn't be toxic. Probably.

Removing the blister pack and instructions, she was shocked by how tiny the pills were; the smallest she'd even seen. How could they possibly be effective? The instructions seemed standard: one a day with a glass of water after a meal. Do not take if pregnant

"Chance would be a fine thing," Natasha quipped to herself.

She pulled her weighing scales out from under the sofa and stepped on them, 22 stone and 6 pounds. This wasn't her heaviest, but neither was it her lightest. It was the weight she settled at when she wasn't self-medicating with food or on an extreme fad diet.

She'd eaten about an hour ago, but Natasha thought this would be fine. Carefully, she popped out the tiny pill, desperate not to break or drop it before placing it in her mouth. The taste was sour, nearly meaty, but unlike anything she'd had before. It was neither pleasant nor unpleasant, just strong, even more so considering the meagre size of the solitary pill. Natasha gulped down a glass of water and the deed was done. She was on the first step to her new self.

*

It was 3am and Natasha woke abruptly, her stomach was grumbling loudly. A sharp stabbing pain sent her bolt upright clutching her belly. Sweat was pouring from her brow as she launched herself out of bed and quickly crawled on all fours to the toilet just in time before her bowels erupted. A constant stream of liquid faeces splattered the toilet bowl. As her bowels emptied, the pain gradually subsided. She sat more upright and breathed heavily, feeling some relief. What had she done? Why was she so stupid?

After an initial flurry of gas and excrement, her stomach settled down. She cleaned herself up and went to find the FatBGone packet. She rifled through the side effects listed on the back of the instruction insert.

"In the first 24 hours some diarrhoea and discomfort may be experienced, this is perfectly normal and will have completely cleared up by day three. If symptoms persist, please stop taking FatBGone and consult with your GP."

This was normal then. Natasha felt relief she'd not shit herself but wished she'd flipped the instructions over to see what she could be expecting. If these pills did nothing else, they proved to be an efficient laxative. She returned to bed to find Renton had taken her spot in the warm patch. She forcibly moved the cat and tried to get back to sleep.

*

***

Renton rudely awoke Natasha batting her face with his furry paw. After the previous night's emergency bowel evacuation, Natasha had managed uninterrupted sleep. She was a little sweaty but otherwise felt fantastic. She was hungry, but that wasn't unusual. Renton again batted Natasha on the nose; she wasn't the only one feeling a pang of hunger. But first things first, a weigh-in.

Natasha pulled the bathroom scales out from their resting place and stood on them, waiting for her weight to be displayed. To her delight, she was eight pounds lighter than the previous morning. Before patting herself on the back too hard, she recalled the less than calm nighttime toilet trip. She was lighter; she'd expelled a lot of waste and no doubt dehydrated. She had far cheaper laxatives in the medicine cabinet that would produce comparable results. So, if this was FatBGone's weight loss solution, she knew it was doomed to end in an expensive failure.

She carried on to the kitchen to get Renton's breakfast and fix herself something light. Renton's breakfast comprised the usual protein-rich luxury kibble. Natasha's light breakfast evolved from a scrambled egg on toast to eight rashers of bacon, four sausages, another six pieces of toast, an additional four eggs fried and two tins of beans. If the local cafe had put this on the menu, it would probably have had a name such as a "Gut Buster." With the feast polished off, Natasha felt the usual shame but was still hungry, and sweaty. Pouring through the fridge, she pulled out and rejected an apple, throwing it to the floor along with half a lettuce. She then opened up a milk carton and downed it without taking so much as a single breath. Dropping the drained vessel, she reached back into the fridge pulling out a lump of cheese and a stick of butter which she promptly chowed down on.

21

Four years and not a moment or opportunity wasted. Gareth had spent tens of millions of Cahill's money, a special fund, not linked directly to NewU Pharma, set aside especially for bribing and extorting. His favourite use of the money had been a 19-year-old rent boy they had set up with a 50-odd year-old prominent married cabinet minister. They had tapes of the intimate encounter and arranged a viewing at a local private cinema for its star. Gareth hadn't been present himself, but this encounter too had been filmed. He'd never seen a man produce so much vomit. At first, he vomited upon seeing the encounter, then when told the boy was only 15, which was a lie but a plausible one, vomited more.

The MP wasn't just looking at a ruined career and marriage, he was looking at a prison sentence and a lifetime on the sex offenders register. He agreed to help them, use his influence to bring the obesity epidemic to the fore. Gareth's people made it clear he was safe and that the secret would remain so, as long as he did what he was told. He had mused that all this effort, expense and criminality had been wasted on trying to get a legitimate pharmaceutical approved for use. He'd stooped very low many times in his life, but never to these depths and for so long. But after killing Josef, none of this seemed like a line was really being crossed.

The tabloids had been engaged to get the public's blood

boiling at the uncaring government and the greedy pedlars of sugary and fatty foods. It was about knowing the right people at the right red tops and they will get your message across. You could even start a war if that's what you wished.

Over the last two years, everything had stepped up a gear. After the death of a grotesquely obese 12-year-old girl called Jenny, the public was putty in the press and Gareth's hands. "Jenny's Law" had gathered nearly 1 million signatures on an online petition calling for immediate government action, banning of high sugar and highly addictive junk foods. Those behind the petition campaigned on every media stream for serious government investment in curing obesity.

The left-leaning government was a people-pleaser. They overpromised and underdelivered at great expense. Luckily, a particular cabinet minister had a solution. It just so happened that the Health Minister had been working with private industry on just such an answer. Gareth's man did his part and the Prime Minister listened gleefully as they presented their results. The PM knew he'd get all the plaudits, and this could become part of his legacy. It would be so easy. It was ready for distribution and he barely had to dirty his hands in forcing it through. He had public opinion behind him and he'd be the man to fast track this miracle cure for the epidemic of the twenty-first century. He didn't have to aggravate the junk food industry banning certain food types, put draconian limits on how much sugar could be used or tax people's favourite chocolate bar.

The Prime Minister himself pushed through the drug - the trials had all been outstanding, with no long-term side effects and impressive results. Some close warned him against being too heavily involved. Five years down the line if people drop dead with colon cancer, he'd be finished. He didn't need to listen; he knew best. He knew this was his moment to be forever remembered. He was all too eager to stand beside Jenny's parents, with a picture of the overweight tween and shed a tear as he introduced the newly passed Jenny's Law. A law that would enable them to fast track urgent medical treatments if they were in the public interest. It would start with fighting fat but could treat any future illness or condition.

It was too easy for Gareth. It had taken on a life of its own. He spent less money corrupting and more time schmoozing. James Cahill had been keen to share the limelight and there was more than enough for both.

Four years, but here they were on the night of the launch. For several months, warehouses had been full and ready to ship. The government had signed a billion-pound deal to supply the NHS. They had marketing materials and had already reached out to social media influencers, supplying them FatBGone for free, but reaping the benefits of all the attention.

The popularity amongst the pointless internet celebrities had created a black market that shifty warehouse workers and those with easy access were ready to capitalise on. Neither Gareth nor Cahill cared about a few hundred missing boxes. It was all good publicity as word spread about this wonder drug.

The work in the UK almost complete; tonight's launch would confirm that. Contracts were already being drawn up for shipments to the USA, Canada, Australia, several South and Central American countries, pending approvals from the various agencies and governments. In the next two months, they would be all over the world. Thanks to a Prime Minister easily manipulated who didn't just open a door to a country, but the entire world.

A sophisticated venue in central London hosted the night. The media, politicians, celebrities, investors and that fat girl's family were in attendance. Gareth happily stayed in the background and let those who would pay his bonus and decide his stock options to bask in the glory. The presentation felt more like the launch of an expensive new smartphone rather than a drug marketed to save lives. Gareth had put much of it together himself. Two morning television presenters were the hosts, introducing each of the experts and speakers, case studies and the rigorous testing that had been undertaken. Jenny's family featured heavily as did a tear-jerking two-minute video dedicated to poor Jenny. Gareth privately referred to it as "An Ode to Cake" and could barely keep a straight face as it played.

At the end of the presentation, there were tears, cheers, and so much applause. Success.

As Cahill climbed down from the stage, he sought Gareth and gave him a warm hug, "We've fucking done it!" Cahill excitedly claimed.

You've done nothing but open your wallet, you fat fuck, Gareth thought, but he censored himself. "It was a real team effort. Congratulations."

Cahill carried on through the room soaking up the adulation.

22

It had been the best three weeks of Natasha's life. She'd been eating like a horse and had still lost 7 stones. She had spent a fortune on new clothes, her old ones hanging off her or just plain dropping to the ground. She still had some way to go, but she couldn't help but admire herself in every mirror or reflective surface she passed. It wasn't just clothes costing money, Natasha's food spend was through the roof. From 50 to 60 pounds a week, she was now spending over 200. It wasn't a problem, not yet at least.

She was sitting on her sofa, snacking on a large bowl of crisps, Renton beside her purring. Her phone buzzed with a message taking Natasha's attention from the crisps for a moment. Picking it up, she peered inquisitively then her face opened with a beaming smile. It was Joshua. Having met him yesterday morning at her local coffee shop, he was a charming man in his late twenties. He was good looking, out of her league, in reasonable shape and tall. Natasha had never had a man approach her before.

"I can't stop thinking about you. Fancy dinner tonight?" he messaged. She fancied dinner, she fancied him nearly as much.

"Yes! I've been thinking about you too." She didn't want to risk losing her shot.

Then 10 minutes past, and no reply. "Damn it!" Natasha exclaimed. She's already fucked it up, and all it took was one stupid text message. Her phone buzzed again into life.

"Great! Do you know Stefano's, about two minutes from our Costa?" She giggled uncontrollably.

"Our Costa!" Natasha said out loud barely able to contain her excitement.

"Yes, but I've never been there." She hit send and waited. Less than a minute passed before the response.

"Well, let's change that. 8pm?" She couldn't believe what she was reading.

"Sounds amazing!" Natasha launched herself to her feet on hitting send and jumped up like an excited child.

"I'll see you at 8pm!" With that, the date was set.

She stopped and suddenly dread filled her. What would she wear? Would he like her when he saw her again? Saw her eating like a pig? What if he liked her? What if he came back, and they made love? Natasha wasn't a virgin, but she'd only had sex once. It was with a friend when she was 19, and was an awkward exchange of bodily fluids that she kind of enjoyed but didn't feel she had done it right. She hoped that was about to change. These pills were damned fantastic.

23

Late, why was he late? It was 20:23. Natasha had arrived 10 minutes early, but he was now nearly 25 minutes late. Stefano's was a nice, but not an extravagant restaurant. It was family-run, cosy but perhaps slightly dated. Less than half the tables were in use, with couples and small groups enjoying their meals. Natasha had already demolished the first helping of breadsticks and was contemplating getting some garlic bread. Suddenly she realised, was this one big fucking cruel joke? She'd lost so much weight, but she was still a fat girl. A stupid fat girl.

She looked around to check if she was being watched, being mocked. It wasn't obvious, but she suspected everyone. She wanted to cry, but she was determined not to give the unseen arseholes the satisfaction in seeing her upset. When the waiter came to her table again, she would ask for the bill, pay and discreetly leave. Natasha checked her phone one more time before reaching for her bag. She produced a credit card from her purse ready to show to a member of staff, so they knew she wanted to pay, but then a hand rested on her shoulder.

"Natasha! I'm really sorry I'm late. My bus broke down and I left my phone at the flat. I ran the last half a mile. I was having a bit of a mare." Joshua looked a little dishevelled and was catching his breath.

Natasha smiled, a sense of relief washed over her, "You're

here now."

Joshua sat down at the table and the waiter joined them with menus and a wine list. "Are you a white or red kind of girl?"

Under other circumstances, she would settle for a Lambrini, but this was a date and not a night on the sofa. "Normally white but I don't mind red if that suits you better?"

Joshua pointed to an entry on the wine list for the waiter's benefit, "The Pinot Grigio please."

The waiter smiled, took the wine list back and then left the couple to a moment of awkward silence.

"Again, I'm sorry. I really hope you weren't here long?" He seemed sincere. This wasn't a cruel joke.

"Just 10 minutes or so," she lied. They both smiled as they began to thumb through their menus.

"Do you recommend anything?" Natasha liked the look of all of it but pretended that she couldn't eat it all.

"I've only been here once, but I had the Lasagne, which I would thoroughly recommend."

"Sounds good," she closed the menu and looked back at Joshua.

"And I think I'll have the Calzone, garlic bread to share?" Natasha nodded, and they both placed their menus down ready for more awkwardness.

24

It wasn't possible for things to have gone any better. Orders were pouring in and manufacturing couldn't keep up with demand. NewU Pharma had ridden the wave of excitement and already made hundreds of millions of pounds, but now was the endgame. Two huge multinational pharmaceutical companies were fighting it out for the honour of buying NewU. EverGreen was based in the USA but had facilities across Europe and Asia, complemented by deep pockets and a huge portfolio of profitable drugs. Rodgers Taylor Henderson was also based in the US but enjoyed market dominance in South America and Africa. They were constantly in the shadow of their bigger competitor and knew it. Bidding had started at a cool billion, but that was no longer enough to tempt Cahill and his cronies. It was a starting point, but with the money they were making, it needed to double. Gareth's amazing work got him a seat at the table during negotiations. His charisma was an asset and allowed Cahill to sit back and think whilst Gareth did the talking.

Little did Cahill know that EverGreen had already bought and paid for Gareth. The millions Gareth had been awarded in bonuses from Cahill was nothing to what EverGreen's acquisitions team had already syphoned to him and had promised him. He didn't have any morals anymore; they had long since been sold. RTH had also provided Gareth with a bung, although they lacked the skill and experience of EverGreen and undervalued him. He took the money and advised he couldn't promise anything but would influence Cahill and inform on EverGreen's offer so they could gazump it.

In negotiations with RTH, Gareth enjoyed playing cat and mouse with them. He knew they would not win, and he was enjoying the game. He was being paid enough to have fun. With EverGreen, he didn't give them an easy ride, but he made sure that Cahill heard what he wanted to hear. Ultimately, it had to be Cahill's choice to go with EverGreen. They had to appeal to his growing vanity and his greed. Gareth's job was to give RTH enough rope to hang themselves whilst EverGreen would swoop in with a higher offer.

Eva Hernandez was of Latino descent, born and brought up in Texas, a stunning beauty with an amazing figure. She looked far younger than her 43 years. She'd been with RTH for seven years and was their star player. Her career had run very much like Gareth's. Gareth thought she was too old for him, but wouldn't turn her down since he figured she'd be a fun shag, and screwing her would be even funnier when she realised he'd screwed RTH too. She was more fun than Bob Green from EverGreen. His father had founded the company in the fifties, and he'd taken over in the late eighties. He definitely was too old for Gareth and definitely wouldn't have been as fun in bed. But he knew how to bribe properly, Gareth as a man who had paid many people off appreciated that skill at such a high level.

Eva had failed to impress Cahill. Despite his flaws, he was dedicated to his wife, the love of his life, and he found Eva's misplaced attempts to seduce him an insult. Gareth had encouraged her to do this, as much for his own amusement as to damage RTH's efforts to strike a deal. Cahill found her arrogance annoying. He was an old school misogynist and didn't appreciate being sent a woman to negotiate with, especially one who wasn't higher up. Bob, on the other hand, was equipped with the correct genitalia, owned the company and spoke only of money, and lots of it. Cahill didn't want a blowjob in his office, he wanted hundreds of millions in his bank account. Gareth had advised Bob that a big one-off offer would not be enough. Cahill would still want some skin in the game. He recommended either an ongoing profit share or shares in EverGreen. After weeks of negotiations, they agreed on a deal, an outrageously generous one of just over one and a half billion pounds. On top of that, Cahill would receive five percent of all profits for five years, then one percent after that. His board would share two percent and then quarter percent for the same period.

Cahill had instructed the legal team to draw up the paperwork to proceed with EverGreen. Much to Gareth's delight, they tasked him with informing RTH of their failure. Their offer was nearly one and a half billion, but straight cash. Gareth had been encouraging them all the way, advising that their offer was substantially higher than the one EverGreen had been willing to reach. Gareth had chosen a chain Italian restaurant, a low end one on a high street. It would show Eva exactly what he thought of her and the offer.

Eva had already seated herself when Gareth arrived.

"Sorry, I got stuck back at the office," Gareth gave a hollow smile and sat down opposite Eva.

"Cut the shit Gareth. What's going on?" Her wait had done nothing to improve her mood. "I thought we were close to a deal, then I get an asshole from EverGreen gloating that they've got an agreement. What are we paying you for?"

A waitress approached with menus. "We're not eating!" Eva snapped.

"I'll have a gin and tonic," Gareth smiled, the waitress smiled in return and left.

"I said I would put a word in; try to steer the deal in your favour. I told you I couldn't promise anything. If you wanted promises, you should have paid more money."

Eva's anger was boiling over. "We gave you nearly 1 million fucking dollars, and you gave us nothing."

Gareth felt mischievous. "I gave you a foot in the door. Do

you think you would have gone further without me? Your frankly abysmal negotiating and tightfistedness cost you the deal. If you wanted it bad enough, you'd have thrown more money rather than your ageing body at it. Jesus, even 20 years ago I doubt you could have fucked your way to a deal."

Eva stood up and threw her water at Gareth, "This isn't over!"

Gareth wiped his face with a napkin and continued with his aggravating grin, "It really is. Don't worry. In five years time when EverGreen buy up your shit show, Bob might let you drop to your knees and blow your way to a new career opportunity."

Eva moved forward as if she was ready to slap Gareth, then regained her composure, adjusted herself and returned an equally shit-eating grin, "Go fuck yourself."

25

The hallway was pitch black, just a dull light from the beyond the front door bleeding through the gaps. A rustle of keys and scratching at the door interrupted the tranquillity. The door burst open and Natasha came through the door, mouth attached to Joshua's as they embraced. They slammed the door shut and carried on through the hallway to the sofa. Natasha unbuttoned Joshua's shirt as she pulled him down with her, their lips barely separating for a moment as they fumbled and undressed each other.

"Wait, wait," Natasha pulled herself away. She'd allowed herself to get caught up with the moment but only now did her self-doubt re-emerge. Another human hadn't seen her naked ever. Even when she lost her virginity she wore a t-shirt.

"Are you okay?" Joshua was panting.

"Are you sure you want to do this with me?" Natasha struggled to get the words out.

"Too fucking right I do! You're amazing." Joshua re-engaged and Natasha relieved, continued with greater vigour and confidence.

Joshua's hand slipped between Natasha's legs and she let out a quiet gasp before reciprocating and squeezing her hand down the front of Joshua's trousers. The breathing became heavier as the couple allowed themselves to enjoy the experience. Natasha pulled her hand out of Joshua's trousers, undid his belt and unbuttoned his flies before pulling his trousers and briefs down. Joshua was nearly fully erect, his penis a good few inches bigger than the only other one she'd seen in the flesh previously. She positioned him on the sofa and got on to her knees.

"You don't have to," Joshua offered, being a gentleman whilst hoping he didn't just sway Natasha from her current course.

"I want to," and she did. No one had made her feel the way Joshua had done, and if they were going to only have one night, if it was a cruel joke, she at least wanted to give it everything she had.

She licked his shaft and kissed the tip of Joshua's cock before taking as much of him in her mouth as she good. He let out a slight groan of pleasure as he rested his hand on the back of her head offering some encouragement whilst being careful not to force her to do anything. Her action became more vigorous, more energetic. She'd never given a blowjob before and missed the nuances of a technique.

"Slower, gentler," Joshua requested quietly. Natasha took the critique on board and adjusted. Joshua relaxed as she carried on at the gentler pace. After a few moments, he gently lifted her face from his crotch and stood up.

"Your turn."

Natasha led him to the bedroom. Renton jumped from the bed in the shadows unnoticed as Natasha removed her remaining clothes and lay on the bed. Joshua climbed on top and kissed her, before edging down her body kissing every inch, paying special attention to her nipples. He reached her vagina and slowly started licking her clitoris, moving his tongue inside of her at a random speed and pattern. Natasha clutched his head and let out a deep moan as her legs quivered uncontrollably. This was the most perfect experience of her life. Joshua eased himself back up to Natasha's face and kissed her passionately as he entered her which resulted in another groan. As he was slowly thrusting, she again let out a loud moan and dug her nails deeply into his back. This was so much more intense than she'd ever imagined. It seemed like they had been making love for hours but she couldn't tell. Her nails dug deeper into his back as she began to climax, her breathing getting even faster before she came and let out a powerful moan. Joshua wasn't too far behind after seeing his work was done. They were both exhausted. He kissed her again before rolling over to lie by her side.

"Is it just me, or are you really hungry?" Joshua asked, still struggling to regain his breath.

"I could eat." Of course.

26

It had been constantly on Natasha's mind since she first took that pill. The desire to eat, the need to consume. The FatBGone pills were expensive enough, but the amount she had been spending on food was ridiculous. The last few days Joshua had been a regular fixture in the flat and he seemed capable of keeping up with her appetite. Between the two of them, they'd gone through a large week's worth of food shopping, several takeaways and snack runs to the local newsagent. Natasha was looking forward to finishing the pills and then returning to normal. She had at first enjoyed eating anything she wanted, but it was most definitely now becoming a chore.

It was their first night apart since she had slept with Joshua for the first time. She had held back a little with what she ate in front of him. They still consumed gluttonous amounts of food, but she knew on her own she would have eaten even more. She grabbed fish and chips on the way home and polished it off on the bus. She raided the cupboards and finished the last few remnants of food in the fridge, ate the remaining half bag of uncooked pasta as if they were crisps and now stared at two pouches of Renton's cat food on the kitchen worktop. She couldn't, could she? She popped the top off the first pouch, salmon and trout. She didn't like trout, but looking at the jelly covered brown lumps, Natasha didn't think that'd be the problem with this scenario.

What's wrong with her? She didn't want to eat it, but she was so hungry. She scooped out half the packet with her fingers and shovelled it into her mouth, licking each finger clean. It didn't even taste that bad. The jelly was meaty in flavour but not a great texture and taste combination. Renton appeared and meowed a protest at his dinner being eaten in front of him.

"Fuck off cat!" She had no love or tenderness in her voice, just desperation and anger.

She quickly dispatched the rest of the packet, being careful not to waste a drop. Renton again protested and Natasha shoved him forcefully from the worktop. He hit the floor and hissed at her. Natasha tore open the last pouch and ate it even quicker than the first. It wasn't enough. Renton jumped back on the worktop and sniffed at the empty packet before staring at Natasha.

She didn't even think as she grabbed the poor cat by the throat and smashed his furry head against a kitchen cupboard. He went limp straight after the impact. Natasha hit him one more time before slamming his lifeless body on the kitchen counter. What had she done? She stared at Renton for a moment, his eyes open and filled with confusion, blood dripping from his ears and mouth.

Natasha gently stroked his chin as if to comfort him, then launched herself at the tiny corpse. Biting into Renton's neck and chest, she coughed as the fur entered her mouth, but she didn't stop until she had a good mouthful of flesh. She chewed through the tough tissue and swallowed. Sweet relief. Natasha picked out a lump of fur from her mouth and looked at it closely before fixing her gaze on to Renton. She couldn't work out why, but it tasted good. The kitty meat scratched the itch that all other food had struggled to. She didn't feel bad for Renton. She was fixed on him, but not out of love. She saw meat, and she wanted more. She grabbed a large knife and took Renton's head off in one hard chop. Natasha placed it to one side; she'd return to it when she needed to. She hacked at the body and pulled Renton's skin off, not cleanly; it was a gory, slippery struggle. She didn't know the best way to skin a cat but believed there were many alternatives. Hers wasn't elegant, but it did the job. Her mouth was watering, her impatience growing. Natasha licked the blood from her fingers on her left hand as she began sawing through Renton's shoulder blade. About half way through she put the knife down and pulled at the leg twisting it until with a crunch, it popped free. Natasha pushed it against her lips and took a bite. Cat was even nicer without the fur. She groaned with pleasure at the relief.

27

It had been the happiest week of her life since that magical date with Joshua. The sex had only got better. She had continued losing weight and now turned heads wherever she went.

Natasha had never had this kind of attention before and she was loving every minute. Even Joshua had shed a few extra pounds. She was due to meet him that afternoon, and she planned on grabbing a quick bite to eat and then hitting the lingerie shop, a treat for her and Joshua. Their first night apart had been hard, she missed him greatly, but the revelation of Renton had nearly made it worth it. She had thought about the fresh meat, how it scratched that hunger itch that anything else she had eaten had failed to. Maybe she should go to the butchers or get another cat. She left her flat. As she locked the door, she turned and saw Mark. At least Kelly wasn't with him. He was just going into his flat when he saw her.

"Hello sweet thing, are you lost?" Mark had a wide smile. Natasha looked around, unable to believe he was talking to her.

"I live here," she mustered.

"You're the whale's new roommate?" He genuinely didn't recognise her.

"Yes, I just moved in, I'm Nat... Natalie. It's a lovely place. Natasha is lovely."

"If pigs are your thing, I guess. But that flat, it's a shit hole. You should see my gaff, its top-notch. You need to come and have a look, see how sweet these places can be. How about now?" He was eager.

Natasha looked him up and down. He was an arsehole, but he was a fit one. She liked Joshua, a lot, but the chance to shag Mark and rub Kelly's nose in it was too good to turn down.

"I've got a few minutes," Natasha smiled and Mark let her inside.

It was her first time in the flat. Mark wasn't lying, it was nice. Everything was expensive from the sofa to the TV to the rug. She could question some stylistic choices. It was a little too chavvy for her liking, but you couldn't dismiss the money that had been spent.

"It's lovely. What do you do for a living?" She was intrigued. She thought they were council tenants on benefits. This was closer to an investment bankers' pad than that of a job centre regular.

"A bit of this, a bit of that," Mark smiled widely. A thief or drug dealer was Natasha's first thought. Probably both, and nothing that required a great deal of intellect. But damn, that arse was tight. Natasha carried on looking around. She heard her tummy rumble… best make this quick.

"And the bedroom?" Natasha took him by the hand and invited Mark to lead the way. She should have eaten before she left. She wanted him and he was definitely keen too. They entered the bedroom, and she pushed him onto the bed. Mark could not believe his luck. He eagerly unbuckled his belt and slid his trousers down, exposing a forgettable penis.

Natasha placed herself on top of Mark rubbing herself against him; slowly at first as his erection grew until he was inside her. She began building up speed and Mark grabbed her thighs and squeezed. He was already ready, Natasha wasn't; this was far too quick. Natasha stopped and looked at Mark.

"What are you doing. Don't stop. Finish me off!" he pleaded. She slid down. He was fully erect. Mark leaned up and looked at Natasha. She smiled and got on to her knees, pulling him closer. Her stomach again rumbled as she started licking him, before she gently kissed the tip of his penis. Mark smiled and laid down flat. Natasha started sucking. Mark used his hands and forced her deeper on to him. She tried to pull back but wasn't able, so she went with it.

"Faster, faster." Mark was ready to explode. "Look at me, look me in the eye!" Mark was so close.

Natasha obliged. "Ow! Jesus less teeth!" Natasha didn't oblige, she bit down hard.

Mark screamed with pain. He tried to pull Natasha off him and failed. She clamped down firmly until she turned her head and ripped his penis clean off. She stood up in shock at what she had just done and spat out the appendage. Mark grabbed the area, which was streaming blood, but she wasn't done. She jumped on top of him and bit hard into his neck, ripped a chunk of flesh then another. He tried to push her off, but he couldn't muster the strength. Natasha chewed and swallowed the meat, maintaining eye contact all the way through. He couldn't fight back. After the next bite he stopped even trying to resist. He was done. His arms flopped down, and the bed was awash with red. He blinked one or two more times then just stared at the ceiling.

Natasha carried on eating, less frenzied, becoming content. Mark may not have been able to find her g-spot, but he satisfied her in the end. Natasha was no longer shocked or upset at what she had done. She looked at Mark's bloody, lifeless body and didn't feel regret. She felt a desire to carry on eating, which she did.

28

The bathroom was full of steam. Natasha stepped out of the shower and grabbed a towel to dry herself. Her clothes lay bloody, spread across the floor, red smears present on every surface. She walked back into the bedroom. She had covered Mark with a sheet, his face still exposed, his cheeks picked clean of their flesh, bone showing through. A phone rang and grabbed Natasha's attention. She looked around and found it next to the severed penis.

"Hey Josh, really sorry I was called into work. I tried to call but I didn't have any reception," she sat on the bed and continued drying her legs. "Yeah, I think it'll be a late one but how about lunch tomorrow?" She looked back over at Mark and moistened her lips, "That sounds great. I miss you."

Natasha put her phone down as she heard something vibrating. It wasn't her phone. She looked around and saw Mark's. Four missed calls and nine text messages - all from Kelly. Natasha let a wicked smile grow across her face. She looked at some of Mark's previous messages then she began to respond, "Hey babe. When u commin home, ive got a surprize for ya!!" That seemed to capture the tone. She was confident Kelly wouldn't question it. A minute passed then another message arrived. Kelly had taken the bait. She was on her way.

Natasha was clean, but very naked. Kelly was about her new size. She opened the wardrobe and began picking clothes out, throwing them onto the floor in disapproval. It was all so slutty. Natasha loved her new and improving figure, but this was just trash with a label. She found a nice pair of jeans and a top that she thought would show off her breasts, and she placed that carefully to one side and then put on the most ridiculous outfit she could find. She didn't intend on wearing it for long. Natasha looked at herself in the mirror and smirked. She had on red leopard-skin print leggings, a hot pink boob tube, and a blue pair of knee-high boots. Not a combination that should ever be worn together, but she really didn't think the trio were any more ridiculous for being together than they would have been alone.

Natasha made her way into the kitchen. She was hungry, but she wasn't looking for something to eat. She opened a few sets of draws and examined their contents. Kitchen towels? *Next.* Tin foil and clingfilm? Nope. Cutlery? *Getting warmer.* Natasha rustled through the contents and pulled out a steak knife. She gently touched the tip. It was sharp, but it wasn't very big. She placed it on the side, a reserve in case she couldn't come up with something better. She opened another draw and produced a stainless-steel meat tenderiser. *This was more like it.* She gave a few practice swings into midair. It seemed okay, a usable weight. She took a swing at the front of the microwave, the glass panel smashed and the head of the tenderiser was stuck, but a good strong tug freed it. She placed it next to the steak knife. Her arsenal was growing. Where were the big knives? Natasha smiled, "There you are."

A series of knives were held to a strip on the wall. A large carving knife fitted the bill; she checked the sharpness of the blade and was satisfied. She took the knife and the tenderiser to the living room and took a seat. She produced Mark's phone and composed another message.

"In the bedroom babez, close your eyes 4 ur surprise"

Within minutes, a key entered the lock, and the door swung open. Kelly threw her handbag to the floor and removed her jacket as she shut the door behind her. She stopped, adjusted her bra and skirt then calmly walked towards the closed bedroom door.

"Marky babe, I'm ready for my surprise," Kelly entered covering her eyes with both hands. Natasha quietly strode behind her.

"Marky?" Kelly uncovered her eyes and stared in disbelief, not able to process the scene before her. She took one step back and bumped off of Natasha and turned to face her. "Fatasha?" She recognised her. *Good, that would make it more satisfying.*

Natasha smiled as she brought the tenderiser down onto Kelly's temple. She staggered back, surprised she didn't even try to defend herself from the second blow as the stainless steel crunched into her nose and mouth. Kelly crumbled to the floor and tried to scream, but all she could muster was a frightened, muffled sob. She struggled to breathe through her smashed nose, her broken teeth with blood and enamel finding their way to her throat. Natasha tossed the tenderiser to the floor and produced the knife. Kelly's eyes widened as she realised these were her last moments. Natasha pinned Kelly to the floor and held the knife to her eye.

"I'm not fat now bitch," she slowly pushed the knife into Kelly's eye, it popped as the tip entered and the blade slowly slid into the socket. One last push and brain met metal and Kelly's life was extinguished.

Natasha stood back, looking at her work. She saw meat and didn't want to waste it. Moving to the kitchen, she emptied the fridge, throwing the contents onto the floor. None of it was any good to her now. She finally could satisfy her hunger and a jar of gherkins or lowfat yoghurt would not cut it. A slice of Mark and Kelly though, would hit the spot.

29

Without Renton the apartment seemed empty and soulless. For so many years he had been a dedicated companion. He had calmed Natasha when she was upset, made her feel loved and needed. He had done nothing but love her. Now what remained of his carcass was in the kitchen bin, covered in household waste, slowly rotting. Natasha sat silently, waiting for her next meal. She had been ducking Joshua for the few days since she made her first kills, with no intention of seeing him until she had finished with Mark and Kelly. He had kept calling, sounding more and more desperate in each voicemail. He had been banging at the door on and off for nearly half an hour. Natasha remained quiet and still. Calm and relaxed.

"I'm so hungry Natasha, I have to see you. I've done something terrible. Please!"

desperation tinged with anger in Joshua's voice, Natasha recognised it. She wasn't sympathetic. It irritated her. He had been getting progressively louder and desperate. Natasha didn't need the attention so relented and threw the door open, dragging Joshua inside. He looked a mess, his skin was pale, he was sweaty, and his shirt covered in food stains. He ran straight into the kitchen and ransacked the fridge and cupboards.

"Where's the food, I need to eat!" he pleaded with Natasha.

"I don't have any, it's all gone." Joshua continued his

doomed search before slumping to the floor in failure.

"I don't know what's wrong with me. I can't concentrate. I have to eat. Look at me, I'm a fucking mess!"

"What did you do Joshua. What's this terrible thing you did?"

He was like her, she knew as soon as he had knocked on the door. She wondered if she looked as bad as him. Natasha glanced down at her arms. She wasn't as pale or sweaty but she had changed. She had calmed since she had tasted human flesh, so maybe that was it. Maybe she could give him a little of Mark or Kelly. A taste.

"I stole," he quietly admitted.

"You stole?" *What a pussy.* She'd killed and eaten a cat and two people, and he had stolen something.

"Yes, I, I took two packs of sausages." He seemed ashamed, he still had shame.

"That's not too bad," she let out with a breath.

"I ate them raw in the shop. They threw me out." That was disgusting, but still lower league stuff compared to Natasha's recent exploits.

"I don't know what's happening to me," he was tearful. He was pathetic. Natasha pondered. Should she share her meagre meat supplies or just kill Joshua? Use her precious chunks of human flesh or add to it. Joshua didn't look in great shape, but he would be a few meals at the very least.

"One more chance," she muttered under her breath and stood over him. "It will be okay. We're changing. I don't know how or why, but I felt like you. Now I feel, well I feel fantastic. You need to pull yourself together. I can help you, but you need to sort yourself out. Stay here," Natasha left the flat.

Joshua wiped his tears away and struggled to his feet, he had a small tremor running down his left arm causing him to rub it vigorously. He breathed deeply and tried to compose himself.

Natasha returned with a small piece of Tupperware and handed it to Joshua, "Try this."

Joshua took the tub and popped open the top. Inside were

bloody slices of meat. He picked up a slice and sniffed it.

"What is it?" he was salivating but hesitant.

"Just eat it."

He slowly popped it into his mouth and chewed. A smile crept across his face as he quickly scoffed the rest, a disgusting sight. Finishing the meat in double quick time, he licked at the inside of the container and when that was free of blood, he attended to his fingers and the gore spread around his mouth.

"Is there any more?" He finally felt satisfied, but still hungry. The stingy portion he'd been afforded was a snack, and he needed a meal.

"That'll do for now. I don't want you to be sick." Joshua had calmed, sweet relief.

"I did a bad thing too," Natasha confessed. She took Joshua's hand and led him out of the apartment to Mark and Kelly's. At first Joshua was confused, but then he started sniffing the air and became excited, like a hound picking up the scent of a fox.

"This way," Natasha led Joshua from the living room into the bedroom. Blood on the floor, the bed, the walls. Everything soaked or splashed with the deep red claret.

Joshua stepped in and took a deep long sniff, "Where are they?"

Natasha motioned over to the kitchen and Joshua entered eagerly. On the floor, two partially butchered corpses, bloody bones and bits of flesh.

Joshua dived onto the pile and started sucking the meat off of the bones, desperately trying to pick clean the remains and not waste an ounce of the magnificent flesh. Natasha watched. She thought she'd done a decent enough job of removing the flesh, but obviously, Joshua's desperation drove him to try hard for remaining scraps. She'd let him finish then tell him about the meat in the fridge and the importance of rationing it. At the moment, he had to get past that initial hunger.

30

Natasha had instructed Joshua to shower. He had settled since picking clean the two corpses across the hall, but even before the blood and gore, he had looked a mess. She stood naked in the bedroom, admiring her slim physique in the mirror. Her pert breasts, tight arse, long slender legs and perfect waistline. Despite gorging herself, she had continued losing weight, and she thought she looked perfect. She may have become a monster on the inside, but she no longer cared about that, she looked fabulous on the outside. After suffering years of being looked at as a freak, she was enjoying her new beauty. Joshua joined her. His belly bulged with the recent feed, his skin maybe a little paler, his eyes a little greyer.

"How are you feeling?" she enquired without looking away from her own reflection.

"Hungry." It was as much a grunt as a response.

"Take it slowly."

He was still wet from the shower, fumbling with his clothes as he got dressed. He wasn't concentrating on the task in hand, his hunger preoccupied him. Shirt and jeans barely on, he left Natasha to her mirror and left the flat, swiping the keys to Mark and Kelly's along the way.

At the front door, he struggled to insert the key, missing the hole by millimeters several times before he clicked it into place. Joshua smiled instinctively and entered. His nose instantly picked up the scent. Must eat. A few flies had gathered around the bloodstained bedroom and the rotting pile of bones in the kitchen. This didn't bother Joshua as he made his way through the living room to the kitchen. He opened the fridge and there they were, maybe a dozen bloody containers each filled to the brim with meat. *So hungry.* Joshua popped the top off a container and grabbed a handful of meat forcing it all into his mouth, barely chewing as he swallowed. The next tub didn't last any longer. Nor the next. *Eat.* In a few minutes, it was all gone. Every piece of Tupperware and old takeaway container was emptied of human meat. Every drop of blood licked clean. *More.* Joshua was frantic. He needed more; he craved it. The look of desperation on his face was nothing to the look of anger Natasha showed as she stood behind, pure disbelief of the greed.

"What have you done?"

Joshua turned around and snarled at Natasha.

Her food was gone, and just this moron remained. Maybe he would do? He would be several days worth of sustenance and she was already hungry. Time to make the best of a bad situation and Joshua had become that. Joshua bared his bloody teeth as he approached Natasha, his eyes grey, his skin pale, his belly bloated with flesh. She was at boiling point. How fucking dare he turn on her? Who the hell does he think he is? She grabbed a knife she had previously put to good use and stabbed Joshua in the stomach and pushed him onto the floor. He hadn't given up and grabbed a handful of her top and dragged her closer to him, his teeth gnashing, eager to get a bite. Natasha pushed his face away and continued to stab his torso to no effect.

"Why won't you die?!" she screamed at him as she pushed him away and climbed back to her feet.

He scrambled after her on all fours, sliding in his own viscous, discoloured blood, unable to gain traction. Natasha stepped back to give herself room and gave a hard kick to Joshua's head, sending him face-first towards a kitchen cabinet.

He snapped back at her, more determined than ever. Natasha slashed at his face with the blade, opening up several wounds but still, he persisted. Joshua leapt up from the floor and sent Natasha tumbling on to her back the knife falling just out of her reach to her right. He desperately tried to bite her face. She gripped his throat trying to keep him at bay with one hand and reach the tantalisingly close knife with the other, her right hand just millimetres from the blade. Her left hand gripped ever tighter, his greying blood started to run down her fingertips as she dug in deeper. Natasha gathered all her strength and threw Joshua to her left side, ripping his throat partially out, his flesh stuck under her bloody nails. She moved herself towards the knife and grabbed it. Joshua wasn't so much as dazed by his throat protruding from his neck. He was now as angry as he was hungry, the rage spilling out of him at the same rate as his greying blood. In one clean motion, Natasha swung the knife into Joshua's ear through to his brain. He stopped instantly and slumped to the floor, the knife still embedded in his skull. Natasha scrambled away and tried to catch her breath, careful not to keep her eyes off of Joshua. What had become of him? How come she wasn't a snarling beast like him? She had so many questions but nobody to answer them. She had liked Joshua, maybe had even loved him a little. Now she was alone again, and hungry.

Natasha got to her feet and gave Joshua's lifeless body a hard kick to the chest.

"Fucking arsehole," she composed herself and straightened her clothes.

She would have to raid Kelly's wardrobe again before leaving the apartment. Walking back into the kitchen, she hoped he had left her something, a scrap of meat, a piece of offal, anything. There was nothing. Joshua hadn't left so much as a crumb. That selfish bastard. She walked back through to the living room and stared at him. Could she? Should she? What choice did she have?

Natasha pulled the knife from Joshua's ear, a pop signalled it coming free. She kneeled down next to him. He was skinnier than he was when they met. But still some flesh ready to be harvested. She sliced off a small slither of his upper arm, and looked at the meat. It wasn't as appetising as Mark or Kelly; it was discoloured, felt almost rubbery in her hand. She gave it a sniff, and it didn't smell good. Natasha held the slither to her mouth and touched it with the tip of her tongue. Her face screwed up at the foul taste. She was hungry. It wasn't good, but it was all she had. Natasha quickly threw the slice in her mouth and chewed, her face contorted as she struggled with the taste and the chewy texture. She swallowed. Straight away, she doubled over and threw up all over the floor, collapsing in a coughing fit. The vomit tasted much better than the meat, but the experience was still unpleasant.

Natasha sat and looked at the mess as her stomach rumbled. She pondered how Mabel was, and how she might taste.

31

Standing naked, blood smeared down her face, arms and breasts, Natasha looked around the the room. It was that of an elderly person, the decorations and furniture aged but looked after. She licked the blood from her wrist like a cat cleaning itself after a meal. Mabel had been an old girl and had barely scratched the itch Natasha had for human flesh. The meat on her was tough and stringy but it was human meat and it had taken the edge off. But for how long? She was running out of neighbours to eat and knew she'd been shitting on her own doorstep. It had been easy, but the risk would only increase. Her clothes were neatly folded in a corner. She was tired of getting them covered in blood. Mabel, bless her, was stunned when Natasha started stripping off before her. Natasha had been able to calmly approach Mabel before ripping out her throat with just her teeth. She had barely screamed, a mere scared whimper.

Natasha wandered to the bathroom, a terracotta suite that lacked a shower. She started to run the bath, smelling the various shampoos, body washes and bubble bath solutions before finding something suitable to use. As the bath began to fill and bubbles formed, she searched the medicine cabinet, tossing aside toothpaste and pill bottles before finding a pot of toothpicks. Carefully, she plucked out a single pick and began digging flesh from her teeth, looking carefully at each meaty morsel before licking them off of the stick and swallowing. The bath nearly filled, she slipped in, the bubbly water turning pale red as the blood mixed with the suds. She sighed a deep relaxed sigh as she closed her eyes.

Maybe she should fire up a dating app or better yet, a hookup app to find some lonely or horny soul and fool about before a good feed. That might take time, not a bad idea but not one for a quick feast. It was a Friday. Tonight, there would be plenty of suitors out in town, plenty of men desperate to shag her. She didn't linger for long in the bath. It wasn't for relaxation but to clean the thick crimson staining her skin. After a few scrubs of her pale flesh, she stood from the bath, the blood-tinged water dripping from her. Clean enough, she would only get bloody again anyway.

32

The club was full, and the queue snaked around the velvet ropes in front of the building. Natasha wasn't one for queuing anymore. With great confidence, she strode forward bypassing the holding pen to the annoyance of the women, and lust of the men. The two male bouncers allowed her through without so much as a second thought, their female colleague was less impressed but did nothing to halt the injustice to those waiting patiently in line.

Inside, men and women of all ages danced, drank and were having a good time. Natasha had been to a club once in her life, on a team night out at work. She had hated every second of her colleagues enjoying themselves whilst she had done little more than sit in a dark corner drinking bottled cocktails. Tonight was different, eyes were upon her; she'd not be seeking the anonymity of the darkness tonight. A young man gave her a wide smile. She smiled in return, and he approached. Natasha pulled him closer and kissed him passionately.

"I'll have a vodka and coke." He disappeared into the crowd to undertake his orders.

Natasha didn't feel the need to wait for his return before she started grinding against another man who didn't seem to mind nearly as much as his girlfriend. She kissed him and watched him as he was dragged away by his irate other half. She eyed up several other men. Sure they'd be fun, but she didn't need a good lay, she needed a good feed. With a full belly, there would be time for fun. Natasha didn't need a man with a six-pack, desperate and fat would be her prey. The male equivalent of who she used to be. Somewhere in a dark corner nursing a drink had to be a grotesquely overweight man just getting through the night. She just had to find the fat fuck.

Natasha danced through the club as she searched and there he was. A magnificent specimen, late twenties, maybe 6-feet tall, close to 18 stones in weight and importantly alone. He sat at a table on the edge of the club and nursed a bottled alcopop as he stared blankly at his smartphone. She slid up to him with a wide smile as she gently placed her hand on his back, startling him.

"Hi!" Bright and breezy but he was still unsure.

"Sorry, can I help you?" Bless him, he seemed scared.

"I'm Nat, I'll be honest with you. I've always had a thing for bigger men."

"Is this a joke? Did Jon tell you to come over?"

Natasha slid in even closer and placed her hand on his leg and slowly slid it up to his crotch, finding his penis. It didn't take much work to get it fully erect.

"What's your name?"

"Brian."

His dick was an okay size, she thought. But it didn't matter. She grabbed hold of it through his trousers and started rubbing it vigorously. Brian was in shock but enjoying it. She kissed him as she continued pulling him off and he climaxed before their lips drifted apart.

"I'm sorry," he apologised, but Natasha just smiled at him.

"Want to come back to mine?"

Brian nodded enthusiastically at improving what was already probably the best night of his life.

Natasha led Brian out of the club and bumped into the man she last saw disappearing towards the bar to buy her a drink. He didn't seem too bothered as he consoled himself by shoving his tongue down the throat of another girl. He shot a bemused look at Brian before continued with his new would-be conquest.

*

Bloody and satisfied Natasha lay in the bath as it slowly filled with water. The red bubbles turned pink as they increased in volume. She smiled. She had only eaten part of one of Brian's legs. The rest she had butchered with an increasing professionalism and stored in the fridge-freezer. His fatty flesh was so much more satisfying than the well-toned or wrinkly bodies she had so far consumed. Brian would last at least a week, maybe more. She had a couple of days to relax and not worry about her next meal. Maybe she'd go back to the club and find a man for some sexual satisfaction. Hell, she might even try to pull a woman; she'd always been curious.

The water nearly touched her chin as she gently turned off the tap with her foot. She then disappeared under the water. After a few moments, she emerged, eyes closed with a beaming smile. Life was good.

33

Tonight, Natasha opted for a different club to be cautious. It was a quieter night, but she was determined to have her fun. A fresh meal of Brian had set her up for the evening. All she had to do was find a few acceptable specimens that would give her some fun. There was so much she'd wanted to try for so long. Joshua had been fun until he started to change. But he was a normal man. He was someone Natasha believed she would never have had a chance with before her change; but he wasn't special. She wanted to experience it all - muscular, athletic, well hung, women, threesomes, younger, older, everything - and it started tonight. She was intent on having fun in the club and then carrying on the party elsewhere.

She had eyes on her once again as she circled the club before spotting her target - a mixed-race man in his mid-twenties easily clearing 6-feet in height, muscular build and a strong smile. The light caught his teeth; they were bright white and perfect. He would be the start. He hadn't seen Natasha approach, and it was only when she was grinding up against him, did he realise what was happening. He joined in and they all but fucked on the dance floor. They were all over each other. Fellow clubbers gave them space in case full-on intercourse ensued. Natasha pulled his face close and kissed him for what felt like forever before tilting his head so she could gently whisper into his ear.

"Wanna fuck?" He smiled, and she dragged his hulking frame across the club to the women's toilets, bursting past two women exiting without slowing down.

The cubicle door flung open and slammed shut. She pulled at his trousers until she was face to face with his large penis which she immediately took as much of him in her mouth as she could. He placed his hands on her head and guided her pace. She pulled his hands off and he placed them back on. She thought for a second about biting down but decided against it, instead standing up and dropping her panties before bending over and pushing herself towards her lover. He didn't need any further encouragement and began thrusting much to Natasha's pleasure. She moaned and groaned unable to control herself, her ecstasy as much from the excitement of the situation as the mountain of the man she was with.

He spluttered and hunched over her done.

"Can I get a number?" he asked.

They both stood up and attempted to straighten themselves out. Natasha shook her panties off her ankle and stuck them in her pocket.

"You're number one, now head off like a good boy. I need to pee and find number two," she pushed him through the door of the stall and locked it behind him.

He stood for a moment in the middle of the ladies' toilet, bemused by what has just occurred as two girls entered.

"What the hell?" one of them piped up.

Embarrassed he quickly departed.

The toilet flushed and Natasha emerged to freshen herself up. One of the girls turned to her, "There was a guy in here."

Natasha was already reapplying her lipstick. "Fucking creeps everywhere, how do I look?" She turned to face the girls who weren't interested. "I think the word you're looking for is stunning," Natasha flashed them a smile and headed back to the dance floor to find her number two.

34

Brian had lasted for just a week. She had hoped for longer, but she'd been unable to help herself. His tasty, satisfying blubber had really hit the spot and as hard as she tried, the portions she afforded herself continued to grow in size and frequency. She hadn't actively hunted for more food since Brian. She'd had far too much fun indulging in several hookups a night, men and women, old and young. A 70-year-old grandfather proved a far better lay than a young strapping 17-year-old lad she'd picked up. Experience truly was underrated. She had tried women, but it wasn't her thing. She was happy to have tried the experience but would rather suck a dick than go down on a woman.

Her last meal would cover her for a few hours before the hunger would start playing on her mind. She was getting known in the clubs. Women despised her and the men knew she was an easy lay. Getting her next meal at one of the local clubs wouldn't be a good idea. She didn't need to be a missing person's last known sighting. She could pick up someone anywhere, it really didn't matter, desperate lonely people were everywhere. As long as they were fat, they were the best. It didn't matter where she found them or what she had to do to get them back to hers.

She had decided a local board game shop would be her deli for the day. Lonely geeks who didn't look after themselves.

The funkier smells a human produces didn't seem nearly as offensive as they used to. She had passed the shop several times. Its key demographic seemed to fit in with her preferred menu choice.

*

She had been in the shop for a few minutes, browsing the wares and the clientele. A few met her criteria. *Wiry and tall. No, thank you.* She saw one who was short and fat, but why waste the effort of a kill for ultimately fewer meals from a short arse? One boy was a strong contender for her freezer space. Maybe 6-feet tall, a touch under 20-stone and at most 21-years old. She found him repulsive, but he was perfect. She had doubts about her plan. In the confusion of a club she could stalk, entrap her prey and disappear with them and no one would notice. Here there were witnesses, all of whom had spent their time staring at her since she entered. If she walked out with this lad, she'd be the talk of the local board gaming scene. When he disappeared, it wouldn't take long to join the dots back to her.

"Excuse me, do you have the Love Island Monopoly?" She needed her out.

"Sorry, just the ones you see." She thanked the worker and left.

Across the street, a bus stop seemed a suitable place for Natasha to wait. A few people were already waiting, complaining the buses had been delayed. She waited, staring at her meal to be. Waiting for him to leave, to be alone. Then she could make her move.

"It's all gone to hell I tell you. These buses, honestly they've been delayed and cancelled all day yesterday and now today. Then you have these people attacking each other. Honestly, people are just awful. I've only come out to get my pension. I'll be home locking the door as soon as this silly bus comes." This little old dear reminded her of Mabel.

Natasha surprised even herself by not being filled with guilt of her slaughter of that kind old girl. "I'm just waiting for someone," she smiled but didn't want the attention.

"Well, you should be careful. A pretty girl like you needs to look after herself." *I look after myself just fine* Natasha thought. "They said on the radio this morning that these attacks, people are biting each other. Honestly, have you ever heard anything so disgusting?"

Natasha's interest was piqued. It couldn't be, could it? "I haven't seen any news."

"Well, people seem to have gone demented. Honestly, I don't know what's wrong with them. Fighting and biting. My friend Doris told me that the police had taken away her neighbour for eating his girlfriend." The old girl was enjoying being listened to.

"I had no idea." Natasha genuinely didn't.

"Doris is probably off her medication again. She likes to tell stories."

Natasha had been so absorbed with herself that she hadn't been paying attention. With all of her fornicating, she had snogged, and fucked so many men and women, she might have had infected others like she had Joshua. Then others who had been taking FatBGone. Surely they would have had a similar reaction to her. It could have affected thousands. Her next thought wasn't that of fear for humanity, but of how disgusting the infected tasted. She didn't like the thought of living in a world without people to feast upon.

She looked back up to the shop, her target wasn't there. The fat bastard had given her the slip. She desperately looked around and caught sight of him further down the street and immediately gave chase pushing past those waiting in line for the bus.

She was fixed on him as he waddled down the street without a care in the world. Natasha was able to close the distance quickly until she was in striking distance, she slowed so as not to startle her prey. A big friendly smile began to spread across her face, she was ready.

"Excuse me, sorry, excuse me."

At first he didn't turn around. He wasn't used to women talking to him on the street, so he had no reason to believe he was being addressed. Natasha reached out and touched his shoulder causing him to flinch, "Sorry, were you just in the board game shop?"

He was in shock, Natasha loved that expression. It was powerful and something she could never previously achieve.

"Yes," he squeaked.

"I know this might seem odd but I saw you and thought you looked nice. I wonder if you could help me?" She had spent so much of her life lacking confidence it had become easy to replicate. "I'm Natasha."

"Kevin, I'm Kevin."

"Hi Kevin. I was wondering if you'd like to come to my flat and help me," she touched his arm. "I have a few games for my nephew, and I know he'll want to play them with his favourite auntie. Do you think you can teach me?" Kevin was a deer in the headlights. "And maybe I could teach you something?"

Natasha hooked their arms together, and she led him away for dinner.

35

Kenneth Addo was in his late twenties, muscular build and at over 6 feet 6 inches. He was an imposing black man with perhaps the friendliest smile in the whole British Army. His parents were Ghanaian immigrants who welcomed Kenneth to the world three days after they arrived in Swansea where a number of their extended family had settled in the seventies. He was a proud Ghanaian, and a prouder Welshman. His physique making him a forceful presence on the rugby field. He was looking at a professional career until on a night out he was set upon by a group of white men who wanted nothing more than to beat the shit out of a young black man. He was strong and tall back then as an 18-year-old, but he wasn't a fighter then and they didn't fight fair.

Along with the fractured skull, collapsed lung, a broken nose, ribs, fingers and wrist, they had done a job on his left knee. In the next two years, he'd made an excellent recovery, but his knee would never pass a medical examination by a professional rugby club even if he could get in the door. Rugby would not be his future. He missed being part of a team and couldn't find work that he engaged with. His formal education was cut short along with his sporting career. Stacking shelves at the local Sainsbury's was a job, but he wanted to make a difference.

The British Army welcomed Kenneth. He was an excellent

soldier, hardworking, intelligent and brave. No one had a bad word to say about him, and his closest comrades would follow him anywhere. A tour of Afghanistan saw him in action, charging an enemy machine-gun nest, saving his pinned-down squad. He received the military cross and a bullet in the shoulder. After recovering, Kenneth spent a further month in Kabul before returning to the UK for his next duty. It seemed like a step-down, but the assignment was temporary for him and his colleagues. With a heightened terrorism threat because of the West's involvement overseas, soldiers were providing armed guard services to many key intelligence and strategic installations. They deemed the Wellworth Research centre key and worthy of having a contingent of up to 20 soldiers permanently based on the site.

In the heart of the countryside in Lewes, there was a single narrow road in; it was secluded and that suited those who ran the centre. A bus service shuttled civilians to the site and back into the local town just over two miles away. A few locals would cycle in, only the more senior staff members were afforded a parking permit to get through security to the limited parking facilities. Many of the scientists would stay on-site for days at a time if their workload required and Wellworth facilitated this with sleeping quarters.

Kenneth didn't know too much about what he was guarding. But every day, he saw men and women in white coats wandering around the small campus. It was already well protected with a large enforced fence around the perimeter, a protected gate, and more CCTV than seemed necessary. They upgraded the gated entrance, from unarmed private security to a team of four soldiers equipped with their L85A3 assault rifles. They supplemented the outer perimeter fence with a secondary one, smaller but sturdy. An observation post mounted on the four-storey central building that overlooked the single and double floored buildings around it. The OP housed two more soldiers, a sniper and his observer. Two teams of two patrolled the fence line at all times. Private security was still used, but now purely internally. They monitored the screens in the CCTV room, performed standard checks through the buildings, and liaised with the commanding officer.

There was resentment between the two sets. The professional soldiers hated the under-qualified overpaid civilians. Those same civilians hated being replaced by gun-toting Rambos who swanned in and took control. Kenneth stayed out of the petty rivalry; he had a job to do, and he would do it. Whether he was standing at the gate waving through scientists, janitors or politicians, patrolling the perimeter in gale-force winds and rain or getting a numb arse spotting for the marksman, he did his job.

He was coming off his shift from patrolling the grounds and was in the barracks stripping off. The rain had been relentless and even with waterproofs, he was wet through. He'd taken some guilty pleasure during the handover with the dry and happy men about to take over. They had laughed at him and his partner, a little too slow on the uptake to realise they were about to enjoy their own drenching. The corner of the barracks had a TV and two sofas, somewhere for downtime. Normally, one or two of the soldiers would watch some sport or a film. Today, the news was getting their attention. Kenneth walked past, naked with his towel slung over his shoulder. The images gripped the assembled men, police in riot gear deploying water cannons and falling back. The aggressors were not the usual hippies, thugs or impressionable youths. They were a full-on cross-section of society. Men and women, young and old, skinheads and teen Asian girls.

"What are they protesting about now?" Kenneth was nonchalant and had no shame about standing naked amongst the others. They didn't notice or care.

"I don't think they said. Just people being dicks," responded the squaddie.

Kenneth carried on to the shower. He was cold and tired. Shower, wank, food and bed were his plans.

He had only been in the shower a few moments when an alarm sounded. "For fuck's sake," Kenneth muttered, he rinsed the soap off himself and grabbed his towel before making his way to the barracks.

The men from around the TV were busy getting into uniform with an officer screaming orders. "Briefing room in five!" He left the barracks in a hurry.

"What the fuck's going on?" Kenneth asked.

"It's all kicking off. That riot on the TV, it's happening everywhere," efficiently responded a soldier hurriedly tying his boots.

Kenneth began to join the others, quickly getting dressed. His only pressed uniform was balled up on the floor in its own puddle of rainwater and was no longer looking as presentable. He grabbed another. It was clean and dry, but he feared he'd be crucified for the state it was in. No time to worry. He quickly dressed and was the last out of the door.

They made their way to the main building and to the second-floor briefing room. The private security guards were flapping but oblivious to what all the fuss was about; they were to be excluded. Several senior looking men and women in white coats shuffled into the briefing room ahead of the military personnel. Only the soldiers on duty were excused, but several unfamiliar uniformed men were present of varying ranks.

"All, none of what you hear today is to be discussed with those not in this room. Not your girlfriend, the receptionist, your uncle Bob or the rent a wanker security twat you steal money from at poker. This is top secret." The Major wasn't a regular on-site, but Kenneth had seen him before. "You may know of the evolving situation outside. What you have seen on the news and may have heard from friends and family is sadly the tip of the iceberg. The government and our superiors have been putting measures into place to safeguard Great Britain and as many of its citizens as we can."

This seemed pretty unbelievable. Too unbelievable. When in Afghanistan, Kenneth had got used to emergency drills, exercises and tests at the expense of rest and nerves. This had a very familiar smell to it. He'd foregone his wank and dinner for this shit?

"We have begun creating survivor centres throughout the country. Many of your fellow soldiers are there now, digging trenches and erecting fences. Whilst you enjoy your creature comforts, they're actually soldiering."

Fair play to him, Kenneth thought. This Major was enjoying his act and was convincing.

"There is something infecting people, and we know nothing about it. This research facility will be at the forefront in investigating and they will need protection. In the coming days, that fence will attract those looking for safety, looking to officials, soldiers for help and protection. Let me make this clear. That is not your fucking job! Your job is to protect this facility and the people within it."

Okay, this isn't the normal shit. Kenneth sat up and paid attention.

"You will be reinforced with 40 men in the next two days. Your rules of engagement are to do what you need to protect this facility and its people. The private security will be relieved once we are reinforced."

A soldier raised his hand, "Sir?" He nervously spluttered the words out.

"This is not a Q and A at your damn book club." He wasn't angry, it was becoming obvious this was just the Major's manner. "Go on."

The soldier was Bobby, young and very green. Maybe this is why the Major allowed his interruption. "My mother and sister sir, they're out there," Bobby got the words out despite his lack of confidence.

"I appreciate you all have loved ones out there. And we will pick them up if we haven't done so already," the Major gave the most forced, insincere smile, matched by Bobby trying to pretend he was satisfied with the response.

"I will give you orders in due course. Those just off shift, you'll have four hours' downtime. All of you need to check out equipment from the armoury. You are to be armed at all times. Dismissed."

The squaddies followed their order and began departing, leaving the Major talking to the white coats.

"You!" the Major signalled to Kenneth. "Iron that fucking uniform!" Kenneth nodded, cursing under his breath, he nearly got away with it.

36

It had been a busy shift and Amy was well and truly fed up. The world was going crazy, and she found herself filling out paperwork three hours after her shift had ended. Her sergeant had already told her to expect to be called back in so to hurry, finish her forms and to get home to get some sleep. Expect to be called back in? Amy wasn't even sure she'd make it home and was eyeing up a corner of the canteen to get some shuteye.

In the last two days, things had been getting worse. Several frenzied attacks had at first been put down to a new street drug that hadn't yet earned a fantastical name. However, when the perpetrators were everyday average people, mums with their children, middle-aged bank managers, teenagers and would-be brides, something was obviously off. It wasn't just Croydon experiencing this phenomenon - police forces all over the country were reporting the same occurrences. They had been pushed to the absolute limit; all leave had been cancelled. The fact that this was happening everywhere meant no neighbouring police force could support another.

When Amy eventually made it to her makeshift accommodation, the 24 hours news station blaring away in the corner of the canteen was reporting the same stories of frenzied attacks all over the world. Riots on the streets of Croydon was one thing, but aerial footage of small villages suffering the same levels of violence was jarring. A small group of exhausted police officers nursed cups of tea and biscuits, glad to have some relief from being on the frontline. Amy didn't want to socialise. The other officers around her speculated the cause and what the future held, but Amy had no time for such frivolities. Sleep was all she cared about now. Whatever craziness was occurring would be there after whatever sleep she'd get.

37

The ink was barely dry on the contract. Cahill and the other board members had disappeared off into the sunset, prepared only to emerge to pick up their profit share cheques every year. Gareth didn't want to stick around. His job was done. NewU Pharma had paid him handsomely as had EverGreen. He didn't need to work another day ever again. He was now a rockstar in his field. Everything was perfect.

When he picked up the paper, everything was perfect. Flicked on the radio, perfect. Drove to the gym in his classic Aston Martin, the very definition of perfect. It was when Gareth failed to read the story about a spate of vicious attacks. It was when he ignored the news bulletin about the civil unrest up and down the country. It was perfect as he drove past the woman tearing out a teenage boy's throat with her teeth on a deserted street.

The gyms car park was empty. With a fat pill that works, the gym had become a more solitary experience. It was a modern building, a large glass-fronted first floor for the members to gaze out from as they went for a spin on a bike or run on a treadmill. The changing room was empty too, only a solitary attendant was in the building. They had tried to talk to Gareth but he had his headphones and signalled he couldn't hear. Instead, he just walked off and ignored the staff member.

10K on the cross trainer and Gareth was a little out of breath and a little sweaty. The TVs were all displaying the news across several channels. Finally, Gareth stopped to take notice. He unplugged his headphones from his smartphone and plugged them into the nearest piece of gym equipment and changed the audio channel to match that of the nearest screen.

"The public are being advised to stay inside with the Prime Minister due to make a statement shortly." the news anchor looked dishevelled and genuinely scared.

"What the fuck was going on?" Gareth pondered as he mopped the sweat from his face. The other screens had similarly confused and anxious reporters, cutting between footage of scenes more like a war zone than an average British high street. Gareth unplugged his headphones and drifted towards the glass front of the gym.

A solitary figure stumbled down the street, probably drunk. Quiet. So very quiet.

"Excuse me." Gareth turned with a jolt, it was the same staff member he'd seen earlier.

"Yes. What?" he was a little embarrassed for being startled.

"As I said earlier, we need to close early today. You have to leave. Now."

Gareth didn't say a word. He was confused and slipped into autopilot. Walking through the empty corridor to the men's changing room, he passed the female changing room. He could hear a sobbing.

"Not my problem," he spoke softly to himself as he continued. In the changing room he didn't stop to shower, he changed out of his sweaty gym gear into his street clothes, got his keys and checked his phone. No messages: no one to care about him or check if he was okay. In addition he had no one for him to check in on. Home, a gin and watch from his apartment the drama on the streets below until it had all blown over.

He passed the women's changing room, the sobbing continued. Gareth didn't know why he opened the door, maybe it was his natural predator instinct. A woman who was upset was an easy target. He could sweep in as the good guy, make her feel better, fuck her then dump her back where he found her. He didn't care about her wellbeing. She was sat hunched over, sobbing wildly on a bench, facing away from Gareth at the far end of the room.

"Are you okay?" He could still fake sincere when he needed to.

She stopped crying and sat up, pausing for just a moment. "I'm so hungry. I can't stop. I can't bloody stop!" the girl turned to face Gareth. Early twenties, brunette, slim, maybe 5 feet 4 inches tall. She was so very pale; her skin so lacking in colour it looked almost grey. Her lips were bright red, as she spoke so were her teeth. "I don't know what's wrong with me," she rose to her feet and faced him. In her hands she had a human foot, much of the flesh had been torn away, the bone exposed.

"What the fuck?!" Gareth edged back, and she started moving towards him.

"I need to eat. I can't stop. You have to understand. I need it," she dropped the foot and approached him gaining pace. "Help me, please!" Her voice was fearful but there was something else, something more malevolent.

Gareth backed out and slammed the door shut, running as fast as he could. He ran to the end of the hallway and turned back to see the girl giving a slow pursuit. He threw the door open to reception area and continued running. The staff member was in the reception locking up the office, and Gareth narrowly missed him as he ran past.

"Arsehole," the staff member muttered under his breath.

Gareth burst through the exit and was halfway to his car. He fumbled for his keys, looking nervously around. A loud scream erupted from within the gym. This gave Gareth added focus. With the door open, he was sitting down and starting the engine within seconds. He looked in the rearview, the staff member came running out, blood pouring from his neck. The girl followed at a slower pace than before. Gareth threw the car into gear, released the handbrake and put his foot down.

He whipped out of the car park to an eerily empty street

allowing him to put his foot down, driving far beyond the speed limit.

After a couple of miles he slowed down, but he still drove faster than was legal. He whipped through crossings and traffic lights. He didn't know what was going on but guessed that what had happened to that girl is happening elsewhere. He didn't want to be on the streets; he wanted to get back to his apartment and barricade himself inside until the police got their shit together. As he was thinking of the relative safety of his apartment, his attention wandered. He didn't see the small red car coming across the roundabout.

He just clipped the back of the Ford Fiesta which spun around and hit a lamppost side on. Gareth's Aston spun and then flipped, landing on its roof skidding slowly to a halt against the curb on the other side of the junction. Gareth was stunned but conscious, finding himself suspended upside down, blood dripping from his head to the ceiling beneath him, pooling amongst the broken glass. He looked around but there was no help coming. He placed his left hand amongst the glass and blood and with his right, he released the seat belt and crashed down amongst the debris. He groaned with pain as he tried to re-orientate himself and force the door open. Scrambling out onto the road, it took him two attempts to get to his feet, stumbling back down in between, his head betraying him if he moved too fast. The small Ford was wedged against the lamppost. The driver was trying to get out but couldn't. She was a blonde girl no older than 20. A deep cut across her head covered her face in a thick gloss of blood.

"Please help, the door won't open."

Gareth wandered over, still not completely with it himself. He opened the passenger door, the girl reached out to him and he moved back nervous about what she might be.

"Please, the door won't open, and my leg is stuck." Her leg was indeed pinned between the steering column and the warped door.

"I'll get someone," Gareth began to walk away. He took out his phone but there was no reception.

"Please don't leave me!" the girl begged.

"I'll get help. Someone will come for you," Gareth continued to walk away. He saw a man walking toward the stricken car. *He'll help her. She's his problem now.*

Gareth looked a state. Blood stained his face and clothes, but he was nearly home. He had avoided people. He didn't know who to trust. The emptiness of the streets made this an easier task than it normally would have been. He was close to his apartment building, a few more minutes, and he'd be inside, have a shower before getting into some clean clothes and fixing himself a drink. Muffled pops took his attention. They grew louder as he rounded a corner onto his street. Two armed police officers, one young and one older, fired with their Heckler and Koch carbines at a group of people standing over an old lady who writhed on the ground covered in blood. Several members of the group pulled and grabbed at her. The bullets ripped through their flesh but didn't stop them. Several turned around to address the annoyance of being shot and began to stumble towards the officers. Their skin greying, their eyes vacant but somehow angry. By luck rather than judgement, a round struck the forehead of one of the people in the group and they collapsed in a heap.

"The head, hit the head!" the older officer barked at the other. They began felling a few more, but there were too many.

"We've got to get out of here," the young one declared as he changed magazines.

They hadn't seen Gareth as he approached. He didn't know what to think of this scene but was sure these people had the same crazy as the girl at the gym and was happy that the police were blasting 9mm holes into them.

"I was in a car accident. I need help," he sheepishly piped up.

They both turned, carbines raised and stared at Gareth. "Have you been attacked?" the older officer demanded an answer.

"No, a Fiesta clipped my car. I ended up on my roof. I have a cut on my head, but I think it's stopped bleeding now." They continued to observe, the older officer signalled to the younger one to cover them against the group. He resumed his shooting.

"We need to get out of here."

"You're not bitten, just the wound from the car accident?" There would not be time for a full interrogation, but he didn't want to leave a civilian in this mess or take an infected person in the back of their car.

"Just the accident, I promise."

"We're pulling out, sir get into the back of the car," he turned and fired several rounds at the group, more of which had decided the old lady meal would be washed down nicely by two police officers and a freshly bleeding Gareth.

Gareth didn't need telling twice as he got into the back of the car, the officers following shooting as they moved to a minimal effect. The car doors slammed shut and the engine roared into life, a screech of tyres as the rubber stained the tarmac.

"What the fuck is going on?" Gareth looked through the rear windscreen and a few members of the mob were following at a slow pace.

"That's the end of the world. These things are pretty much dead. They're not, but they're not alive like you or me," the young officer enthusiastically spoke as if he were talking of his favourite football team.

"They're not dead you plonker. Something has got into the water, or maybe it's a drug sending people bat shit crazy," the older officer tried to correct his young colleague. "Bullshit, people poisoned by dodgy water or shit faced on smack don't walk towards you after taking three-rounds to center mass. They stay down. These things aren't people. They're death walking the earth to devour the living." The young copper wouldn't be swayed.

"Where are you going to take me?"

The two police officers looked at each other.

"Your home?" the younger one shrugged.

"That was my home."

38

The alarm was going off and Amy mashed around trying to find her phone to stop the racket. It felt like only minutes, but she'd managed to get nearly five hours of sleep. Eyes half closed she found the phone, but it wasn't making the loud klaxon. She sat up from her bed of chairs and the room was dark, only a red flash of the station alarm and those illuminating the emergency exit. Amy reluctantly accepted that however bad the last few days had been, today would be even worse. She got to her feet, grabbed her stab vest and gear, then moved quickly to the exit. Today would be worse.

Amy's instinct was to head to the cells in the basement. They were full to the brim and would need to be evacuated. There were only a handful of officers still in the station rushing in different directions. The rest must have already evacuated. None of those who remained seemed in the mood to stop and talk. She reached the entrance to the cells, and it was quiet. Good, Amy thought to herself, they've already been evacuated, otherwise, they'd surely all be going nuts. The emergency generators still supplied power to the secured doors and emergency lighting. Her ID let her through, but she wished it hadn't.

In an ideal situation, each cell would have one prisoner. In times of emergency such as the London riots in the summer of 2011, the cells may hold two or for short periods, three inmates. When Amy finished her paperwork last night, each cell had six people in. Despite the frenzied, violent nature of these offenders, they showed no interest in attacking each other. When this discovery was accidentally made, it seemed like a victory as handcuffing prisoners to radiators wasn't something the IPCC endorsed, and in a world of heightened litigation, it wasn't a great idea to leave yourself open. After the emergency was over - a lot of embarrassed people would reflect on what happened. Sure, they may have taken a chunk out of some bus driver's arm or eaten the neighbour's dog. But if they had been handcuffed to a radiator, they would be the victim. Each cell now contained seven or eight bodies, and blood was everywhere. Beneath her feet, shell casings carpeted the tiled floor. These people wouldn't be suing anyone. Amy slowly edged backwards careful not to slip on the bloody brass. A lot appeared to have happened in the five hours she'd slept, and she needed to know what. Closing the door to the cells, she ran through the building.

As Amy sprinted through the heart of the building, she bumped into a fellow officer and both went flying. He was a young officer. Amy had seen him around the station but didn't know his name, just that he always seemed cocky. Today he just seemed scared. The look of fear in his eyes added to Amy's unease. He stumbled to his feet and carried on running without saying a word. She had no idea what he was running from, but she needed answers and continued to the front of the station. Hitting the front desk, Amy saw her sergeant behind the counter, tending to a wound on his neck that was bleeding freely. In front of him, he had his baton and two unused tasers.

"They're fucking everywhere." He was calm but angry.

"The cells, it's a bloodbath. They were all murdered," Amy stated trying to grasp the situation. She turned and saw the front doors had been barricaded shut, but numerous people were trying to get in. The sergeant sat down holding his wound.

"We couldn't cope. We started losing contact with the guys on the street. Just too many of them, too many." His wound needed attention, but he didn't look like he was about to bleed out.

"The cells?" Amy demanded an answer.

"There was a COBRA meeting, the government announced a national emergency. There's a contagion and anyone exhibiting signs of infection were to be neutralised."

She couldn't believe what he was telling her.

"Murdered," Amy responded.

"Don't let them near you. Yesterday, they were violent humans. Today, they're monsters," he touched his wound, emphasising the brutality. Amy approached him to help.

"No. If I don't bleed to death, I'm probably infected like them," he signalled to his meagre arsenal. "Take that and head to the loading bay, there's a squad of TA soldiers and whatever we have left evacuating. I'll stay here. I'll die or I'll try to eat all of you insubordinate fuckers. Go!"

Amy grabbed the tasers and baton and ran. She turned to see the front doors edge open and half a dozen bloody hands reaching through, but she didn't stop. The station was now empty as she made her way to the loading bay. She burst through the doors and instantly regretted it. Half a dozen panicked territorial army soldiers raised their rifles at her, one letting off a single shot that whistled past Amy's face close enough for her to feel the heat from the bullet.

There can be a certain lack of respect when people talk about the territorial army. These weekend warriors are seen as oddballs, undertrained and not real soldiers. However, in recent years, the regular army has seen an increasing dependence on using TA troops to support them in theatres of war all over the world. Many an IT specialist or banker has found themselves swapping Cisco routers or investment bonds for an assault rifle or Land Rover patrol vehicle. They may not be elite, but they're trained and armed. Amy would have been forgiven for not trusting the ability of these troops having narrowly avoided a 5.56mm round to the face, but this collection of men and women seemed a safer prospect than whatever was forcing its way through the station entrance. She composed herself and carried on forward with her hands in the air. They ignored her as the collection of police, TA and support staff hurriedly loaded up the army trucks. The gates to the courtyard were closed, but hands and arms reached through, groans and gurgles were barely muffled under the sound of the truck's engines.

"Who's in command?" Amy pleaded, but no response was forthcoming. "Who the fuck is in command?!" she screamed, determined for an answer.

An army officer surrounded by subordinates, giving each a task, signalled her over. "You need to get in truck four," he ordered.

Amy looked over and saw the likely candidate truck four with several of her colleagues visible in the back. "I don't understand," Amy mumbled.

"We're moving out in two minutes. You can be on the truck, or you can stay here. I'd rather you got on the truck." With that, the army officer continued organising his team. Gunfire erupted. This time the targets were legitimate. Several of these deranged people, already bloodied and beaten, stormed through to the loading dock.

"Mount up, we're leaving," the officer screamed.

The speed of the withdrawal quickened. Anyone not on a truck quickly made it their priority to be on one. The maniacs kept coming. Amy jumped onto the back of truck four, assisted by two other police officers already onboard. As she scrambled inside, she watched what should have been an execution but turned to be a perfectly fair fight. She'd never seen anyone shot before but was sure an average human couldn't expect to survive three or four shots to the torso. These people did. Half a dozen was now nearly 15. Only three had succumbed to the punishment being inflicted upon them and fallen to the floor. Others pushed forward despite their obvious and horrific wounds.

"Aim for the heads!" the officer demanded as he climbed into the nearest truck.

All but one TA soldier had boarded the trucks. His

colleagues continued to fire where they could from the trucks. It was hard to tell if Private Corby was a brave man, an idiot or just suffered from tunnel vision. Whatever it was, Corby continued to lay down marginally effective fire whilst everyone else got themselves on a truck. They cried out for him to join them, but above the screams, the gunfire and the sound of bullets ripping through flesh and bone, he didn't hear them. As the things got closer, he fumbled for a new magazine only to turn and discover he was standing alone, the trucks starting to leave. Priorities changed, and Corby abandoned reloading his service rifle to run for his life, but the trucks were already moving away from him.

Amy's was the last truck out. It was going slowly enough that Corby may have caught up to it. Its inhabitants pleaded the driver to stop, but the driver ignored them. She had orders, and the best she was willing to do was drive as slow as possible. An armed police officer opened fire with his G36 carbine at the pack closing on Corby but found little more success than others had done. Corby was agonisingly close. Had he realised a few seconds sooner that he needed to run, he'd have made it. It wasn't one of the things from the police station that got Corby, it was one from the courtyard gate. It had found itself flattened by the convoy of trucks smashing through the gate and its peers, but this one wasn't helpless. Its legs were pulp, but its torso, arms, and head were in perfect working order. It grabbed Corby's leg, sinking its nails in without remorse and wouldn't let go. Corby tried to release himself but fell on top of the beast. He screamed as its teeth sunk into his hand.

Corby threw himself over, now on his back; now he could see what everyone on truck four could see. He sobbed with fear, he knew it was over. Inside the courtyard, 100 creatures descended upon Corby, outside several dozen more moved towards their meal. Corby disappeared below the monsters, his screams lasted seconds before ceasing abruptly. Truck four now picked up speed; the occupants stunned into silence. Only the diesel engine and the intermittent sound of flesh meeting motor vehicles could be heard as they headed through what used to be Croydon.

39

A field somewhere near the village of Chipstead in Surrey isn't where you'd expect to see a full-on refugee camp spring up. Events had been moving fast, but mass evacuation of the population wasn't possible unless you had somewhere to evacuate them to. The fences were high and plentiful with the camp designed in sections. Numerous guard towers and checkpoints existed on the perimeter and all the way through to the camp's core where the scientists and military leaders were based. Each layer offered an escape into the next, so if one were to fall, inner areas could be sealed and protected. Even as Amy's truck arrived, work continued on building up defences. Men and machines were hard at work digging trenches and creating bunkers under the watchful eye of dozens of snipers and machine gunners. With the firepower on display, nothing was getting in that hadn't been invited. The corpses surrounding the perimeter with various parts of their heads missing testified to the skill of the men in the towers.

Camps such as the one in Chipstead were being rapidly created throughout the country. They weren't pretty but would suffice for the perceived needs. They'd keep people in, keep the infected out and provide the authorities with operating bases in areas where they might otherwise have no presence. An hour ago, Amy didn't think the world could be saved. Seeing the scale of this endeavour, she decided perhaps there was hope. Society wouldn't fall, just yet.

In front of their convoy of trucks were civilians being unloaded from a collection of buses, trucks, and vans. They shared Amy's look of terror and hope. The army trucks passed by and ushered directly into the camp. The trucks had become a bloody, pulpy mess from their escape from the streets of Croydon. The looks attracted by the sight were not of shock, but acceptance. Every person who'd made it to the camp had fought hard to get there. It may have been barely 12 hours since the shit hit the fan, but no one had been spared the violence or the gore.

The trucks pulled into a service area and the order to disembark given. A team of soldiers and personnel in hazmat suits greeted them. The command was given for the truck passengers, a collection of soldiers, police and civilians to stand in line ready to be given the first of their examinations. The routine was still being perfected, but the welcoming party had the basics down. They separated new arrivals into civilians, VIPs, and non-civilians. Non-civilians were army, police and anyone with medical training. Civilians like those at the first gate were escorted to a holding enclosure, secure from the rest of the camp and had armed guards looking in, rather than out.

VIPs were escorted to a similar enclosure, but with a few more creature comforts and would be seen to before the civilians. The VIPs were politicians, the rich, and the famous. That a pop star with a few top 10 singles to their name was entitled to more when the world was falling apart sat well with no one. Likewise, money was on the verge of being worthless and yet the rich carried on with their privilege. Those with money or a recognisable face tasted just as good as a poor nobody to the dead. The non-civilians were prioritised, the returning soldiers needed to be cleared for duty straight away. They were stripped and given a visual inspection for wounds. If clear they would return to their barracks to await orders. Police and medical personnel were submitted to a similar check, but then briefly interviewed for their personal information and experience. They would then find themselves assigned a role. Anyone with a wound would see a part of the camp they would rather not have. They were escorted, calmly, for treatment in the camps central research and treatment centre. There, they'd receive a vaccine. Shortly after this, they'd pass out. Eventually they'd wake. Strapped to a table unable to move, surrounded by men and women in white coats and masks, and armed soldiers. They would be subjected to many tests and treatments, but the result would always be the same, they'd turn. The camp hadn't been in place long, but the scientists had already found a good supply of test subjects to poke and prod. They were no closer to finding a cure, but at least they had plenty of samples.

They grouped Amy with her colleagues. After the brief humiliation of stripping for their inspection and an interview, they were assigned a tent and given instructions to clean up and meet in the HQ tent in one hour. Their new home was sparse, a bed and a box each in a large tent housing 20 other adults. The box was superfluous since most were wearing everything they owned. The bed was small but still looked like an upgrade on the alternative. They were shown to the shower block, where they washed in cold water and got back into their dirty clothes, enjoyed 20 minutes of sleep or rest before being summoned to their induction.

The camp was calm, the arse had fallen out of the world in less than a day and the mood was quiet, but relaxed. Besides the continuous construction work, there was an unnerving peace. Everyone here had seen the horror and felt saved and they let themselves believe everything was okay and they'd be all right. Then a shot would ring out and remind everyone that there were things outside the wire that didn't want them to be safe. Amy joined her fellow police officers in the HQ tent. Some she recognised, others were from different stations, the ranks were mixed but they all shared the same bemused look. In front of them, a middle-aged woman smartly dressed, a senior police officer and an army sergeant.

"I need not tell you, we are in trouble," the smartly dressed woman was a master of understatement. "We are currently the main London South survivor centre. We are running constant rescue missions in the local areas and bringing those we find here. We have a limited military resource and their job is to defend the camp from the external threat and rescue those who need saving. This camp is growing hourly and we don't have the resources to police it, fortunately for us, we have many officers such as yourselves. And we need you."

The senior police officer stepped forward, "I understand this is a hard situation, but we need you to do your job maintaining law and order inside of the fence. People are scared and desperate. Without you the camp will descend into a chaos that could rival the streets we saved you from."

Almost as if rehearsed, the army sergeant stepped forward to say his piece, "You won't be armed, you will have a radio and you will be a visible presence. If you get in trouble, you call my team. We are in charge of internal security, and we will step in and restore order where you're not capable."

"Questions?" The smartly dressed woman appeared keen on wrapping up the briefest of briefings. The audience looked around at each other. No one appearing willing to ask a question except for Amy who raised her hand to the irritation of the three presenters.

"Yes?" the senior police officer snapped.

"What's the plan for tomorrow and the day after? We're just going to wait for those things to arrive in sufficient numbers until we don't have enough bullets to put them down?"

"The situation is fluid. We're not alone. There are many camps like this throughout the country and we are in communication with them all. Today, we're regrouping, tomorrow we will be on the front foot." The woman was obviously a politician, but not one she recognised.

Amy guessed the important ones were safely squirrelled away in the most high-tech of bunkers and not slumming it with the proletariat in a field behind a few chain link fences.

"This camp is very impressive. We were getting the shit kicked out of us on the street for the last week. Why, when you knew what was happening, didn't we receive more support? We were left on our fucking own." Amy enjoyed swearing casually to help hammer home her point, especially with superiors. It worked better with the bosses who knew her best.

"Officer! You are out of line." Amy's superior wasn't impressed with her choice of words, he wasn't familiar with her.

"We appreciate mistakes may have been made, but we are working tirelessly to rectify them. We're all in this together." Definitely a politician.

Amy wasn't impressed, but still knew she had a duty to help. There were no further questions.

The senior officer wound up the briefing, "You will be summoned in small groups and given your assignments. I wish we could give you a break, but you're needed. People need the reassurance of seeing you doing your jobs; they need to feel safe."

With that, everyone got up and drifted out, awaiting their next instructions. Amy attracted glares from those in charge as she left, but all made no further comment.

40

The promised reinforcements hadn't yet made their way to the research facility, forcing the soldiers to spend the last two days pulling extended shifts. They spent any time in the barracks sleeping or speculating on the state of the world. Morale was in the toilet and tiredness abounded, mixed badly with fear and confusion.

Kenneth was making his way to relieve Bobby; the soldiers now patrolling solo rather than in pairs and the young lad was on edge. They met at the perimeter fence and greeted each other with a smile.

"You okay there kid?" Kenneth could see Bobby was struggling, but he couldn't offer much more than some sympathy and the promise of some kip.

"You know how it is Kenny. I think about me ma' and sis. I thought I saw one earlier," Bobby signalled towards the field beyond the fence.

"Your family?" Kenneth was confused.

"No, a man. It looked like he was eating something, a rabbit or something. I don't know."

Kenneth got closer to the fence and looked out beyond. Long grass, a few trees and that was pretty much it. As far as the eye could see nothing but greenery. "You head back mate, get some sleep. I hear our relief will be here by the morning and then we can all start getting some proper rest. This shit will blow over soon." Kenneth wasn't lying, it was pretty much what he'd been told, and he hoped it was true. Bobby started walking back and Kenneth patted his shoulder as he passed, "It'll be fine."

"Perimeter A2 checking in," Kenneth spoke into his radio as he started walking the well-trodden route in the growing grass.

"Copy that," a crackled radio voice responded.

Kenneth checked his rifle as he walked, a habit from Afghanistan. It was a warm and dry day but not up to Afghani standards, distinctly less dust and sand blowing around to work into well-oiled moving parts of a clean rife. Still, he never wanted to fire his weapon on British soil in anger, but if he needed to, he wanted to make sure it was ready. He and his fellow soldiers had been given very little detail on what was happening outside of the fence. From what they'd overheard from the research bods and seen on the news, the soldiers had wasted too much of their too little spare time speculating. A chemical attack on food or water supplies seemed to be the popular theory, turning the population into frenzied maniacs. Bobby had stated it was down to smartphones; either China, North Korea or both had programmed the signal to drive people loopy. He said it explained why a lot, but not all people, were affected. If the head sheds hadn't confiscated their personal phones, it was likely Bobby would have destroyed them himself.

Whatever it was, it hadn't found its way to them yet. The official government line was very much one of denial and downplaying of the facts, but it was becoming obvious that this would have to change soon. Sky News had footage of one of the survivor camps being built. It looked impressive for a few days' effort, but this appearance only led to other sightings. *It can't be more than another day or two before it's all official and the shit truly hits the fan,* Kenneth thought.

A car horn and shouting came from the gate. Kenneth naturally wanted to run over and see what was going on, but his training and experience told him to keep patrolling, to not be distracted and to remain alert. With those at the gate distracted, the rest of the site was vulnerable. This wasn't Kabul; a car bomb would probably not go off, mortar shells wouldn't rain down, a sniper wouldn't start picking off high-value targets and an assault probably wasn't about to begin. This was East Sussex. However, a desperate person may try to get access, cut through the fence, maybe try to climb over it. It wasn't Kenneth's place to question the wisdom of sending civilians away into the unknown. He was a soldier. He followed orders.

Kenneth carried on following the fence line, occasionally glancing at the gate between concentrating on his job. A man holding a child, maybe two or three years old, stood beside a red Ford Focus. There was shouting, but it was impossible to tell what was being said. It was easy enough to detect fear and anger. The soldiers held firm; he wasn't coming in.

Kenneth stared back out to the fields. He could make out something maybe a kilometer from the facility.

"OP this is Perimeter A2." He awaited a response from his radio. Kenneth glanced back to the front gate then to the thing in the distance. He strained to make out what it was when his radio screeched into life.

"Perimeter A2, this is OP."

"I can see something one klick out of the west fence, do you have a visual." Kenneth's optics on his rifle didn't offer much in the way of magnification, but he could see it was two people. They were unarmed and looked exhausted, slowly making their way to the facility.

"Perimeter A2, covering entrance gate. Continue to monitor and we'll assist when we can."

Kenneth wasn't surprised, but he needed to report it. He continued walking, switching attention from the two distant figures, the gate and any other potential threat. A soldier at the gate screamed a command at the man.

Then the shot rang out. Followed by three more. Kenneth crouched to one knee and raised his rifle towards the gate; the man carrying the child was slumped against the car and the child motionless in front of him. A woman emerged from the car in hysterics and ran towards her downed family. She screamed at the injustice, the loss and with great anger. The radio erupted with several panicked voices.

She kneeled by the child and picked up the lifeless body. She scrambled with it to the man and hugged them both, crying uncontrollably. The commanding voice of the Major demanded calm on the radio and then silence. Kenneth stood up and looked back out to the field, the figures in the distance were making slow progress, not put off by the sound of gunfire. He turned back to the gate, and the woman was remonstrating with the soldiers standing over the bloody corpses of her loved ones. She strode forward in anger. The soldier fired in fear. She was with her family.

Kenneth's radio screeched back into life, again the Major's voice restored calm. He was on his way down. The command was simple: all soldiers to hold their position. Kenneth looked back over the field; the two figures he could see were now a group of nearly 10. He glanced up at the observation post, gave his head a slight shake, and concentrated on the job in hand. He knew the reinforcements should have been here and things were about to get really shitty. They were just going to have to let it play out.

41

The camp had grown in three days. Hundreds had turned to thousands, the perimeter fence had been pushed out ever further, and the resources stretched to bursting. Although the rescue teams had been successful in bringing in civilians, key workers were in exceptionally short supply. Medical personnel, military and police were at the sharp-end of the outbreak; many either joining the ranks of the infected or becoming a feast for them.

Amy didn't feel tired anymore, she was beyond that. Policing the camp was tougher than the streets. The hours were longer, the people more violent, scared and all about to snap. Fights would break out over water or tinned fruit, often with deadly consequences. After two members of the camp's police force were beaten to death, the military had relented and armed them, albeit with batons and pepper spray only. Firearm trained police officers were moved to defend the ever-growing perimeter as the numbers of soldiers dwindled through increasingly dangerous journeys beyond the camp.

Amy had enjoyed two hours' sleep and set off with her partner, PC Derek Jones. Derek was a good man in his early thirties. At a touch over 6 feet tall and with an athletic build, he was the poster boy for a modern police service. He was also a father and husband with his family still unaccounted for. When they had downtime, this was all that occupied his mind, but when they were on patrol, he was a fully focused professional. Amy liked that about him. She thought it was a shame about his family. She fancied him but she knew a shag and some intimacy was what she needed, Derek didn't.

The camp had grown by layers, resembling the circles in a tree trunk, every section was fenced off to the one it bordered. The further in the camp went, the more important the occupants, gates were manned but not secured until you reached the innermost level. Today, they assigned Amy and Derek to patrol the outermost level. These were the newest guests of the camp and often the most traumatised, having spent more time surviving in the wild than others. Fights here were commonplace and more vicious. It was hard to adjust from caving in the head of a vicious monster to sharing your water ration with another desperate soul. They were still on edge, not able to trust the safety the camp offered. It would be a tough shift. Amy and Derek had their gear and started making their way through the camp. The first gate was relaxed, and they were waved right through. This part of the camp the people smiled, laughed and life seemed almost normal. They reached the next gate, tension rose, but it was no worse than a Palace vs Brighton game at three o'clock on a Saturday. The people didn't smile; they kept their heads down and their belongings close.

As Amy and Derek approached the final gate, the atmosphere changed completely. The gate was closed, several armed soldiers stood wearily on either side keeping a close eye on anyone who dared to get within 10 feet of them. Amy and Derek stopped and waited to be invited to approach, a soldier signalled them as he opened the gate. They walked through to the last section and the first sight that greeted them was a woman, in her forties, kicking a child firmly in the back. The child crashed to the floor and turned in shock to see the woman bearing down on him. He was maybe seven, white as a sheet and stared open-mouthed as she reached towards him and grabbed a chocolate bar he had in his top pocket. The tears started to stream down his face. She didn't hear Amy approach, but she felt the baton strike the back of her leg behind the knee sending her crumbling to the ground.

"What the fuck is the matter with you? All of you!" Amy screamed as loudly as she could. The woman writhed in pain clutching her leg as Amy picked the chocolate bar up and handed it back to the boy. "You should eat this sooner rather than later sweetie."

The boy took the bar and scrambled to his feet before running off without saying a word.

"You like the new rulebook, don't you?" Derek smiled at Amy.

"It's simpler, everyone's a dick."

Derek offered a mischievous smile.

"What about the boy?" Amy returned the smile sarcastically.

"He didn't say thank you, did he?"

Amy and Derek started their patrol leaving the woman struggling to get back to her feet. This level of police brutality might normally draw a crowd, but in this part of the camp, in these damned times, it didn't even warrant a second glance.

The odour in the air was that of death. The camp was overcrowded and water not in good enough supply for washing. The corpses piled up around the fence line; there were not enough soldiers to deal with the problem and a distinct lack of volunteers amongst the scared civilian population to assist. The military or the police patrols concerned few civilians; most appreciated they wouldn't beat them half to death for a bread roll. However, some were scared. Amy had noticed it the previous day. Just one or two people acting suspiciously. At first, Amy thought they were up to something, then she realised these people thought she was up to something. The streets of Croydon had taught her that not everyone trusted those in authority. Today, a few more people acting in this way.

"Have you noticed them?" Amy asked.

"How long have you been in the police force? If a few people giving you the stink eye bothers you in a world where people are eating each other, maybe it's time to find another profession." He allowed himself the light-hearted moment; he couldn't afford many.

"The last time I looked, resignations weren't being accepted. And besides, where else offers the perks of luxury accommodation, exotic tinned food and the opportunity to meet and interact with interesting people?"

They walked at a leisurely pace, there was no need to rush anywhere and it was a nice day, a light summer's breeze that would be pleasant if it wasn't for the stench it carried.

"But you have noticed them, right?" Amy was sure she wasn't going mad.

"Yeah, I've noticed. I've heard them too. There are stories - it's all bullshit - of us and the soldiers snatching up people and taking them for the white coats to experiment on."

"You're shitting me?" Amy half laughed.

"People just don't believe they're safe. They won't let their guard down. Nothing is coming from the outside through those gates so they're turning their fear inwards. I don't blame them. Some of those white coats and their bosses, our bosses, they don't seem like good people."

"There aren't many good people anymore."

"Yeah, but these fuckers, I don't think they've ever been right. For all we know, they started this shit." Derek half-believed his own accusations.

"Now you're sounding like the one who should consider their career choice."

"Hey, there's lots going on and we know nothing, especially of what goes on in the treatment tents." He'd become more serious. "You've seen those things, they can't take any chances." Amy hated the turn in the conversation, she didn't enjoy defending the regime; she knew it stunk too.

"But what do we know, nothing? This didn't just happen, somebody did this, why not the government?"

"We know we're safe, and they did that for us." Amy had always been endowed with a huge sense of loyalty. Those in charge were the government. She'd seen firsthand them saving lives and all those ungrateful bastards milling around had them to thank, but never did. She found the idea that someone would hold them responsible as repulsive. Sure, Amy felt she'd lost many friends because of the lack of initial response, but this wasn't a typical crisis. This isn't something that could be drilled for. Derek was certain this conversation was spiralling and tried to draw a line under it.

"Just be careful." It was too late, Amy was getting progressively more pissed with him.

"I've always been fucking careful. My only concern is the shit heads on edge ready to ruin what we have."

They continued in silence, concentrating on the job in hand, hoping something would clear the air. The wait wouldn't be long. A woman screamed from inside one of the makeshift tents before two children ran out in tears. Derek and Amy ran towards them, batons in hand and ready. A woman, early thirties, dirty but still retaining some glamour, fell through the open doorway clutching her blood-covered arm. A man came out following her, clearing 6 foot 3 inches, full of rage, blood dripping from his mouth and his skin shimmering with a grey hue. He threw himself onto her and bit down on her cheek, ripping a chunk of flesh exposing her jaw, her scream muffled by the blood now pouring into her throat. Derek reached him first, jumping on the man knocking him off of his victim. They wrestled on the ground, Derek tried to strike the man with his baton, but they were too close. He was wild fury. The woman dragged herself a few feet away to safety, whimpering with pain. Amy had her pepper spray out and pointed at the men.

"Stop resisting!"

The man paid her no attention. Derek wrestled himself free as the man snapped at him with his teeth and clawed at him with his hands. Amy discharged the spray. Derek coughed and wiped at his eyes, but it did nothing to its intended victim. Amy dropped the spray and swung with her baton, connecting cleanly with its eye socket sending the thing face-first to the ground. With barely a pause, it was back to its knees, scrambling towards Amy.

She didn't hear the first or even the second shot, but the third one made her duck. The monster's head popped open and its chest split. Amy hit the ground an instant before its lifeless body did.

Four soldiers approached, assault rifles raised screaming orders at those nearby. Amy couldn't understand what they were saying. She looked over at Derek and the woman. The soldiers didn't give the creature that attacked a second glance. They pointed their weapons at the two police officers and the victim.

"Stay down, all of you!" The soldier sounded scared; this was the first time one of these things had got inside.

The checks until this point had been completely successful. Another soldier called in for support and another dozen soldiers were rushing to their position already. They started setting up a perimeter around the gruesome scene, looking outwards onto scared civilians.

Amy crawled over to Derek. He was still, lying flat on his back staring into the sky.

"Are you hurt?" Amy was concerned but couldn't see any gunshot wounds.

"I'm fucked is what I am," Derek held up his hand. It was missing two fingers, the stumps dripping with his fresh blood. "It doesn't even hurt, it just tingles."

Amy was in shock more than Derek.

"You're okay. They're working on a cure, it'll be fine."

Derek smiled.

"Sure, I'll be fine. They'll take me to their big fancy tent and make me better. That's how it works." The bastard had to get a last shot in on their argument.

Another four soldiers appeared with two stretchers; they were allowed through the defensive ring. They spread themselves between the woman and Derek, scooping them up onto the stretchers and restrained them, neither resisted.

"Can I come with him?" Amy put her hand on Derek's chest.

"Were you injured?" The soldier was hesitant.

"No, I'm okay."

The reply was a firm, "No."

The soldiers picked up the wounded and quickly made their way back through the camp, Amy tried to follow but was stopped by the muzzle of a rifle pushed into her chest.

"I'm one of you for fuck's sake!" Amy got into the face of the soldier.

"Get back in your box, you blue bitch!"

He withdrew his muzzle and smashed the butt of the rifle into her face. Amy crumbled to the ground, blood seeping from a small gash below her left eye. She started climbing to her knees as the soldiers all withdrew at pace. She looked at them in shock and hatred.

A woman approached, "Are you okay?"

Amy looked at the woman as she tentatively touched her wound, unsure of what to say.

42

Being a good soldier who's 6 foot 6 inches had its drawbacks. They had pulled Kenneth from patrol duty to help clean up the mess at the gate. All soldiers had their rifles in hand and were stationed on alert. The private security was still being kept busy, but their resentment had grown. They hadn't been allowed to leave and hadn't been given a reason. They had all seen the news, heard the rumours and wanted to go home. The shooting at the gate had made up most of their minds and now presented an opportunity. It distracted the military, several junior scientists and other civilians were as in the dark as the security team, and they saw their chance. The soldiers may have thought they were superior, but they didn't have the numbers or inclination to stop a dozen or civilians walking past them.

    Kenneth helped another soldier move the last body, the young boy. The bullet had entered his skull through his cheek. The entry wound seemed small, but the eye above solid crimson alluding to the internal damage. They picked up his limp body and a flap of scalp swung free, matted, bloody hair and a chunk of skull hanging from the back of the head. They carried the corpse about 20 feet from the fence line and placed it on the body of its mother and father. There wouldn't be a burial, not yet. The number of people approaching was now nearly 30, and they'd be at the gate within minutes. The car was pushed to one side, and the men returned to what should have been the safety of the facility. In the minutes since they'd been rushed to action, the restless civilians had massed at the gate, the soldiers inside struggling to contain them. One or two of the soldiers even wishing to join them as they hadn't signed up to shoot unarmed civilians, to shoot children.

The Major fired his Glock pistol into the air then pointed it towards the crowd.

"Anyone crosses that threshold and you will be spitting a nine-millimetre bullet out of your fucking cranium!"

There was a hesitation in the crowd, but their numbers gave them confidence. They surged forward and knocked the Major to the ground before he could get a shot off. Kenneth stood back and held his rifle in the air to show he wouldn't stop them, the other soldiers did likewise as the crowd surged past. The crowd left the relative safety of Wellworth's fences, some on foot, a couple in cars, several soldiers followed them, not in pursuit but joining the departure. Young Bobby was amongst them, he'd had enough and wanted to be with his family; they must surely need him.

The Major scrambled to his feet and took aim at Bobby with his pistol, "I will shoot any soldier leaving!" This was a desperate threat from a man whose authority was waning; the crowd and those soldiers leaving didn't so much as slow.

Anger grew in the Major as he began to squeeze the trigger. Kenneth jumped in front of him. "Sir, don't! If you shoot one of ours, that's it, none of us will stay. This isn't what the British Army does!"

The Major's face screwed up, and he lowered his Glock and holstered it. "To any cowardly cunt who wants to leave, go now! Get the fuck out of my facility," he pointed towards the outside world. "The rest of you, seal the damn gates before we're really in trouble." Those who remained obliged.

Over a dozen civilians had left, all the private security, a few scientists and a couple of general office staff. Three soldiers had also defied the Major and deserted their posts. The remaining soldiers began sealing the gate and resuming their duties.

The Major looked more furious than normal. He grabbed Kenneth by the arm and yanked him clear to talk to him privately, "Lance Corporal, the men know and respect you. I need you close. Reinforcements aren't coming." The Major's demeanour had turned quickly to concern taking Kenneth off guard.

"Sir?"

"Our resources are too few and need too great. Up and down the country, we are fully stretched. The territorials have been helping but a few weekend warriors with rifles aren't enough. Those overseas are being recalled, but it's too late. The survivor camps are filling as cities and towns are abandoned." The Major pointed towards the group approaching the camp, on a collision course with those fleeing, "They aren't people, they're not refugees looking for help. They're infected looking to eat the living."

Screams suddenly sounded from the road leading through the field. The observation post opened fire at the approaching figures as they began attacking the deserters. Those in cars drove on, not daring to stop to help. The soldiers in the field tried to protect themselves and the others but were taken by surprise and overwhelmed. They began running back to the Wellworth Research Center, desperate to return to the safety of the gates, the fence, the armed soldiers. As the sniper punched holes in the bodies of the aggressors, they momentarily were felled before getting back to their feet and continuing. Two pinned down a young woman in a white coat, thrashing at her, the white coat becoming red with her blood. Others turned to see the gruesome sight, and this only strengthened their resolve to get away as quickly as possible.

The panic spread, and the young began to push past the old and the weak. A woman in her early sixties and a man of the same age fell and couldn't get back on their feet before they were set upon. Two of the deserting soldiers came to their aid, Bobby fired at one monster striking its throat. It didn't so much as pause. When they completed enveloped the two civilians, the soldiers fought them with the butts of their rifles and wrestled them off.

"They're not staying down," cried the observer in the OP over the radio. But all could see the fight playing out too close for comfort.

More gunshots in the field, Bobby and another soldier could see they'd picked the wrong fight and began to retreat with the civilians, the third soldier emptied a magazine into the creatures, missing with more rounds than he hit. Those finding their target not much more effective than the ones harmlessly whizzing past. As the people started flooding back to the facility, the soldiers began to open the gates.

"No!" was the command from the Major. "They've been exposed!"

The soldiers looked to Kenneth for direction. "Seal them, no one enters." He had to back the Major. This wasn't a democracy, this was a military operation. He believed in obeying orders from his superiors, and he'd make damn sure his fellow soldiers would too.

Hands gripped desperately to the wire fence, pleas and tears streamed into one indistinguishable sound, broken only by a moan from one of the things as they drew closer.

Bobby pushed his way to the front. He was bleeding from a wound on his face, "Let us in. Please let us fucking in." Kenneth had his rifle raised at the group. Bobby looked him in the eye, tears rolling down his cheeks.

"Get back Bobby, you need to run!" Kenneth pointed his rifle directly at Bobby, but Bobby didn't move. The creatures drew closer, covered in a greying red blood from their multiple ineffective wounds.

They were not getting back in. Those who realised this first ran in the opposite direction. Too many were slow to grasp the situation they had put themselves into. The soldiers inside the fence looked on in horror, the monsters too close now to get a clear shot on. There were maybe 20 of these things now pushing up on those stupid enough not to flee. Screams of fear replaced with those of pain as the teeth bit down. The hands clawed. Flesh pulled apart. Bobby was still holding on to the fence staring at Kenneth as a monster sunk its vile teeth into his neck and ripped a chunk of flesh free. Bobby didn't cry out in pain. He didn't fight back. He just held on, resigned to his fate, to never seeing his mother or sister again. Kenneth put a single round through Bobby's skull. He fell back onto the creature behind him pinning it to the floor.

"Light them up!" Kenneth screamed and the soldiers now wilfully shot at the civilians and creatures alike. They couldn't let them into safety, but they could give them a quick death and free them of the fear. The civilians collapsed as their bodies were subjected to the tiny explosions of the bullets entering them. The creatures remained more resilient. At the closer range, Kenneth took aim and shot one in the head, it popped open and it fell to the ground motionless. "The heads, you need to shoot them in the head!"

In the next minute, they neutralised all the creatures, except the one beneath Bobby. Kenneth popped in a fresh magazine and was about to finish the job when the Major pushed his rifle away.

"No, the white coats will need to take a look. Secure it." None of the men moved, the smoke still clearing from the hundreds of spent rounds, the cases littering the ground around them.

"Sir, it's not safe," a soldier sheepishly announced.

"Private, you heard the Major. That is what this research centre needs to examine," Kenneth pointed to the snarling creature. "This is what's out there, attacking people. This is our job." Kenneth approached the gate, and a soldier opened it, two more followed in behind him, "We'll need some rope to secure it and a bag for the head."

They carefully exited, rifles at the ready as they stepped between the bloody bodies of former colleagues, civilians and the creatures. Kenneth looked closely at one, he was sure it was safe. Its head split in two courtesy of a 5.56mm round to the cranium. The skin tone struck him, the thing was formerly a black man, that much was obvious. But his skin whilst still dark, took on a grey, nearly metallic hue. His clothes were loose, splattered with dry blood underneath the new still wet patches. Its mouth was open, the teeth chipped, the eye that hadn't been obliterated was cloudy.

They cautiously approached the surviving beast under Bobby's body.

"How do you want to do this Kenny?"

"We'll bag its head, get a rope on each arm and drag the fucker to the gate. We can do a proper job in there."

The two soldiers did as they were told and the three of them dragged it in; its feet kicking and flailing, the noise of its teeth slamming together and its angry moans. As they made it through the gate, it was quickly closed behind them and everyone stood back not brave enough to get too close in case it broke free. Kenneth took off his belt and bound their captives' legs. It continued to thrash ineffectively as Kenneth stood back.

"What do you want us to do with them?" Kenneth pointed towards the bodies along the fence and gate.

"Take three men, move them to the other bodies and burn them all." The Major started walking back towards the main building, "Perhaps keep one creature out there, in case the white coats want to poke at a dead one."

43

The lab was working 24 hours a day. Diane was one of its workers. She was in her forties, a plain-looking woman, with a slight build with mousy blond hair, who had an engaging personality. Before the outbreak, she wasn't career-driven and rather junior in her department at the local water company. Testing water samples and jars with a lump of excrement in them wasn't an exciting life, but there was no pressure, and that suited Diane. The fact she found herself in a military camp as the world looked doomed was luck rather than judgement. No more jars of shit for Diane. Now it was various tissue or blood samples, but the pressure was on. The water company was as relaxed an environment as you could hope to have been in. The government and military were more highly strung.

She avoided direct contact with the subjects but saw them entering the treatment zone. It was by the end of the first day she realised none of the patients were being treated. They were being held, sedated, and either euthanised or taken away for testing before they turned. Diane wasn't comfortable with what was being done, but she trusted in her superiors. It was always harder when the patients were children. Diane was just starting her shift when two patients were being brought for treatment, a woman whose face and arm were bandaged and a policeman.

A doctor called her over, "You, you're in research, right?"

Diane slowly walked over, hoping she would be dismissed.

"Yes, I'm just a scientist. Quite junior," she hesitated but answered honestly.

"Come with me, we're short-staffed." His authority made sure it was a command, not a request. "I'm not medically trained." She hoped that would dissuade him, let her get back to her microscope.

"You can hold a tray, swab a wound and apply a dressing, can't you?" He sounded condescending.

"Yes." He would get her to help no matter what she said. *May as well just get on with it.*

"Well, this way then please."

Diane followed the doctor into the treatment zone and taken aback. She'd never entered before and wasn't expecting to see so many patients, strapped to beds and sedated. She'd assumed there might be double figures, 15 tops but there were around 50 people with half a dozen armed soldiers keeping a watchful eye on them. The doctor led her to the two new patients. He looked over the woman. She was unconscious and her wounds, despite being bandaged, were seeping. He instructed the two soldiers to take her to the research. Diane knew what that meant, a live test subject for vivisection. The doctor next looked over the policeman. He was conscious and calm; his hand was bandaged and it looked like he was missing some fingers.

"PC Derek, Derek Jones. You were in the camp when attacked?" the doctor was making notes as he spoke.

"Yes, one of those things got in." He was calm, resigned.

"And it took two of your fingers? Bite?" He already had the information but was testing his mental state.

"Yes, it happened in a second, bit them clean off. I think it swallowed them whole." Derek seemed almost impressed it could do such a thing.

"Derek, you know the prognosis isn't good?" He held the notes down and made eye contact with Derek.

"I know," there was a tinge of sadness in his voice, but he'd accepted his fate, he'd be with his family soon enough.

"You will become one of these things. There won't be any physical pain, none more than you've already experienced, but the infection will take hold and reach your brain. It's there already. You'll start having urges and you will lose control. At some point, you'll cross the line and not be yourself; you'll be something else."

"So what happens? Do I wait it out?"

"Well, you can, but I wouldn't recommend it. You can be anaesthetised and knocked out cold. You won't feel a thing, we'll run some tests then humanely end your suffering. You will be at peace."

"No third option?"

"Well, we can give you a strong anaesthetic but you'll remain conscious. We'd open up your skull and monitor your brain whilst running a series of tests. It'd help give us a huge insight into what is happening."

"You're a doctor?"

"Yes, but I'm also a scientist. We can't treat anyone until we know more. We've got plenty of infected who are too far gone and corpses to test on. But we can only learn so much. You're newly infected. What we could learn from you over the next six hours could help save humanity."

"I won't feel anything?"

"Nothing at all. You'll be conscious and we'll be talking to you throughout. We can increase the pain relief if you begin to feel any discomfort."

"I guess I can't say no."

The doctor finished writing his notes and gave them to Diane before calling over two soldiers, "This one needs to go to research. She has the notes; she'll assist."

"I don't do this kind of work," Diane muttered to no effect.

"You think I did? This is new to us all, you're a fucking scientist. Go help with some fucking science. We all have to get our hands dirty."

44

Kenneth hadn't been in the lab before, he didn't relish it. The smell was something artificial and not at all pleasant. His reward for hogtying the creature that had condemned him to shoot his friend in the head, was to accompany it and keep guard. It was a waste of his ability, but the Major had insisted. This was a dangerous thing that needed watching, and might need putting down. Kenneth was the only man the Major had seen display the attributes that might be up to this task on his own. They couldn't spare a second guard when they were already spread so thin.

The creature hadn't calmed down at all since they secured it. Now tied to a gurney, the hood remained on its head as it struggled to get at the mass of people around it in their protective masks. The scientists were eager to examine the creature. The lab wasn't originally set up to take a live subject, but as the crisis loomed the lab took delivery of more expensive equipment and those trained to best use it. They had been struggling with a few old samples sent across from the first recorded cases. The well-prodded tissue sample and the small vial of blood had yielded no breakthroughs and they had learned very little. Now, they had an infected live specimen, and a freshly slain sample to do with what they wished. But how to get started?

The giant soldier didn't speak, didn't move. He just stood

over the creature; rifle ready to shoulder so he could kill it. He was both reassuring and a worry for those present. They'd all just seen the execution. They understood. They were men and women of science and too aware of the importance of their work. There was a contagion and one of the few things they knew was the method of infection, transmission of bodily fluids. This wasn't their discovery; this had come in the briefing pack. They trusted it, but not enough to readily breathe the same air as it without a mask.

Dr. Jana Srnicek was the woman in charge. She was born in Czechoslovakia in the sixties, moved to London in the seventies and stayed ever since, raised two children, and now a grandmother. She was good at her job and this terrifying reality they were living in was a challenge that stimulated her immensely. She couldn't think of her family beyond using them as a motivation to succeed and to do so quickly.

Whilst the others stood back pondering, Jana stepped forward, "Shall we get to work then people. I want fresh samples. I want a CT scan now and I want everything documented, that includes video."

The white coats began scurrying around immediately putting into action her demands. Kenneth respected her authority and calmness. He'd dealt with civilians in Afghanistan and found he could put most into one of two categories: "twats" or "useful twats." Dr. Srnicek was definitely in the latter group. His orders from the Major were simple, but not pleasant. If it escapes, put two in its head. If it bites, scratches or spits on anyone, they would receive the same treatment. Dr. Srnicek knew of these orders, but Kenneth doubted anyone else did. He'd rather have been outside with his fellow soldiers, not inside with the nerds.

"Would you like a seat, Lance Corporal?" an attractive young woman in a lab coat offered him a chair with a smile.

"No thank you ma'am."

"Maybe a cup of tea?" she meekly responded.

"No, thank you." Kenneth wasn't keen to fraternise with the girl, she was beautiful, and Kenneth thought or at least hoped she was flirting with him. At best there would be flirtation and nothing else. At the worst, be might have to use two of his bullets on her. There was a moment of awkward silence before she sheepishly got back to her business.

Dr. Srnicek had noticed the exchange and approached Kenneth, "That was a little cold soldier. She's just a girl trying to be nice when the world has turned decidedly nasty."

"I have my orders, Dr. Srnicek."

"Call me Jana, and as I recall, your orders aren't to be a prick to my staff."

"But..."

"But nothing, I know you might want to keep a personal distance for fear of questioning your orders to eliminate any threat should you have to. But I want you to question it if the time comes. Our world is seemingly full of unthinking, uncaring creatures. Do you think you really should be aspiring to that?" Kenneth didn't get a chance to respond before Dr. Srnicek walked off.

She approached the girl and patted her on the shoulder before whispering something in her ear. They both looked at Kenneth who looked away out of shame.

45

Amy sat slumped against the fence, close to where the attack happened. The civilians gave her and the corpse a wide berth. She figured that someone would probably come and clean it up eventually, but it was dead, and no one would dare touch it, so it was hardly a priority. Looking at the wire, she could see another section being constructed; the workforce quickly assembling a new fence line under the watchful eye of the soldiers. Surely this would be the last expansion? Each fence was more hastily assembled than the last. The new addition was a little over 12 feet in height of chicken wire with a few fence posts. So eager to get the job done, they cut corners, not even clearing bodies, hoping someone else would do it. At least the previous section had barbed wire and was corpse free.

The number of people coming into the camp had dropped in the last day. Trucks coming in held only a handful of survivors. Those coming in on their own had completely stopped. The soldiers too were taking a battering. She stood up and brushed herself down. Her baton was on the ground and she bent over and picked it up. Looking at it in the light, the blood had a greyish hue to it. She walked over to the fallen creature and wiped the blood on its trouser leg before giving it a firm kick with her boot.

She started to walk away as a woman approached her

distressed, "My daughter, she's not well!" She was in a panic.

Amy's professionalism overtook her anger, upset and frustration. "It's okay, where is she and what is wrong?" Calm and friendly.

"I think she's turning. She's eaten all our food. She's sweaty and angry. She's not right!" The woman was failing to calm down.

"I'm sure she's okay. Can you take me to her?" Amy tried to give a reassuring smile before talking into her radio, "Checking on potential infected, assistance required. Low priority."

The radio crackled into life, "Confirm and med team will assist as required."

They would send no one further out into the camp unless they absolutely had to. The woman led her to a tent, Amy was hesitant to enter. If this girl was infected, she wouldn't want to be in a confined space with her. The tent's flap was open and she could see inside. The girl was maybe 14, slim and plain. Her clothes hung off of her and she was agitated. Her hands and feet were bound and were sore.

"Are you okay, honey?" Amy was nervous.

"I'm just hungry. I need to eat." She was desperate, but she didn't sound angry.

"Do you have anything you can give her? Anything at all?" Amy looked to the mother.

"We don't have much left. We haven't been given a lot, and she's already eaten almost all of it." She started rummaging through bags. She got to the girl's bag and pulled out some clothes, a toothbrush, sanitary products and a box of FatBGone which took Amy's attention.

"Is she on any medication?" Amy picked up and examined the FatBGone box.

"No, that's some silly internet thing she wasted her birthday money on." The mother was apparently unhappy at this decision.

"Do they work?" Amy seemed genuinely interested.

"It did, she lost 7 stone. She was a big girl."

"So, it wasn't a total waste of money?" Amy felt it was an exaggeration, but obviously it had worked to some extent.

"Well, it was over 500 pounds. She didn't tell me that. All her birthday money and she sold her iPad. She didn't tell me that either. All to lose weight for a month. Bloody kids." The mother was exasperated. Despite everything going on, she still had her motherly frustration at watching her child wasting money.

"500?" Amy couldn't believe it.

"500," the mother confirmed sternly.

Amy placed the box back on the floor, "I'll get a medical team to take a look." Amy put her radio to her mouth, "Control, I'm…"

The mother stopped her, "Will they take her away?"

Amy knew the answer. This kid was infected. She was already showing the signs they'd been told to look out for. She'd be dragged away, to the same place as Derek, never to be seen again. She couldn't remain here; she was doing the family a favour. The girl would go fully insane, attack her family and condemn them too. No, there was only one thing to do.

"They will check her over, may take her in for some antibiotics but she'll be fine, I promise," Amy lied. It was the kind and necessary thing to do.

Amy called it in, and she waited with the woman and her daughter. Waiting for them to be separated forever, for this teenage girl to live out her last hours scared and alone. Amy put her arm around the woman, wishing someone would put their arm around her.

46

A cacophony of muffled groans, moans and whimpers filled the air. Only two soldiers were guarding this area, both in the corner next to the entrance facing into the room. A small pile of sandbags gave them some cover and a place to perch their general-purpose machine guns. If there was trouble, these two men could shred everyone in the room within seconds. This did not give Diane any comfort. There were maybe 20 people strapped to gurneys, some heavily sedated, a few nurses, doctors or scientists keeping themselves busy. Diane was walking behind the two soldiers moving Derek to a space in the middle of the tent. They locked the gurney into position and the soldiers returned to the treatment room.

"So, what now?" Derek was still calm, but perhaps a little nervous.

"I'm sorry, I have no idea. I don't normally do this. I'm much more examine a glass of pee kind of lab technician." This was probably nearly as uncomfortable a situation for Diane as it was for Derek.

"I can pee in a cup if that makes you feel better?" he smiled.

"You're okay, thanks."

A man in his late sixties wearing a lab coat approached and motioned for the notes and started thumbing through them.

"Ah, very good. I'm sorry Mr Jones, but you will help us greatly. I know this is tough, but I can't stress just how much you'll help us learn." He tapped Derek's upper arm in a half-hearted attempt at comfort.

"Are you a doctor?"

"No. I'm head of research here. Call me Andrew." Technically, Andrew was Diane's boss, however, in her few days in the camp she'd never spoken to him. She had been in briefings, received a group bollocking and observed Andrew at the top table with those in charge. He never came across as friendly, so it impressed her he even bothered to try with poor Derek.

"Are you a nurse?" Andrew abruptly asked Diane.

"No, I'm in the sample evaluation team." He didn't even recognise her.

"Well, what are you doing here? Shouldn't you be testing samples?"

Diane couldn't agree with him more. "The doctor, he told me to bring him in." She would have been happy to get back to her job. This was not a nice place to be. What if one of these patients broke loose and infected her? What if those soldiers with the big guns got jumpy and opened fire? No, back in her little makeshift lab was perfect.

"I'd like her to stay," Derek smiled at Diane, oblivious to her discomfort.

"Well, then she'll stay," Andrew scribbled his own addition to Derek's notes and placed them on his legs.

"We'll be back shortly and get started. Can we get you anything?" Andrew couldn't do comforting if his life depended on it.

Derek thought for a second, "I'd kill for a burger."

47

The research area was very well lit, uncomfortably so. Diane now wore full protective clothing, gloves, a mask, and an apron. Others had come and fitted all manner of monitors and probes to Derek, the top half of his scalp had been removed and a man in a white coat gave it his full attention only glancing occasionally over to various screens set up around him. Derek was becoming agitated. Hours had passed since he'd been taken in. Diane hadn't left his side for more than a few minutes, mopping his brow, feeding him the meagre rations allowed and putting the straw to his lips to take the allowed small sips of water. Diane hadn't found the courage to look at Derek's exposed brain. She didn't see the need to.

"How's it going?" Diane asked. She knew, but she needed him to speak, to say the words.

"I've been better Diane. How's it looking back there?" If Derek could have squirmed with discomfort, he would have done so.

"I'm sure it's fine," Diane looked at the man in the white coat who made momentary eye contact revealing nothing.

"Can you take a look?"

Diane resigned herself to looking at an exposed brain in a live man's skull. She walked around and looked but wasn't shocked or disgusted. She'd seen such sights before, never in a live subject, but it wasn't that much different. She looked closer and something took her attention. A greying residue had formed around the hypothalamus. She couldn't be sure if this was normal, as normal as it could be with an exposed brain, but it didn't look right. "What's with that?" Diane pointed at the affected area.

"That's it. We've taken a sample, and it's being tested. It started developing around 40 minutes ago and is increasing. That part of the brain controls hunger," the lab-coated man carried on writing his notes.

"Is it just on the surface?" Diane tried to adjust her angle to see.

"No, from what we've seen from expired subjects, it is in the brain, the liquid you see is coming from inside." He wasn't as interested in talking as Diane. It wasn't his job.

"Is that even possible?" Diane seemed doubtful.

"I'd say so," he pointed at the residue to suggest that was evidence enough.

"How's it looking Diane?" Derek had been listening and didn't seem so much interested as worried. He didn't know how much longer he'd still be himself. Diane walked back around to where Derek could see her.

"Honestly, it's spreading and fast."

"Okay. I guess this is the final straight. Has this helped?" Derek didn't want to die in vain. He wanted his life to have meant something. He couldn't save his family, but maybe he could save some others.

Diane looked up at the lab-coated man, who again made brief eye contact saying nothing. She smiled as if she'd received a positive response and looked back at Derek. "Yes, this has been a huge help," she lied. Derek smiled.

"Can you do me a favour?" Diane half expected him to ask her to end it now, he could see his usefulness was drawing to an end and must have some kind of desire to keep a little dignity.

"Of course Derek, just ask and I'll see what I can do." She was sincere but prayed to herself he just wanted a sip of water.

"My fellow officers, Amy in particular, you need to warn

them. They don't truly believe that we're fucked. There are some good people. They just need to be ready and they're not. Just talk to them. Please do what you can so they know it's not all foil hat; that trouble is coming," Diane nodded. It could have been so much worse.

"I just need a few minutes fresh air. I'll be back shortly."

Diane made her way towards the treatment area, removing her protective gear as she went, as she approached she attracted the attention of the two machine-gun-toting soldiers who trained their weapons on her. She halted, frozen with fear before both acknowledged she was no threat and pointed their gun barrels in a different direction. She carried on through until she reached the treatment area, discarding her gear in a medical waste bin, she didn't stop to look around. She knew what was happening. She walked outside and took a deep breath of what passed for fresh air.

She missed the jars of shit.

48

Diane had spent most of the day with Derek, but he was changing rapidly as the hours passed. The transformation had been quick. He hadn't completely turned but was now full of anger and hunger. He had been heavily sedated, and Diane knew the next step would be the last one. She didn't need or want to be around for that. Returning to her small lab, expecting to see some familiar friendly faces, she was surprised it was empty. Equipment in place, a cup of tea still with steam rising from its hot contents. She began to worry that in her haze she'd missed an alarm or warning. Perhaps there was an incident and she needed to get out of there. She turned straight into a mousey white-coated woman in her thirties.

"Diane, the briefing is about to start. Where have you been all day?" It was Carole. Diane was relieved to see her but didn't have a clue that there was a briefing.

"They reassigned me," Diane offered with a forced smile.

Carole led Diane to a courtyard between the various makeshift labs. They had gathered most of the scientific and medical staff, and a few soldiers surrounded them. This didn't look good, but Diane had become used to the sight of armed men and women watching over them.

"We have perfected a test that will help us identify anyone infected, including those showing no obvious signs. We are sharing this information with the remaining camps we can maintain contact with. Unfortunately, we've had confirmation two of our sister camps have been evacuated. Our military colleagues are preparing a team to reach out and aid survivors. Order has fallen at a third camp and we are looking to support them soon." It was the usual parade of important-looking members of the camp, military, political and scientific. Those who controlled everything and had links with whatever was left of a government. It was the politician who took control - the smartly dressed woman who mastered understatement and would not be shaken.

There was a noticeable murmur amongst the assembled crowd. It was hard to think beyond the fence of their own camp, but to hear other similar sanctuaries had succumbed to either the things outside of the people within, was difficult to ignore.

"We will test some of you after this briefing, then you will assist with the remaining support personnel and he VIPs before we begin with the public." The politician saw it as very simple. It was down to everyone else to implement it.

"What happens to anyone who fails the test?" Carole had sheepishly asked, showing her inexperience and naivety of what happened in the camp.

"We must do everything to protect those not infected. The safety of this camp and its healthy inhabitants is my utmost responsibility and we will do what we need to do." A politician too experienced to say that she was authorising the murder of civilians but making those present certain it was the only way.

"Are we any closer to determining the source of this outbreak or finding a cure?" Diane couldn't see who had asked. The voice sounded old and croaky. It must have been one of the old GPs. None of the scientists would have bothered to ask a question they knew the answer to.

"As you know, we've been mainly occupied with producing a reliable test, but with your hard work we have fed good data back to Wellworth. We understand they are making tremendous strides towards a cure, but still require us, and the other camps, to assist them." Gee up the troops, but don't answer the question.

Few of those assembled could believe a cure was close. This thing was so aggressive, so quick to evolve a cure would be months away, if at all.

"Do we know what happened at the other camps?" Diane this time felt empowered to ask a question.

"We're still determining that. Our teams will assist and find out what happened. There are many dangers. We need to remain vigilant, on both sides of the fence." The military representative knew the living were as big a threat as the dead.

They wrapped the briefest of briefings up, those in attendance knew that their camp probably wasn't as safe as it felt. A new method of detection was about to be rolled out and that would lead to a number of people being led away to their deaths. At worst it wouldn't be hard to imagine full-scale riots.

Diane was on the list of 10 to have the test applied. They were led to a tent by another white coat and four soldiers. It was unnerving as they all knew the ramifications but didn't know for sure that they weren't infected. They were all scientists or medical staff and Diane stayed close to Carole, the most familiar of those around.

"The test is simple and quick. You will perform this yourselves so please pay attention." The test administrator wasn't familiar. She probably worked closely with the top brass. She was older and had a comforting authority to her. A young man was invited forward to take a seat on a stool, with the tester continuing to issue instructions.

"Please turn your hand and I will prick your finger." No more warning was given, and the young man winced as the small puncture was inflicted. A small drop of blood began to gather and once sufficient, it was scooped onto a glass slide with a drop of a thick white liquid placed next to it. It was then placed under a microscope and examined.

"Clear."

The young man breathed a sigh of relief, as did the other

nine members of the test group.

"The blood is exposed to the solution, a simple mix or lard with an off-the-shelf protein powder. I believe this one is vanilla." A bottle of the liquid was passed amongst the group.

"The solution doesn't react with the blood sample; the sample reacts with the solution when this microbe is present. Much as those infected grow an insatiable appetite, the microbe seeks sustenance. The fatty protein-rich solution is effective in provoking a reaction, and we can see this clearly. The same blood sample looks clear until it contacts the solution. In more advanced cases, the blood sample is swimming with the microbe and the test isn't required. I'm sure those of you have either seen those samples or the infected know that."

If they weren't trying to eat you, the advanced cases were using every ounce of what was left of themselves to resist tasting your flesh. If this test worked, it would at least mean those harbouring the infection wouldn't have the chance for it to progress or pass it on to loved ones. People such as Derek wouldn't be attacked and condemned for trying to protect others.

"Next."

Diane obliged and stepped forward. She was subjected to the same test and invited to look at the sample.

"Another pass." Smiles all round. This was easy, the mood lightened as everyone began to relax.

Carole emboldened by the clear tests felt confident to step up next. She reached her hand out and received her finger prick. The sample was taken, and the solution added. She waited for the all-clear. The sample was checked and double-checked. The confidence Carole had shown was quickly eroded.

"It's nothing to worry about, we need a bigger sample by the look of it. Can you go with the Private who will take you back to the lab? If they're not running too far behind you might get back for the end of the session."

Carole was filled with fear as the soldier approached and

stood by her. "Can I go later?" The words could barely pass her lips.

"It's best to get it sorted immediately. It'll be fine." The administrator signalled to the soldier who took Carole by the arm and began leading her away.

"Please!" Carole was crying but nobody would help; they were all too scared of what she might be infected with or what might happen to them if they got involved.

Diane stood wishing she'd had the courage to help, but the same fear gripped her as the others.

"Next please," the test administrator carried on, stride not dropped. There was a lot of testing to do, and over the next few days there would be a lot of failures. No need to get hung up over one poor woman.

49

In a time full of bad days, this had been one of the worst. Amy cut a lonely figure as she made her way through each checkpoint. She couldn't look the soldiers in the eye as she made her way slowly back to get some rest. She couldn't get Derek and that girl out of her mind. What a waste, what a tragedy. What a fucking day. She got back to her bed space, determined that her immediate future would be a shower, food and some sleep.

"Amy, debrief in the command tent, now," the voice came from nowhere and made Amy jump. It was another police officer, but she didn't know them, at least not well enough to be on first-name terms.

She didn't question the order, she followed. The command tent had several police officers and a white-coated woman. It was Diane. She approached Amy.

"I've been with your friend, Derek."

"How is he?" *Finally, some good news*, Amy had hoped.

"He doesn't have long I'm afraid. He volunteered to be studied, and the infection has taken hold."

What the hell? Why has this woman come over to tell her what she already knows? She could be grabbing sleep rather than being reminded that Derek is slowly turning into one of these beastly things.

"So, what do you want? Why come here and tell me that? I

know he's fucked. I saw him get bitten. Coming here doesn't help him and it sure as hell doesn't help me!" The days frustration and anger finally erupted from Amy as she barged past Diane to leave the tent.

"There are more, too many more," there was sorrow in Diane's voice.

Amy paused, "When did you get to this camp, before the evacuations, before the towns and cities fell? Before neighbours attacked neighbours, mothers feasted on their children? Of course, there are more. This isn't over because we've got a big fence and men with guns protecting us, this is still the start." Amy couldn't calm down and she didn't want to. "Your lab, that treatment area, I'm guessing there are hundreds of the same throughout the country, maybe the world, and they're the lucky ones. At least here they won't turn on those around them. I had a young girl picked up today; she was infected. What I did was a kindness to her and her family! She won't have to live with the guilt for killing them and they will survive!" Amy resumed storming out.

"More are infected. It doesn't always show immediately, a bite brings it on quicker, but there have been others, emaciated, weak, no bites or wounds but very much infected. One creature even appeared to have been perfectly healthy and lucid. Her husband woke up with her ripping a chunk of flesh from his arm with her teeth. Both are now tied to a gurney. Anyone could have it. In the next day testing will begin. First with us and then with the rest of the camp and anyone who shows a trace will be dealt with." It scared Diane.

"That's a good thing." Amy couldn't see the problem, they're dangerous and need to be separated from healthy people.

"When half the camp is taken away to be euthanised, do you think the other half will allow that? It's one thing taking away an odd infected person here or there, but mass removals? There will be a riot, more will die, become infected and we will fall, and we wouldn't be the first camp to do so." Now it was Diane's turn to be angry.

Amy was bemused, she well knew that most information was need-to-know, and she didn't need to know. The casual dropping in of the fact that other camps had been lost wasn't to be washed over.

"Camps have already fallen?"

"Two. And contact with a third has been sketchy at best as they are under siege from those they're protecting." Diane didn't have an awful lot of information to share but didn't see a need to censor any. It would make sense. People are scared, hungry and tired with an unknown threat lurking everywhere. Suspicion was high and knowing people, Amy could completely understand. She knew what desperate people were capable of. Whether it was a junkie needing a fix or a father defending his family. She could see the distrust in the eyes of the people in the camp. The gratitude of being saved was being quickly replaced by anger at the conditions and those taking away loved ones, never to be returned.

"Does the test work?" another officer got involved.

"As far as we can tell. We assume those without bites and displaying no symptoms are healthy but that isn't always the case. The test has already identified the infection in outwardly healthy individuals. When isolated and monitored, the infection continues to grow, and the victim shows more obvious signs before having to be sedated before they are eventually euthanised."

"We're a few police officers. We don't have any influence. We don't have any control. I don't know what you expect us to do?" So much information, so little use for it.

"You need to be ready. When this camp suddenly descends into riots, you need to help people get out, you need to protect them. We should all be putting some supplies to one side."

50

The treatment room was brimming with patients in various states. The soldiers manning the machine guns surveyed the potential targets and the two staff in the room. Diane had felt the need to see Derek one more time. She knew he would be sedated, waiting for his life to be ended, but she would feel guilty if she just abandoned him. She stood open-mouthed as Andrew placed his hand on a female patient's forehead and looked closely at her, then nodded to himself and inserted an object, a pointed metal rod resembling a shiny knitting needle into the ear of the unconscious patient. There was no movement as the victim lay motionless. Then a thick grey liquid slowly oozed from the ear. Andrew smiled as he wiped the rod on the gurney and approached the next patient.

"Andrew no, you can't." Diane was horrified. She saw this coming but witnessing the brutal clinical act of it shook her.

"You shouldn't be here," he briefly checked the file of the patient and then inserted the rod forcibly into the ear, again a thick grey liquid ran free. She knew these people were too far gone. She knew this had to happen. But they were still as much a person as they were a monster.

"You can't just kill these people. They're still human. We might be able to help," her voice quivered. She didn't believe they could be helped but hoped the head of research may correct her.

"We're running out of room and resources. Come the start of the testing, we will not be able to cope. You need to leave," he cleaned his implement and approached victim number three: Derek. He was barely alive and looked like shit left in the sun for too long, but he stirred. They covered him in dressings and bandages from the many experiments he had consented to and a few more he hadn't. Now he was worse than useless; he was a drain on resources. He'd provided as much data as they could rinse from his failing humanity and now, he was just a burden. They had sedated him and now was the end for him. Diane stood between Andrew and Derek.

"We can't just give up. We can't."

Diane pleaded but Andrew just shook his head and signalled for a soldier to join him. He reluctantly left his GPMG position and put two hands on Diane forcing her to one side. Andrew stood over Derek and looked him up and down. Something caught his attention on Derek's upper lip. Andrew produced a set of latex gloves and forced them on. He got in close to examine the grey scarred tissue and what looked like a boil. There was another under his chin and the back of his neck. He hadn't seen this before. It could just be a boil, or it could be something else. Certainly worthy of further investigation, Andrew moved in closer to it and gently prodded the boil on Derek's neck with his gloved finger.

Derek's eyes shot open and looked angrily on Andrew. In a split second he threw himself forward and bit down hard on Andrew's arm. He pulled away in pain, but Derek hadn't lessened his grip. The flesh ripped from Andrew's arm and Derek gulped down the small mass of meat. It hit the back of his throat and he wanted more. With all of his might, Derek pulled himself up and out of one of his restraints. He grabbed the soldier and pulled him closer, tearing a chunk of flesh from his throat. Diane pulled back as the soldier screamed. Other patients in their beds stirred and started wrestling with their restraints, spurred on by the scent of blood and closeness to fresh meat. Most hadn't tasted flesh, but the instinct was there and being so close was too much. Several broke free and rushed to join in the feast.

The sound of a metal bolt being cycled went unnoticed. The first gunshot didn't.

Andrew and Diane threw themselves to the ground as the remaining machine gun went to work on the room. Those who had freed themselves and those that hadn't were chewed up by automatic gunfire. Within seconds, several soldiers and an officer had entered, weapons drawn. The machine gun fell silent as the casing from the last round from the belt spun into the air and landed on the floor on top of the other spent brass. Diane cowered under a gurney. Andrew was clutching his arm a few metres away. His own blood trickling down his arm and his neat white coat speckled with the greying blood of those slain around him.

"You need to get me help, I've been shot," Andrew signalled to his arm. Diane was confused, stunned by him and could only stare at him.

"You were bitten, weren't you? Derek, he..."

"No I was fucking shot. Don't you say anything. I was shot. Shot! Shot and I need help!"

The GPMG was being hastily reloaded as the other soldiers covered the room. The officer held his pistol calmly in front. A few of the patients squirmed, wounded but not dead.

"If they've been injured, one in the head. Call it before you do it."

The soldiers carefully made their way through the room, paying close attention to those strapped down.

"I've got one," one soldier proudly proclaimed.

The remaining soldiers stopped as the first made his kill with a single shot. With the job done, they continued sweeping the room.

"I've got one too," a female soldier motioned with the end of her rifle under a trolley.

"Please don't shoot," Diane carefully came out of cover and stood with her hands in the air. "I'm not infected. I work here." The officer carefully approached.

"Anyone else?" Diane pointed towards Andrew who stood

up.

"I've been shot. I need medical attention immediately."

The officer looked him up and down. "That's the gunshot?" Andrew nodded. "You two, go stand by the entrance, tread carefully." They moved as instructed under the officer's watchful eye. Once in position the soldiers continued clearing the room.

"You have to tell them," Diane spoke in a whisper.

"Shut up, I'm fine." The anger was palpable. Another shout from a soldier, another gunshot followed.

"You might be infected. They need to know." Andrew stared at her.

"No."

Diane stared at Derek. A large part of his face was missing courtesy of a standard-issue 7.62mm full metal jacket bullet.

"You'll turn too, and quickly. We both know too well that will happen to you." Andrew looked down at the wound, it bled steadily, and he winced with pain. "If you say anything you're finished, I will have you thrown out of this camp and you won't last five minutes outside of the fence. You will die horribly and alone." He did everything he could not to scream at her, to display his anger through harsh but hushed tones. Another gunshot as another patient was put down.

With the room cleared, the officer approached them holstering his pistol, "Sir, I apologise that one of my men wounded you. We'll get you to our medical team right away." Andrew nodded. "Are you okay?" the officer enquired after Diane who nodded and wanted to speak up. But Andrew's glare drilled right through her. The officer called over one of his men, "Get a clean-up team here, maintain a presence and inform medical we have a GSW incoming." The soldier started relaying the orders into his radio. Diane couldn't keep quiet any longer. She stepped back and put the officer between herself and Andrew.

"He's bitten. That's not a gunshot, it's a bite." The relief was intoxicating.

"That's a fucking lie," Andrew exploded and moved

towards her, forcing the officer to step forward. He grabbed Andrew's hand and pulled his arm towards him.

"That looks nasty, maybe we need to treat you here?" They all knew infected were looked at in this treatment area, kept away from the more usual cuts and scrapes of the medical tent.

"No, I'm fine. It's a gunshot. I'll get it seen to." Anger replaced with fear. The officer removed his pistol and held it by his side.

"You will be seen to here, sir."

"No, I'm fine. I'll get treated now in the medical tent. I can get there on my own," Andrew made his way out of the tent and the officer followed.

There was shouting, a command to stop, a single gunshot.

51

Five hours' sleep after some rations and a wash at a sink. Amy still felt tired, hungry and dirty. It reminded her of being in the Met. She looked around at the other bunks, colleagues all in much the same state, albeit less of them than the day before. Two men were rummaging through a crate at the end of the bed next to Amy's. She vaguely recognised them, but it wasn't their crate. Her most recent neighbour had been a woman called Lou, in her early forties, physically and emotionally strong, an experienced police officer.

"What are you doing with Lou's stuff?" She was groggy, but slowly waking. One of the men looked up.

"Lou's been taken away. She ain't coming back. Do you want her tampons?"

Amy nodded, and the man tossed her an open pack. They continued routing through, pulling out some food items, socks, a pack of cigarettes and pocketing them all. Finished, they dropped the lid closing the crate and walked off. Amy approached gingerly and opened the crate. She saw a few personal photos, some used underwear and an Arsenal shirt. All useless to Amy. Lou had been lucky enough to have some possessions in camp, but that luck had run out. A shudder of shame crawled down her spine. She regretted invading Lou's privacy and regretted that it was a useless act. Diane's words of warning still bounced around her tired mind. Amy had started pocketing some of her rations. She figured in a week she'd have enough sealed supplies to last a couple of days if she had to flee the camp. She would use her patrols to find weaknesses in the perimeter and seek useful tools or resources. She would save her energy. Prepare, that was the plan.

Still perched on her bunk, several gunshots erupted. Not from the towers overlooking outside the fence, but from the heart. A full-on firefight in the centre of the camp close to where the infected were being held. Amy and her fellow officers grabbed their gear and began rushing towards the action, eager to help. Amy stopped for a moment and grabbed her meagre supplies, just in case. If this was it, if Diane was right, she didn't even have enough food for a day. This was too soon.

The gunfire slowed down as Amy ran towards it. Several soldiers blocked Amy and the other police officer's path, pushing them back at gunpoint. A soldier took charge and addressed the unwanted help.

"Stand back. This is under control, return to your duties!" The police stood their ground as Amy moved towards the front of the small mob.

"We're all supposed to be on the same damn side. We're here to help." The soldier raised his rifle and rested the end of the barrel against Amy's forehead.

"This is an Army matter. If we wanted some jumped up police cunt to help, we'd fucking tell you to. Get the fuck back or we will open fire!"

Several of the police officers backed off but Amy refused, she stood firm staring down the soldiers. She'd had enough of this shit.

The shooting had stopped. A man Amy vaguely recognised, one of the important research bods she thought, emerged from the infected treatment area, he clutched his blood-soaked right arm as he stumbled out in shock. An officer calmly followed him out, closing the gap until he was barely a foot away. He commanded the wounded man to stop. He didn't. The officer raised his Glock pistol and put a single round in the back of the man's head. The body fell to the floor and the officer already turned his attention to the green and blue standoff.

"Stand down, now!" His calm demeanour had gone. He was angry, and he wasn't just addressing the police officers. He quickly put himself in the middle of the fray and shoved aside army and police alike.

"Officers, thank you, but your help is no longer required. We had a breach and several subjects broke loose. They have now been neutralised, as have their victims. Please return to your business."

Amy slowly backed off with her colleagues, not daring to turn her back on these armed psychopaths until she was a safer distance, beyond the range of a 9mm service pistol.

"He just shot him, in full view of everyone," one of the blue mob quietly spoke up.

"I think he'd been bitten," another offered in defence.

"It doesn't matter. They can't just shoot people. Infected or not, if they've given up hope for a cure, we're all a whim away from being snuffed out," Amy replied. She had heard the warnings, she saw hints of what might happen and now she'd seen it. An execution plain and simple. Amy didn't know some of these police officers. The ones she knew she didn't know well. Their numbers had thinned over the days and trust was a commodity in very short supply. They were no longer brothers and sisters in blue, they were just people trying to survive. Scared individuals, feeling very much alone.

52

It had been another two days. The Wellworth fences had held, the creatures had continued to turn up but left unchallenged. After the initial large group, they now appeared more frequently but in smaller groups, first twos and threes, then fours and fives. Everyone was tired and irritable, but the initial shock had worn off and now everyone knew their situation. The TV had become an emergency broadcast with no information, electricity flickered on and off as the generators kicked in when the grid faltered.

Kenneth was the envy of his colleagues. Whilst they were outside doing laps of the facility, he sat in a nice cosy lab with a bunch of civilians being fed biscuits and cups of tea. That's how they saw it. He saw it as boring. The creature had been thoroughly prodded and probed. Fluid samples and scans, an arm had been amputated after the speed of the healing of wounds had been noted. The blood had clotted nearly instantly. The wound scabbed over then took on a near rubbery finish within an hour. Amputating the arm, the creature didn't flinch, and the wound, much like the smaller ones inflicted with prior sample removals, bled a little then healed, as much as you could consider it healing. The flexible scab had become as strong as skin within an hour. However, the most disturbing aspect of this was that the now severed arm acted in the same way. It had healed. It didn't move. It didn't take on a life of its own, but it survived in the same state as the rest of the body. Comparing samples from the first they had been provided, they could see a similarity, but this was something else. An evolution, or at least a strain that differed from the original. It had set off on a different evolutionary path. But how was this possible in such a short space of time?

"If you took off its legs and the other arm, I could get out of here and do some soldiering, Ma'am." Kenneth had been thinking about this since the amputation, but boredom finally forced him to suggest it to Dr. Srnicek.

"But Lance Corporal, if you're not here with your rifle, who will boost morale amongst my staff?" she smirked, even if she didn't want him there, the Major insisted on an armed presence.

Only Kenneth and one other soldier had been entrusted with this duty. The other soldier, a private, seemed happy to sit inside drinking tea and munching digestive biscuits. Kenneth's shift was nearly over. He'd get a few hours' downtime, enough for some food, a kip then back out. He hoped to talk the Major into changing his duty. He wanted to walk the fence. Maybe even go scouting beyond to see what was happening. Fresh air and a chance to do some real work for a change. The lab's phone rang, it could only be internal since the external line had been down for a day. Dr. Srnicek answered it, muttered a few words before beckoning Kenneth over.

"It's for you. It's the Major."

Kenneth looked relieved. Surely, he would be assigned a new duty. He took the handset and pressed it to his ear.

"Sir?" He listened keenly. "I'll be right out." Kenneth hung up the phone and turned to Dr. Srnicek, "You're to stow the creature back in the freezer. I will need to lock you all in the lab whilst I assist with an incident in progress." He ordered her, and she knew to not fight it.

A few pops of gunfire could be heard from outside, adding to Kenneth's urgency. He oversaw the creature being moved, then with the freezer door shut, he closed the scientists in the lab.

Running through the building, the gunfire picked up its pace, as did Kenneth, chambering a round in his rifle. He threw himself through the building door and was greeted by the sight of hundreds of creatures pulling on the fence. It stayed firm but the soldiers' nerves weren't as they fired more and more rounds at the things desperate to taste their flesh.

"Cease fire!" the Major was screaming at the men and slowly they followed the order.

Maybe 10 of these things were lying either neutralised or severely incapacitated, a few sporting fresh wounds but so many more massing. Kenneth rushed to the Major.

"Sir."

"We have two rows of fences. We have one small cache of ammunition. We cannot fucking waste bullets on every stinky bastard who licks its vile rotting lips in our vague direction!"

He had a point. They may have started with a few thousand rounds of 5.56mm, a few hundred 7.62mm for the sniper and the Major had probably two mags for his Glock. They were not a fighting unit. They were not in a war-zone; they were guarding a bunch of nerds in a lab. They couldn't afford to waste the little ammo they had when they had no guarantee they'd receive any more any time soon.

"Lance Corporal, I need you to use that brain of yours to improvise something sharp and pointy to insert into a few hundred skulls. Take two men and start clearing the outer fence, thin out their numbers a tad." Kenneth was finally given something useful to do.

"Yes Sir!" Kenneth ran towards several soldiers and tapped two on the shoulder, "You and you, with me."

The three men raced to the fence line and slung their rifles over their shoulders. There was a small stash of building supplies, offcuts mainly, from the improvements to the fence and front gates. Random bits of concrete, electrical wire, scraps of wood and bags of unused screws and bolts. A small stash of rebar seemed the most useful of these leftovers. Some were only a few inches long, others over a metre. Kenneth sorted through and put anything usable in a separate pile.

After a few minutes, he had built up a cache of nearly a dozen pieces of rebar of what he deemed usable size. They had nothing strong enough to cut through the zinc-plated steel bars, so anything too long wouldn't be of use. Picking out six of the best pieces, ranging from 2 to 4 feet, he handed them to his two men and took two for himself.

"These aren't particularly sharp so aim for the eyes. Don't get any blood on you, that's the queens uniform. She doesn't want it sullied with their filthy fucking grey crap."

The three men approached the gate to enter the void between the fences, another soldier unlocked and let them through. There wasn't a shortage of monsters ready to be test subjects for this most primitive of weapons. Kenneth stepped forward and was watched by 100 hungry eyes and a few dozen scared ones behind him. He picked his target, a pig ugly woman gnashing her teeth at him, her grey skin crusted with blood. Probably a fair mix of hers and some poor victims. Kenneth lifted the bar up and gripped it tightly as he began to take aim, he braced himself as he plunged the bar through the fence striking the thing squarely in the forehead knocking it back a foot into another creature, pissed off but otherwise unharmed.

"Nice shot Kenny!" one of the soldiers laughed as the creature pushed its way back to the front of the fence. Kenneth struck out again, this time the end of the bar pushed past the eye and into the skull and brain. Its body crumbled to the floor.

"That's one-nil to me you wankers. Get yourselves in the game. First one to 25 gets the last can of Coke I've stashed away."

Kenneth was pleased the simple weapon had worked. It would be a long day, but it would be a long day doing a soldier's work.

His two colleagues stepped forward and started ramming the metal bars into their rotten victims' skulls. Pops and crunches added to the sound of flesh slumping to the ground, bouncing off the wire fence.

53

Amy was patrolling alone. Civilians had continued to trickle in at a very slow pace, but experienced law enforcement officers hadn't. The civilians were increasingly feral. If not showing early signs of infection, they were desperate and interested purely in self-preservation. This led to more police officers being injured or killed, adding even more pressure on the remaining few. There had been talks at higher pay grades of arming the remaining police with firearms, but this was quickly turned down. Training issues aside, losing a police officer is one thing, losing a firearm would be disastrous. They supplied a few police issue tasers to those on the more dangerous patrols, Amy being one beneficiary. It was better than nothing, but anyone unlucky enough to come up against an angry mob would find its use limited.

The outer ring got worse every time Amy had to venture into it. The strong preyed on the weak, and humanity had shown its ugly side in only a few weeks. Rape, murder, and drugs piled on the misery. With food running low, it was the weakest who suffered. The very young and very old had their rations and belongings stolen. Underage girls forced to exchange sexual favours with disgusting older men just to get some food for themselves and their families. One or two of the soldiers took advantage. It was a tiny subset, but it bothered Amy the most. She had happily cracked the skull of an offender amongst the civilians, but the soldiers were a law upon themselves. They left no doubt that any action against them would be brutally avenged.

Amy was cautious and tried not to stray too far from the sight of the soldiers at the nearest gate. She had her baton in one hand and the other never further than a few inches from her taser; she didn't trust anyone anymore. She carefully surveyed the area for victims whilst determined not to become one herself. It was quieter than it had been. She had stopped to speak to a few of the familiar friendlies and received her updates. Hope was sliding further into despair. Since the action in the infected treatment tent, many rumours had taken hold themselves or enforced others. Amy didn't know what happened beyond the vague breach details given to her and her colleagues. She knew there had been some deaths. She knew of the execution of the senior white coat, but that was it. The rumours were rife, mainly centring around a mass execution of large groups of anyone showing the slightest sign of infection. These were the daughters and sons, the mothers and fathers of the camp's inhabitants. Scared and confused quickly turned to anger. The most outlandish rumour concerned the mass murder and butchering of the infected to provide meat to the hungry masses. Cannibalism was rife outside by the infected and the most suspicious didn't put this past those in charge to save the good food for themselves.

A man stood gazing at Amy. She didn't recognise him. Maybe he was a new inhabitant or perhaps he'd been lying low. Clearing 6-feet in height, he was slender and pale. He had lots of space around him. The other civilians wisely gave him a wide berth as if he had the benefit of a force-field repelling anyone foolhardy enough to get close. Amy rested her hand on the taser. She could have it drawn and fired at this man in half the time it'd take him to get to her. They stared at each other. She was certain she was seconds away from his attack. She edged back and felt a blow to the back of her head. She was down on her knees, taser in hand and baton in front of her. Amy tried to turn around and bring the taser into play and everything when black with a second strike to her head. She felt a brief shot of pain and then everything was numb, her head fuzzy. She wanted to open her eyes, but she couldn't muster the strength, her whole body refused to cooperate. She knew she was being dragged. She could hear it and sense the movement. This was it. Since the day this mess started, she knew she was counting down the hours until she would be dead.

Muffled voices surrounded her, but she couldn't make out what they were saying. Amy thought it sounded like at least one male voice and maybe two women or even children. Feeling started to return; the numbness began to wash away. The pain grew as the feeling returned. She still couldn't move; they had bound her arms and legs with wire. As Amy opened her eyes, she saw her captors a family of three, a mother, a father and a young boy. They had taken her back to a tent. It was probably a six-man tent. It was dark and dirty.

"What do you want with me?" She was groggy, the words were slurred. Amy looked around the tent. There were two adult sleeping bags, a Crystal Palace children's sleeping bag and a pink one with a unicorn printed on it. "Where's your daughter?"

The father examined the taser and pointed it at Amy.

"You took her. You're supposed to protect us, not take a little girl from her mother. From her family." A sad anger ran through the father's voice as the mother gave the boy a loving squeeze.

"I didn't take your daughter. If they took her it's because she's infected; they will treat her. They'll do everything they can to make her better." Amy remained calm as she began to feel more like herself, but well aware of her situation.

"They are executing people. We all heard it. We've seen the bodies and the breathed the stench from the fires. Don't tell me you're helping people. You're fucking murdering us." The father stood up and looked outside the tent checking for anyone who cared about the brazen abduction of a female police officer. The camp continued as usual, with nobody sparing a shit for anyone else.

"We will trade you for her. You're one of them. They'll give Maggie back to us for you. She's my little girl." The mother was desperate but protective, not willing to let go of her son.

"They won't do it. I wish they would. I wish they could but the number of infected is increasing. If your daughter is infected, they are your only hope. If she isn't, they will bring her back. I promise."

"That's bollocks. Either they bring her back or I'll slit your throat in front of them." Anger now overtook any hint of sadness in the father's voice.

"They will let you do it. Then kill you, your wife, and your son. Their priority is maintaining authority in the camp and that is it, if you stand up to them, they will stamp you down! Let me go. I'll see if I can find out some information about Maggie," Amy held her hands out towards the father, hoping he'd see sense and free her. He picked up the baton and struck Amy in the head. Again, a sharp pang of pain and numbness. Again, everything went fuzzy. Again, everything went black. Amy didn't know if she would ever wake again, but there was nothing she could do about it.

54

The father hugged his wife and son in the tent's entrance. She was crying, and he tried to comfort her but failed miserably. She rested her hand on the boy who just stared at Amy, gagged and bound. She was coming around.

"Please don't. She might be right," the mother pleaded, the father had made his mind up.

"That's why you and Liam are staying here. I have to try. I can't... I can't just do nothing. If I don't come back, stay strong for him, look after him. Do whatever you need to do."

The father ruffled his son's hair before hoisting Amy on to his shoulder. He had the baton hanging out of his belt, taser shoved in his pocket and he picked up a crude blade. It was rough, as uncomfortable to hold as to look at, created from used tin cans and wood offcuts. It wasn't the work of a fine craftsman but of a desperate man. As a stabbing implement, it would be unlikely to be effective for long, but he'd made sure the blade was razor-sharp, slashing was its purpose. And for that it would prove perfectly adequate should the need arise. He gazed upon his remaining family and left the tent hopeful it wasn't the last time he'd see them; aware it probably was.

Walking through the overpopulated camp, the other civilians upon noticing Amy bleeding and slung over the shoulder of a knife-wielding man, wisely gave way. The soldiers at the checkpoint had become far too lazy and relaxed, a grunt toward the average civilian sent them scurrying off back to the hole they had dared to creep out of. They smoked and talked amongst themselves. The reserve soldiers lost a little discipline every day, much like the civilians. They hadn't noticed when a strange man approached and stood only 15-feet away. The father stood and waited to be noticed, and waited. After what seemed like an eternity, he dropped Amy roughly to the floor. She stirred but wasn't conscious as he pulled her up and held the blade to her throat, he announced himself.

"You have my daughter. I have one of yours!"

The soldiers turned and raised their rifles at him, but seeing all he had was a police officer, seemed less panicked, less concerned.

"Slot her, I don't care," the young soldier wasn't battle-hardened, but like everyone else he'd seen a lifetime's worth of misery and suffering. He no longer felt the need to pretend everything would be okay, or that any of these people mattered.

"I'll do it! I want my daughter back now!" Their attitude shocked him, but he only had one hand to play and he had to play it.

"I don't give a fuck if you're demanding the fucking Queen. If she's infected, she's in there and she ain't ever coming out."

The father dug the blade into Amy's throat, a single drop of blood ran down her neck as he pulled her hair back so the tiniest of wounds was more visible.

"Look mate, I don't give a shit about her, but we will shoot you. Your girl is gone, killing that copper will not change that. But it will give me an excuse to put a round in your fucking face. I've only shot those hungry bastards, a fresh one like you will be much more fun." The soldier shouldered his rifle and pointed it at the man taking two steps forward, "Walk away. Now!"

The knife began to feel very heavy. He held it firm, but he could feel it beginning to slip from his grasp. A father loved his family, he loved his daughter and even if she were to die, he was damn sure he'd do everything he could to make sure she didn't do it alone.

"I just want to see my daughter. She's only four. She doesn't understand."

The soldier had grown tired. He pulled the trigger once; a round entered the man's throat forcing him to stumble back letting go of Amy and dropping the knife. He clutched his throat, but it did no good. He was already dead. He collapsed to the floor, coughed and spluttered then stopped moving entirely.

Any civilian foolish enough to have stayed to witness the interaction now made it their business to run and hide.

"For fuck's sake Jimmy, now we will have to clean this shit up," a soldier pointed out.

"Matt, call it in. They'll get it sorted."

One of the soldiers approached Amy who was face-first on the ground, he lifted her by her collar and turned her to face the others.

"Marks out of two, I'd give her one." A few childish laughs from a few of the soldiers as Amy was dragged clear from the body and dumped unceremoniously on the other side of the checkpoint. The incident was being called in as Jimmy stood over Amy.

"Kyle, what do you reckon?"

Kyle approached and eyed Amy up and down, "I don't know Jimmy, she's a cop."

"So? You didn't have a problem fucking that 15-year-old girl or that mother of three in front of her kids. She's got a cracking arse and is already tied up. Sounds like a win to me." Jimmy copped a handful of Amy's buttocks and nodded in approval.

"Okay, let's do it," Kyle relented.

"We're taking her in, back in 20." Jimmy announced to the other soldiers.

"Maybe 25." Kyle corrected.

They made their way through the camp.

"Where do you want to do this? Same place as last time?"

Kyle already wanted the deed done. Every moment with her risked discovery, carrying her through the camp would look suspicious, but easily explained. Taking her to a tent in a civilian area might look odd, but as long as they weren't seen by anyone official, they would go unchallenged.

"Nah, I've got a new place. Smithy set it up last night. Nothing but junkies and scum. They won't bother us." Jimmy was confident.

The tent had tape all around it, a warning to avoid entering. It was enough to dissuade any civilian but meant nothing to soldiers, police or anyone else in authority. There they could have their fun.

55

For the second time today, Amy was regaining consciousness. This felt so much worse than the last time. Her head pounded, she couldn't see anything but she was sure her eyes were open. She couldn't hear properly, everything was muffled, breathing was hard, and she felt a pain between her legs.

"Bollocks, I think she's waking up."

Amy was bent over, face buried into a pile of bedding in the tent's corner, her hands still bound underneath her. Her trousers had been removed and her top ripped open. Jimmy was behind her, on his knees with his trousers down by his ankles, he was reaching forward and fondling Amy's breasts as he continued penetrating her.

"Jimmy, I think she's awake!" Kyle was panicking, he tried to pull Jimmy away from Amy, but Jimmy swung back.

"Fuck off, I'm nearly done!" he continued thrusting at Amy.

She started to realise what was going on. She tried to scream but the blankets obstructed her mouth. She threw herself to the side and could see Jimmy, a sweaty disgusting mess of a man. She tried to fight him off but struggled to get her bound hands to lash out with any strength. Jimmy easily held them as he continued raping her, but now her screams filled the tent. Jimmy punched her in the face, but she didn't stop. If she couldn't fight him off, she was making damn sure someone might hear what this animal was doing.

"Jesus Jimmy, stop!" Kyle paced up and down.

"Shut up, shut the fuck up!" Jimmy was hurrying his pace and getting angry. Kyle couldn't take it anymore and ran out of the tent.

"Just us now officer," Jimmy got in closer.

Amy tried to connect her head to his face, but he pulled back and treated her to a cocky grin.

"Get off me! Get the fuck off me!" Amy tried to remain strong, not cry. She wasn't used to feeling helpless, to be unable to look after herself, and had never felt so betrayed by another human being. She didn't know this man, but he was committing the most heinous action against her for no other reason than he was a horny arsehole. Jimmy was nearly there, he knew it. Amy feared it.

Jimmy's throat exploded as the buckshot entered the side of his neck and exited the other side. Amy was splattered with blood as Jimmy fell limply to the side. She looked at the tent's entrance, a man, a civilian holding a sawed-off shotgun. Christ knows how he got it into the camp but thank God he did. He was old, grizzled and rough around the edges. He picked up a blanket and covered Amy.

"Filthy fucking rapists. I never had any time for them then, and I don't now."

He bent over and pulled out a knife from Jimmy's scabbard and handed it to Amy who struggled to free herself but succeeded. Amy put her trousers back on and fixed her shirt before staggering to her feet, still covering herself with the blanket. She looked in disgust at Jimmy and stamped hard several times on his exposed penis.

"Sorry I put his throat out so you couldn't do that why he was still breathing. Are you okay?" He seemed genuinely kind, with a touch of the old school villain about him. Amy didn't think she had been crying but wiped her eyes just in case.

"Thank you."

"Boris, everyone calls me Bo," Amy nodded. Bo picked up Jimmy's rifle and looked at Amy. "I guess keeping this is out of the question?" He handed it to Amy with an additional magazine from Jimmy's body and helped himself to a pack of cigarettes, a Yorkie and a packet of boiled sweets. "You might not let me take the shooter, but you wouldn't deprive an OAP of a few fags, and something sweet for her indoors?" He gave his best east end charm.

"Do you have somewhere I can go. I can't go back. Not yet." Amy was shattered and didn't trust anyone, but this ageing crook with his illegal firearm seemed like a safer bet than the authorities. Bo smiled.

"It's not pretty and you'll have to put up with my old lady, but it's better than here," Amy finished straightening herself up and covered the rifle under the blanket. Bo popped his shotgun under his coat and led Amy out of the tent.

Considering that this was a layer of the camp that was a level closer to the centre, it was just as bad and desperate as her usual patrol. They walked through the camp and Bo nodded to various people he was obviously familiar with.

"Those pricks, they'll kill us all. I've told Babs, we were better off outside, but she says we're old. I told her, we're old, not daft. You can't trust people when everything goes to shit. You don't want to be relying on people you don't know. But you know, *we're old*," Bo put on his best fake whiny voice and shrugged his shoulders.

They arrived outside a tent, tatty green canvas. Besides a single potted plant, a pink rose that had seen better days, it was much like those around it. Bo widened the opening and announced himself.

"Babs, I hope you're decent. We've got the old bill here, someone's reported your cooking as the cause of the plague. I've agreed to testify in exchange for some clean socks and a Kitkat."

Bo and Amy entered. It was clean and tidy. The few available surfaces had pictures - some of Bo and Babs, others of children, grandchildren and random friends throughout the years. Where possible, homely touches had been installed - an old blanket doubling as a rug, a poster print arranged on the wall with two old cardigans to take on the appearance of curtains surrounding a window with a beautiful view of the countryside.

"Was that you and that stupid bloody pop gun?" Babs wasn't angry, she was frustrated.

"Some blokes were going at her. I had to help, didn't I?" Bo looked to Amy for confirmation. Before she could respond Babs cut in.

"You're a daft old man. You should have got one of those nice young soldiers or a policeman."

"They were soldiers," Amy piped up.

"And she's one of the filth. No offence." Bo added.

Babs offered a smile and gently took Amy by the hand and shoulder.

"I'd offer you a cup of tea, but we don't have any. Would you like a glass of warm water with a slight plastic aftertaste?" Babs led Amy to a white plastic garden chair. She gratefully took a seat and placed the rifle on the ground.

"You can stay here as long as you need love, but at some point they will find that prick without the throat and figure they're a pig down. No offence." Bo sat on a simple camp bed and broke open the shotgun and removed the spent cartridge carefully before replacing it with a fresh one. "I've been thinking Babs, maybe it's time we looked to move out of the city, head to the coast for our last few years. We always liked Bexhill, that sea air would be good for us."

"I'll pack up the flat and start getting the Marina loaded up, shall I?" Babs retorted.

"What do you need sweetie? Is there someone we can talk to for you?"

Amy thought for a moment, there was only one person. "A scientist, her name is Diane." Amy wasn't sure, but she was short on people she trusted.

"Is she a friend?" Babs smiled, hopeful.

"An acquaintance," Amy corrected. "But she seems like good people, I think."

"What's her full name?" Bo got back to his feet, the work of a retired villain was never done. Amy felt embarrassed. The only person she felt she could even remotely trust was a woman whose surname she didn't even know.

"I just know her first name. She's a white coat. She's in her mid-forties, dark blonde hair."

Bo shrugged, "I guess I have some asking around to do then. You stay put sweetheart and Babs will take care of you." He stashed his shotgun back under his coat, gave Babs a peck on the cheek and left the tent.

56

Diane was back testing samples. She had insisted upon it. She was done with dealing with the dying, those turning and the aftermath. She hadn't been afforded any time to recover from her ordeal, not that she wanted it. The clock was ticking, and she had nothing to do except stare at samples through a microscope. She knew that a cure was too far away, that no matter what they did, it would be too late. The boils on Derek were above Diane's pay grade. That sample was taken to a more respected team and they seemed excited. It was just another sample that would show what the damned plague was, but not how to stop it. Having given up, she was just winding down the clock, slowly getting used to the idea there were only days left. She just hoped when it happened, it would be quick. Maybe if she had got in the way of a stray bullet, it could have all been over already. A younger man in a white coat approached Diane, tapped her on the shoulder, startling her.

"You're wanted at the front. Something about your uncle."

Diane had an uncle. A lovely gay man who lived in Montreal with his Canadian husband. She had very much enjoyed the wedding and had visited uncle Jack and uncle Corey twice. However, they were very much in Canada when she spoke to them a few weeks before the outbreak. The likelihood of either of them turning up here seemed remote.

The chances of them somehow making contact was equally unlikely.

"My uncle? Are you sure?"

The younger white coat shrugged his shoulders.

"Aunt, cousin, I dunno. They'll tell you."

Diane thought twice about going, but it couldn't be any less fruitful than looking at more samples. She made her way out of the tent.

She walked up to the entrance to the research area, a soldier was waiting for her. He motioned for her to follow him and she complied.

"Your uncle is a colourful character," the soldier smiled. Jack was certainly that. "He's had the boys in stitches, we needed a laugh and he's giving it." Diane was puzzled. They walked through another level of security and she saw several soldiers standing around an old man enjoying himself, holding court. It wasn't Jack.

"Diane sweetheart, I can't believe it's you!" Bo gave a big smile and beckoned her in for a hug. "Your cousin Amy has been worried about you, she's with your auntie Barbara. Do ya think you can pop out for a visit?" Bo looked at the soldiers as if asking permission.

"Uncle, it's been a long time. I barely recognise you. How is everyone?" She played along.

"Amy is very upset. Seeing a friendly face might help her." The soldiers didn't seem to care if Diane went with Bo or not. She stepped forward and they let her through. Bo gave her a big awkward hug and Diane received it in the same spirit it was given. Bo led Diane away from the soldiers into the camp.

"Amy was attacked, she's fine. Well, not fine but she's breathing. The dirty fucker who attacked her not so much. She's with the old girl and doesn't want to go back, not yet anyway. She wants you." Bo had such a relaxed way about him it was hard to comprehend he was discussing a rape and subsequent killing of the perpetrator.

They passed through another checkpoint, the soldier acknowledged Bo.

"This one will come back in a bit. She's one of your boffins." The soldier nodded, and they passed through unchallenged. This was as far as Diane had been since she arrived at the camp. She knew conditions were bad but witnessing them was different from hearing about them. The inner circle of the camp was a paradise to this third world hell hole.

"One more checkpoint and we're there. You okay love?" Bo, ever the gentleman, felt the need to check.

"I'm fine," Diane lied. She had basic medical training. No more than a first aider, so hoped she was being called upon for little more than applying a plaster.

The next checkpoint the soldiers were a little rougher than the previous two. Subject to more abuse, taught to be wary of everyone and left alone to do their job as they saw fit. Bo approached with a big smile.

"Me again boys, can we get through?"

"Here we go. You only paid for a one-way trip. Is that one your payment to get back in? Bit old, but Gerry might be interested. Gerry!" The soldier was perhaps joking, but he wouldn't be the first rapist masquerading in her majesty's uniform Bo had met that day.

"Come on lads, you know me," Bo pleaded.

"I know you can get things old man. What can you get me?" Bo produced the cigarettes and Yorkie chocolate bar. Fuck them if they thought they were getting his boiled sweets.

"That's it?" The soldier wasn't impressed.

"That's all I've got on me. This one will come back through. I'll send her back with something good. You a Scotch man? Maybe Vodka?" Bo would promise anything right now.

"Tequila." Excellent, the soldier had named a price. It didn't matter if Bo could oblige or not; they were through.

"I know a man, Tequila shouldn't be a problem. Maybe another 20 fags too for you and your mates." The soldier nodded in approval and led Bo and Diane through.

Three men were fighting in the middle of a crowded thoroughfare between the gate and the mass of tents. The soldiers didn't bat an eyelid, and those present did little more than give a little extra space as they passed the bloodied men. Bo and Diane got closer. It appeared they were fighting over a tin of sweetcorn, none of the men were willing to give up their claim.

"First time in our little piece of paradise?" Bo asked but knew the answer, Diane nodded. "Shithole ain't it? I guess your digs are a bit nicer, not so crowded, probably fewer beatings and thievery?" Again Diane nodded, "Don't worry. I'll see you back safe." They arrived at the tent and Bo lifted the opening so Diane could enter. Inside, Amy and Babs were waiting. Amy mustered half a smile at a familiar face.

"We need to get out. Now."

Not a 'hello', a 'thanks for coming' but a declaration that it's time to abandon the decreasing safety of the camp and brave it with the things that were on the other side of the fence.

"I'm not sure we're there yet." Diane knew the day was coming, but she wasn't ready.

"I'm fucking there. I'm not going back. I'm getting out of this cesspit tonight." Amy had been keeping it together but was beginning to unravel.

"How are you going to get out? Tell me, I'd like to know. Even from here, you have two levels before you get to the fence. Let's say you get there, make it over, under or through the fence. The snipers or machine guns don't get you. The things out there fail to get a taste of you. Then what? I can assure you five miles in any direction have been picked clean of supplies or deemed too hazardous to try." Diane knew the camp would fall, but it wasn't the time. They needed more people, supplies and a vehicle. Amy, Diane and these two pensioners with a few scraps of food wouldn't survive for long out there.

Amy was quiet and stared at the floor like a scalded teenager.

"Just give me a day, 24 hours and I'll get us out, all of us." Diane didn't have any idea what she would do, but she needed time.

"One day. Then I'm gone." Her determination left no one in doubt she'd be leaving or die trying.
Bo turned to Babs, "Fancy a trip to the seaside love?"

57

Amy had tried to sleep, but it had been no use. Too many thoughts tumbled around her head - of that cunt who raped her, his friend who had gotten away, the desperate family, Derek. The state of the world. It wasn't helped by random bursts of gunfire directed outside and occasional screams inside the camp. There was no danger they would discover her. The security and soldiers had their hands full keeping order. No longer could they spare boots on the ground to win hearts and minds or prevent people spilling each other's blood. She sat in the corner of her host's tent and examined the rifle she had won from her ordeal. She had been clay pigeon shooting before but otherwise not had much experience with guns beyond what she had seen in films. She fumbled around it, careful of the trigger but otherwise familiarising herself with the gun for when it would be needed. She released the magazine and inspected it. It felt lighter than the spare Bo had handed her, no doubt a few rounds had already been fired in anger. The safety was easy enough to find. Amy worked it several times, same as the fire selector. She brought the rifle to her shoulder and stared through the sights.

"Preparing for war sweetheart?" Bo had been quietly observing as Babs snored away. Amy put the rifle down and covered it again with a blanket.

"I was born in the thirties. I was a boy during the war. I was probably six or seven when I prayed a dirty Nazi would cross my path so I could slot the bastard. It didn't happen. When I got the Queen's shilling, it was in Egypt for that fucking canal. National service throwing a 17-year-old kid across the world with a few weeks training to be shot at by rag heads. Sorry, Arabs. It was shit, but it was nothing compared to now. The Arabs just wanted us gone; these fuckers want to eat you. I killed a lad in Suez. He was maybe 15. He had shot my mate Julian in the back of the head, his face was a mess. Big hole, an eye hanging out and teeth just missing. One moment we were chatting about football, the next he was a lifeless lump of meat. I caught the kid, and he was petrified, I was too. I shot him. I said nothing, I just shot him. He was the first. It'll always stick with me. He killed my mate, but he was a kid, so was I. I know you're the filth, but I don't mind telling you I've killed a few since. They all deserved it and less innocent than that boy." Bo seemed disappointed in the life he'd led, his bubbly persona waning as he talked. "There are plenty of fuckers out there now who deserve it. You will have to be willing to kill anyone who deserves it. Sick or just a prick. They're all dangerous and not many good people are left, fewer with the means to make a difference," Bo took a moment to admire his shotgun, empowering himself with virtue.

"Are you a prick Bo?" Amy asked the admitted murderer.

"One time, yeah, you'd have had to watch me. Now? Nah, my kids didn't change me. Their kids did. Now some of them have kids too. I didn't want to be a great-grandad and a crook," Bo cracked a small smile at the thought of all his family.

"And just like that you're a good man?" Amy was sceptical.

"I didn't say I was good did I, sweetheart? Just said I wasn't a prick. When you go, I want me and Babs to come with you. We might slow you down a bit, I'll admit that, but I can be useful and Babs she, she's a good girl," Bo offered his most charming smile.

"Bo, anyone who wants out can come. I can't promise anything better than this. I don't think there is a utopia out there and we will just be swapping one hell for another. But we will at least have an illusion of control and not at the mercy of our betters to do with as they wish."

Babs stirred, "Will you two stop your nattering and get some sleep. Bo, you know you get cranky if you don't get your full eight hours."

Bo shrugged his shoulders at Amy, "I'll drop off soon love, don't you worry." He laid back down next to Babs.

"Will you be ready tomorrow Bo?" Amy wouldn't be delayed further. She had a day to find a plan, but she'd tunnel out with her bare hands if she had to.

"You might not need to wait that long. People are getting desperate. There's talk of fighting back and rescuing loved ones. They're getting organised but they're almost as patient as you, just itching to do something silly. Get some kip," Bo settled down and breathed heavily as he eased into sleep.

Amy laid down on her makeshift bed, she closed her eyes but struggled to sleep. Too angry. Too scared.

58

Dawn was still to break, and the camp was quiet, the tent filled with the sound of Bo and Babs snoring, which added to Amy's frustration. She wouldn't have been able to sleep anyway, but that fact didn't soothe her anger. A scream roared from within the camp, followed by maybe a dozen more. Amy couldn't work out what they were screaming above the noise of Bo snoring, but it was followed by several gunshots, then several more.

The altercation had turned into a full-blown firefight. Bo sat up aware something was happening, just unsure what.

"It's all right darling, it'll be fine." His first thought was to comfort his much-loved wife. The second was to reach his shotgun, "Amy sweetheart, you ready for your big move?" Amy drew the rifle to her shoulder and checked the safety. A young lad, no more than 15, burst in Amy took aim but didn't fire.

"Bo, it's all kicking off! They've taken three gates and pushing!" The kid was excited, not daunted by the bullets flying around, the loss of life or the plague affecting the world. His enthusiasm wasn't greeted with equal cheer.

"Sam, you keep away from the trouble lad. Those fuckers will put a hole in you just as quickly as one of those big bastards giving them a battering. Look after your sister." Bo was stern, Sam nodded and left. "Babs, get your coat, you've pulled," Bo slowly stood up and hobbled over to pick up a holdall which he slung over his shoulder and a woman's handbag which he handed over to Babs. "Make sure you have your lippy love. We're not coming back." Amy stood at the opening of the tent carefully peering out, rifle ready to be put to use. "You might want to keep that to yourself until you need it." Amy took one last look outside before holding the rifle awkwardly under her top. The three were ready and moved outside where the chaos didn't show any sign of calming.

People ran in different directions, clutching family members close. A large fire was taking hold across several tents, thick black smoke bellowed through the mass of people adding further to the confusion. Amy led the way. Bo was close behind clutching his shotgun under his jacket with one hand, dragging Babs close behind.

"Bo, I want to go back." Babs wasn't sure about leaving. The camp wasn't perfect, but it wasn't outside the fence with monsters.

"Don't be a silly moo," Bo turned to give her a wink and pressed on, eager to not fall too far back from Amy who seemed determined to reach the first fence.

They had dragged a soldier into the open, his face a bloody mess, but he was alive. His helmet had been removed, his equipment stripped, his body armour half gone and uniform ripped. Two men and a young girl approached him as he reached his hand up as if asking for help, all three started kicking and stamping on him. Amy changed direction to help the young soldier, but Bo momentarily let go of Babs to grab Amy.

"You can't save them all. We need to keep moving." He let go of Amy and reached back for Babs, but she wasn't there. Bo panicked. He'd only let go for a moment, they'd only moved 10 or 15 feet. Bo stopped dead and looked around the panicked crowd for his no doubt equally panicked love of his life.

He caught sight of her for a second as a small group passed

in front of her.

"Babs!" he squinted as he tried to see her again. "Babs!" His shouts became louder, fear entered his voice.

"Bo!" Babs appeared from nowhere and hugged Bo.

"Bloody hell love. You trying to give me another stroke?" He turned back to Amy, and they carried on their way.

The fires continued unchallenged, the soldiers and personnel who might try to extinguish them found themselves fighting for their lives. Amy, Bo and Babs reached the first gate on their way to the outer perimeter. It had been abandoned, whether the soldiers had left under their own power or had been dragged away half dead was uncertain. They didn't stop too long to contemplate. Gunshots intensified as a resistance to the insurgency became more organised, if still struggling for effectiveness. Amy climbed a fence to look at the way forward, and glimpse at the struggle behind. Two Warrior Infantry Fighting Vehicles joined in the fight using their 30mm cannons sparingly to carve large channels in the mass of rioters. They turned the fight. The desire of those fighting soon disappeared when a row of 15 people 2 feet away suddenly exploded into body parts or having large cavities appear where chests or faces used to exist.

"We need to move." Amy could see the tide had turned back to military strength and firepower. A stream of civilians piled both ways through the fence, hoping the other side would be better. Amy looked in the direction they were going; the next gate was clear and there appeared to be an opening in the next fence to the outermost ring. She jumped back down, and they continued their escape with Amy leading the way. The riot was being brought under control, but the soldiers would take some time to brave the outer rings where the armoured vehicles would struggle to support them.

They moved amongst the confused, scared and angry until they got to the last fence separating the camp from the outside world. The watchtowers hadn't turned their guns inwards, they stayed steadfast to their job of watching beyond the wire. Snipers, machine gunners and riflemen had held their discipline even when coming under attack. A single tower fired into the camp, but it wasn't shooting at the civilians, the fire was ineffective, sporadic but targeted towards the authorities. The two nearest towers had taken hits, the men inside lay wounded and bloody. More civilians began ascending those towers, encouraged by the surrounding mob. It took the 30mm cannon of one of the Warriors to dissuade that action. The tower exploded and lit up the whole area. Rounds cooked off and whistled in multiple directions adding to the panic. Those looking to take one of the other two towers by force thought better of it and merged back in with the mob.

A large section of the perimeter was now completely unguarded. Others had realised this and decided to take their chances with the hungry ones rather than the remains of civilisation. Large areas of fencing had been cut open and peeled back. Bo smiled when they reached their exit. He and Babs were out of breath but didn't look like they would be stopping. All three headed out into the darkness of the field with the other fleeing civilians.

59

Diane sipped a mug of tea as she sat in the darkness looking up at the night's sky. With much of the power grid down, a clear night like tonight offered a spectacular show without the interference of streetlights and other man-made illumination. The camp operated on minimal lighting. Sitting outside of the thick canvas lab tent in the early hours of the morning, the world seemed nearly peaceful with just the comforting hum of a generator. Hell broke loose.

Screams and shouts brought Diane to her feet. Several gunshots brought her back closer to the floor. People, confused and dazed, poured out of various directions. Soldiers began appearing with no better idea of the situation than anyone else but ready to act. The dark skies began to fill with smoke and light from the fire that was taking hold. More gunshots and more soldiers running blindly towards the action without an idea of what was happening or what they'd do. An officer appeared and called his men back, beginning to organise them.

"Unless you have a fucking rifle, I suggest you get your pretty little arses back to bed and await the all-clear!"

Many of the civilian workers obeyed. Why wouldn't they? Diane had other ideas. Amy was certain to be making her move to get out of the camp and she had to join her. Diane followed the soldiers at a distance slipping past the first gate with them unnoticed. She ducked behind a pile of sandbags as two soldiers fell to the floor a few feet in front of her, one looked dead, her eyes staring vacantly through Diane. The other held his bloody stomach and tried to crawl backwards to safety but the strength drained from him as the blood oozed from his wound. Diane stayed still, realising she was still holding her mug before dropping it to the floor.

The shouts and screams continued. They might have been chanting but Diane couldn't make it out. Gunshots continued with the soldiers struggling to effectively engage any meaningful targets whilst being picked off by aggressors merged with the angry crowds. Diane crawled on her knees to move further forward, her white lab coat illuminating her, but she hoped it would convince those with guns she wasn't a threat. She carried on determined not to stop. She passed the two downed soldiers but didn't look at them for fear she'd be further shamed into helping them. The soldiers still in the fight had now sought cover and no longer pushed further forward. The nearest checkpoint was a mere 20 feet away, but it was the frontline. The soldiers who manned it were nowhere to be seen but their service rifles were being put to good use by the angry civilians.

Several rioters had attempted to get through the checkpoint and had met with their ends quickly. Their corpses serving as a deterrent to any others considering this short-sighted plan. Other checkpoints were no doubt suffering the same fate, and several sections of the fence were being targeted with makeshift wire cutters. From nowhere, a group of four rioters armed with homemade bats set upon two soldiers from behind. The soldiers didn't see them coming as the bats beat them mercilessly. With the soldiers incapacitated, two more rifles had switched sides and began engaging olive green targets. They weren't trained marksmen and only found one target before the soldiers returned fire with greater effectiveness. But their brief attack had added to the confusion and panic amongst the ranks.

An officer grabbed a radio, "We need the armour in play

now. They're everywhere. I have several men down. Get me a fucking tank here now!" He had his Glock in his hand and blindly put two rounds towards the checkpoint.

He saw Diane slowly crawling and signalled for her to go back. They made eye contact, but she instantly looked away and continued. He looked on in disbelief as this moron crawled towards the angry mob.

As she got closer, she moved through blood, bodies and spent shell cases. She suddenly wondered what she was doing, looked back behind her then forward to see which was the best way - give up and go back or push on forward? She slowly climbed to her feet and began a feeble jog towards the checkpoint. As she got closer, she could see the angry faces trying to break through. They looked beyond her; she wasn't a threat, which was obvious. They did not understand what she was doing or why, but they didn't care. Diane merged amongst the crowd and carried on through it. She felt a huge sense of relief she hadn't been shot or beaten to death but didn't dare to let her guard down. She picked up the pace as she progressed through the camp. What little power and lighting there had been was now out, only the moon and the growing inferno within the camp lit the way. She bounced off several people and several more bumped into her as she pushed through towards the next checkpoint. As Diane moved further away from the soldiers and towards the outer rings of the camp, she felt less safe. To those duking it out with the soldiers, she was just a lab rat in a white coat, to those rioters further away, she was part of the authorities responsible for taking their loved ones. As a scientist, she would have been experimenting on them.

An angry woman spat in her face, "You fucking cunts took my whole family!"

She wiped her face and began to slip off her lab coat as a teenage boy shoved her in the back, Diane struggled to remain on her feet and stumbled a few feet forward before regaining her balance. She dropped the coat to the floor and hurried further on.

She made it through the next checkpoint. Nearly there. She looked forward and strained her eyes. She thought she saw Amy climbing a fence but couldn't be certain in the light. Several extra loud gunshots echoed through the camp. That was something big and the reaction was equally loud. Screams of panic filled the crowd behind her. Diane waved to get the attention of Amy ahead, a shove from behind knocked her to the floor. Three figures stood over Diane, two girls, neither older than 10, and a boy maybe 13 or 14. They were all filthy, skinny little things, bruised and angry. The boy had something in his hand, but Diane couldn't see what it was.

"Please I just want to leave, please," Diane pleaded.

Neither of the children said a word. The boy crouched down and repeatedly struck Diane in the stomach and chest.

The pain. She had never been punched before, but it hurt, damn it hurt. The children scurried off into the crowd, despite the pain Diane felt some relief. She tried to get to her feet but couldn't. The pain had her on her knees. She looked down at the blood, all over her stomach and chest. She began to panic. Something was sticking out of her stomach, she pulled it free - the handle of a toothbrush, the head filed down to a point. It was soaked in her blood. The little bastard. She lay down on her back.

"Help, someone, please." No one came to her aid.

A man tripped over her and she lifted her hand towards him, but he looked back then ran off. Diane hadn't noticed before but it was cold. She was so tired. It would be okay. Someone would help her. Diane closed her eyes. Just for a moment. Just until someone would come to help her.

60

The Surrey countryside looked beautiful as dawn began to break, the green fields illuminated as the birds sang. A dozen or so civilians rested in the open with Amy, Bo and Babs amongst them. They had nowhere to go, but they couldn't sit in a field all day. Several had already set off alone, the strongest generally had taken this option; the weakness of the group was obvious and they decided they'd be better off going alone. Those left behind were the youngest and oldest, the weak. Amy had in a matter of hours found herself the accidental leader of the group. Bo was more than happy with this and none of the others had the desire to take the responsibility, at least whilst they were in the open and vulnerable.

"I don't think they'll follow us. They don't have the manpower or inclination to do it. We just have to worry about the feeders," Amy climbed to her feet and stretched her stiff muscles readying herself to continue the trek.

"What next then love?" Bo was already standing. He dared not sit down for fear of not getting back up again.

"Carry on south. When we hit a road, we'll get a better fix on our location."

"That's great, but what are we doing? What's south? I don't know if you've had a chance to look around, but some of these folks make me look like bloody Usain Bolt. If we're lucky, we'll do another couple of miles, but no one wants to be in the open after dark again. Fuck knows how many we lost last night in the darkness. We all heard the screams. This group is a miracle. Jesus Christ himself must've been watching over us, but the fucker probably won't do it again. We should find somewhere defendable for a few nights, get some supplies, sort ourselves out. And we'll need motors," Bo helped Babs to her feet.

Amy looked around at the group. Bo wasn't wrong. Not a fighter or runner amongst them. They must have been truly desperate to choose this over the camp. Bo was right, but they had to push on. The army would have scouted anything of any size nearby, shelter might be achievable, but decent supplies would be less likely.

"What do you think happened at the camp?" Amy had a tinge of remorse in her voice. Maybe it was because many had died or possibly that this group would likely meet a grizzly end.

"It might help in the short term. Fewer people to watch, less food. If you're looking to regain authority, putting down an uprising, and doing it hard has the desired effect." Bo sounded like a man who in his prime had seen authority regained with the use of brute force.

"Diane. I hope she is okay." Amy tried not to think about it. "Time to get going everyone," she started strolling and checked if others were following. The group slowly got to their feet and followed.

61

A week had passed and the bodies at the fence had been growing steadily. The sight was grim and the civilians, no longer allowed outside, wouldn't dare to pay too close attention from the building windows. Half of the local town must have become infected and wandered to the facility looking to feast and finding only a tall fence, a pile of corpses and a soldier ready to dispense a cure to life. The soldiers moved with little more ease than the creatures that besieged them. They slowly shuffled about their duties, whether that was patrolling, guarding, or inserting increasingly grim-looking metal bars in the skulls of the things. The Major and Kenneth were having a briefing in the grounds slowly walking as they talked. Like the rest of the men, they looked tired and had little time to sleep. Niceties such as shaving had gone out of the window and both sported several days worth of growth.

"We might need to organise a long-range patrol. I'm still hopeful we'll be resupplied and maybe even reinforced, but we need to plan for a scenario where that won't happen."

The situation they were in had a calming effect on the Major. He knew shouting and screaming were no longer the appropriate methods for dealing with his men. He spoke softer, listened and whilst maintaining discipline, he did so more like a father than an army Major.

"We can't spare a single man, sir," Kenneth stated the

obvious but felt it had to be said out loud.

"I know Kenny, but I think we might have to spare two. I can't send a single man out there. I can't imagine too many volunteers for that duty," the Major surveyed the fence line, one or two of the creatures still to be dealt with.

"I could do it sir. I could take a rifle, one of the cars and make my way to the nearest camp." Kenneth didn't mind being out on his own.

"A big bastard like you would make a lovely meal for one of them," the Major allowed himself a smirk as he patted Kenneth on the back.

"I could do it." Kenneth was absolutely serious.

They hadn't heard from the outside world in two days. The base in Southampton was still broadcasting its automated message inviting survivors to seek refuge, but no longer responding. They were the last contact, smaller camps had gone quiet a few days before. If Kenneth or another soldier were to head out, Southampton would be the destination. It would only take an hour and a half by car normally. However, it could take days the way things likely stood. Roads would probably be blocked, towns would be no-go areas. Swarms of these things could take a day to evade and navigate. It wouldn't be easy, but between Lewes and Southampton were several camps. They may have fallen, they may just be without power or have equipment failure. They may also just be a mass of bloody bodies and creatures feeding on them. There would be only one way to find out.

"Sir, I could take the Landy, a days supplies and head to Southampton, scouting between us and them for survivors or resources. I'd be back in two days." Kenneth was eager to get moving.

"We'll keep that in our back pocket Kenny. If I decide to proceed, you will be my man. In the meantime, we need to make more improvised weapons and train some civilians. Those not working in the labs can help patrol. I wouldn't trust them with a rifle, but a piece of lumber or blade from the kitchen to protect themselves is fine." The Major was a pragmatist, soldiers, rifles and ammunition were in short supply, but they had a good number of civilians and many potential makeshift weapons.

Another week of this and his worry wouldn't be the creatures outside but the exhausted men inside who might decide a service rifle under the chin was preferable to carrying on.

"Talk to your pal Dr. Srnicek and get a list of non-vital civvies who she can spare, we can start training this afternoon."

"I can train them to blow a whistle, but I can't promise you an elite fighting force?" Kenneth liked the idea of help, he just couldn't see what he could teach anything useful in an afternoon to an assorted group of science nerds, canteen staff or IT geeks. If they saw one of these things, they should run. At best they could scream for help for someone useful to do something.

"Teach them not to cut themselves, how to swing a lump of wood and what to do on patrol. We're not looking at soldiers, we're looking at pairs of eyes. We could all be in this for the long haul." The Major was right, but Kenneth couldn't help feeling he'd be more useful driving to Southampton looking for supplies and reinforcements.

"Yes, sir."

62

A grand total of nine civilians had been put forward for training. A 57-year-old canteen worker, a 19-year-old cleaner, and a 4-foot-11 girl who worked in IT, no older than 25. These were the star pupils. They were focused and able to swing a lump of wood without giving themselves a splinter. The others just didn't want to be there. They just wanted to do their office or lab jobs and not patrol a fence close to the teeth-gnashing end of the crisis. But the Major was adamant. Every available "swinging dick or tit" was to be utilised. Out in the grounds, they had given the group an overview of what they were to do on a patrol, the importance of their role and given the opportunity to go to town on a few hastily built dummies. Hit the head and run was Kenneth's advice. Getting into a physical confrontation was exhausting and trying to slug it out with one of these beasts wouldn't end well for any of these people. The tiny IT girl was the only one in any shape. Her running 10k a day was great, but fighting was a different fitness. It was decided that to avoid them stabbing or cutting themselves, makeshift spears were produced, some were little more than a wooden chair leg with a paring knife attached at one end. It made the blades more manageable and gave the user a little range.

The session was drawing to a close, the 18 eyes stared at Kenneth just as scared now as they were to begin with, maybe a little more. Kenneth had made sure it scared them. He didn't need them taking any unnecessary risks. It was far better they were petrified and ran away screaming than be killed without raising the alarm.

"Questions?" Kenneth announced, glad to be done with this duty.

A young man stepped forward, "When is our next class?"

Kenneth could have laughed. "Next class? That was it. No more classes. You will patrol with a soldier. You can ask them questions and they will make sure you do what you need to do."

Obviously, the forced volunteers were under the incorrect impression that they would be on the fast track to special forces training.

"Just listen to what you're told, and you'll do fine. We have two good fences and weapons. We're in pretty good shape. You're just extra eyes and ears to help us. We fully expect to be reinforced soon, so enjoy your patrols, you may not be called to do too many."

With that the class was dismissed and they wandered back towards the main building bemused. Kenneth's mind had been made up. He was going to Southampton, recce for supplies and survivors en route. Even if he didn't bring back reinforcements, he could bring back weapons, medicines, and food. He wouldn't go AWOL, but he would make it clear to the Major this needed to happen, and now was the time.

The Major was taking a moment to himself, sitting down drinking a black tea as he closed his eyes and enjoyed the silence at a picnic table in the growing grass 20 feet from the fence. Kenneth didn't see the Major was resting his eyes and launched straight into his pitch

"Ammunition is low, food will run out within a week and we're only seeing more of those things approaching, not less. The generators may have another couple of weeks of fuel, but if we don't secure a larger supply, the white coats won't be able to do anything useful."

The Major sat up and rubbed his eyes, "Kenny, I know. If I

send you out, everyone will know that help isn't coming and that we're on our own. But that doesn't change the situation." He took a swig of his tea that had gone cold and stood up, "We'll ready a Landy, a half day's rations and we'll set you off in the morning at first light. We'll tell the men you're rendezvousing with a SAS team working out of Chichester. You head to Southampton, but swing by the camp in Chichester then divert up to Petworth first. If you find help before Southampton, you're to appraise the situation and head back if it's useful. Useful is guns, ammunition, soldiers and food. Civilians at this moment in time are no good to us and we're no good to them. Don't take any risks Kenny. I'd rather you back here empty-handed than not at all."

Kenneth beamed. At last, he could do some soldiering. Him, a 4x4, water, a few supplies and a rifle. He relished being in the combat zone, the monstrous appearance of the enemy wouldn't bother him. Over the last few days, he'd pierced enough of their brains with a piece of metal to know what they were like. Beyond the fence, he didn't plan on getting that close and he really didn't plan on discharging his rifle. He'd take the Landy off-road where he could, stash it and move on foot if he needed. He would complete his duties, get some sleep and head out as soon as it was light. At last, they were doing something and not just waiting.

63

He was ready; the car was ready. The soldiers lined the fence and attracted the beasts away from the gate. There were maybe 50 now and each eager for a taste of the men inside. They weren't hard to attract. A few soldiers thinned their numbers a little more, as they gave a 20-foot clearance either side. Kenneth helped to roll the Land Rover into place to not attract attention with a running engine. His rifle slung across his back, he took two full magazines from a pouch on his belt and handed them to another soldier.

"I've seen you shoot. You'll need these more than me." They were gratefully received.

"If you're not back it two days, I'm getting your shit."

Kenneth patted him on the back as he approached the Major for one last check-in.

"Godspeed, Kenny. I wish we had good comms but you'll be on your own, I can assure you, we won't be going anywhere." The Major carefully handed Kenneth something, eager to make sure none of the other men saw. "It's our only one, I don't even know why it was here, but I trust you might need it more out there than us in here."

Kenneth examined it - a hand grenade. If it got too bad at least he could take a few of them with him. He placed it in a backpack and moved his rifle to the front passenger seat as he jumped in. The soldiers stepped up their distraction, shouting and screaming, banging against the fence with their rifles as the gate was quietly opened.

Kenneth turned the key and started the engine. He threw the car into gear and slammed his foot down. He was off through the gate and worked his way up the gears. A dozen of the things gave a slow pursuit of the car as the soldiers slammed the gate shut and secured the perimeter. The Land Rover didn't take long to disappear into the distance, its moronic pursuers not giving up on their chase. Kenneth checked his mirrors as the centre disappeared behind him, it was good to be out, but now he had to have his wits about him. He'd already decided to bypass the town; that would surely be suicide. He'd stick to the country roads and take it easy, even then it should only take a few hours, three tops, to get to Chichester where he'd scout for supplies and either stay the night or head to Petworth which might take another hour. He had memorised the route but had the map ready to reference. Making his way to the junction, left for town, right to head deeper into the countryside, a quick glance confirmed his suspicions. The bus was small, but on its side, a small blue Hyundai had crashed through the roof and only its rear end visible outside of the bus. Dark stains of blood had soaked into the tarmac and splashed against the dented bodywork of the bus. Kenneth had only just left the safety of government land and already the road showed the chaos that was awaiting him. Several of the creatures, aroused by the diesel engine, appeared from the other side of the bus. Kenneth didn't wait for more to make their way towards him. Through habit, he indicated as he made the right turn and put his foot down.

*

The road was mainly empty. He had passed two other cars in half an hour that were parked up at the side of the road, Kenneth hadn't stopped to investigate; he kept on at his steady rate. It was so peaceful. It didn't feel like the end of the world. If it wasn't for the lack of cows or sheep, the absence of wildlife, it could be any drive in the country. An overturned tractor stopped the good progress. The Land Rover was well suited to off-roading and a gap in the trees through the wooded area allowed Kenneth to get around the obstacle. Getting back on the road proved more difficult. The woods were sparse, allowing for the car to move freely between the trees, but the natural path took him further from the road. Kenneth put his foot firmly to the brake, and the car stopped. He picked up the map in frustration. The woods didn't go on forever but it would be impossible to tell if he could progress further through them or whether he was better off heading back and finding another way around the tractor. Maybe even trying to drag the tractor to the side of the road. Fuck it. Carry on and hope for the best. He drove more slowly, looking further ahead, hoping for a path back to the road. Some movement caught his attention towards the road, a dozen of the things feasting on a horse. Poor thing, it was already dead and providing a meal and distraction, but suddenly the road was less attractive. Kenneth glanced back to the map and decided to punch through to the other side of the woods; it should be a big open field that should have a gate that should lead to a road. There were a lot of *shoulds* in there, but better than the definitive of the feeders on the road.

Within minutes he was out. The field was full of sheep carcasses. This place had been picked clean, but the creatures hadn't stuck around. Maybe they were the ones devouring the horse. The gate was open, and Kenneth made his way towards it, nervous as to what might be on the other side of the hedgerow. A dead farmer. That was the guess, he looked like one. He had a shotgun still resting under his chin, the top of his head was gone. He looked reasonably fresh. His flesh hadn't been touched by any of the things. Maybe the loss of his herd, the fall of humanity was too much, and he took the easy way out. Kenneth knew it was an option, but he wasn't there yet and pretty sure he never would be.

Chichester was well signposted even on the side roads. As he got closer, he saw more evidence of the carnage that had taken hold. First a few more cars, then the odd corpse missing a limb or stripped of flesh. He saw the first of the monsters as he got closer to the camp. He had hoped maybe it wasn't as bad away from Lewes, but he knew it was. As soon as he got close to a densely populated area, signs of trouble grew. It had taken three hours to get close to the camp after a few forced detours. The camp was less than half a mile away, the creature activity had picked up and it wasn't looking good that the camps had held. He'd seen many dead civilians hobbling aimlessly on his trip, but few military, and maybe only a police officer or two. The diesel engine would attract too much attention so Kenneth stowed it at the edge of a field, a few hastily cut pieces of hedge scattered on top to make it a little more difficult to spot. Rifle in hand, he began to make his way towards the camp that should be a little over three fields and a small woodland away. It was painfully slow going. Kenneth knew he was alone, outnumbered, and no prisoners would be taken. He began to be hyper-aware of every sound - a snap of a twig underfoot, a faraway hungry cry from one of the things. "Keep it together, you're nearly there," he muttered the words he'd been thinking since he left the relative safety of the car. He didn't dare cross the middle of the field. He'd be far too easy to spot. His major concern was obviously being eaten, but it had crossed his mind he might become prey to other survivors. Someone might find his assault rifle and ammunition worth killing for. Carefully walking close to the hedge line was slow and cut down his visibility but better that than being shot by an unknown sniper or attracting a group of those hungry fuckers.

The first field down, and no incident.

The second field was a little bigger, knee-high grass, also free of any cattle or obvious threats. Kenneth stuck with his plan of following the perimeter. He clutched the rifle tightly but knew he shouldn't fire unless he absolutely had to. He hadn't had a bayonet issued since Afghanistan. He wished he had one now. A kitchen knife would have to suffice. Half-way around the field, he could see some movement at the far end.

He dropped to his knee and observed through his rifle sight. He saw a woman wearing a nurse's uniform. Some blood stained her clothing, but it didn't seem to be her own. She didn't move like one of the monsters. She moved with caution. Fear dictated how she acted, not tactics or training. She was making the reverse journey to Kenneth and cutting straight through the field. Kenneth's first thought was to help her, but that wasn't his mission. His second was of fear that she might find the Land Rover. He had the keys, but she could still uncover or damage it. Such thoughts didn't have time to linger. Maybe 10 of them followed her at a reasonable pace. Kenneth had the leading monster in his sights. The woman began to run. Kenneth flicked the safety off and slowly applied pressure to the trigger. Before he could apply the final squeeze, the nurse screamed and fell to the floor, trying desperately to get back up. Kenneth moved his sight back to her, something in the long grass had grabbed her and wasn't letting go. He didn't have time to react as the first pursuing creature was on her toppling her back to the ground and top of whatever had grabbed her. It was too late.

The rest of the pack ripped hungry chunks of flesh from her body. A large one came from the gate and let out a bone-chilling cry. The others stopped as it approached the kill. Kenneth couldn't take his eyes off of it. Its grey skin and bloated body were horrifying, large boils on its face looked ready to pop. Its dominance over the others was equally disconcerting. It ambled over and with one hand, picked up the remains of the nurse. Her uniform now completely crimson, her body torn and tattered, the left arm dangling with only a tendon keeping it attached. It looked at the prize then chomped down onto her neck, taking two large greedy bites before tossing the body back to the floor and allowing the others to feed. It looked around and Kenneth ducked down hoping it wouldn't spot him. Seeing nothing of interest, it trundled back through the gate. Kenneth breathed deeply. He tried not to shake, he might need to shoot and didn't have enough rounds to miss just because he was on the verge of shitting himself. After a few seconds, it was obvious they were occupied, and Kenneth gave his surroundings a quick check to ensure he wasn't about to join the poor girl. Surely, the nurse was from the camp. Was there any point pushing forward? Even if there were survivors, they'd have their hands full, looking for help rather than offering it. There would be more of these things and if there were any more of those fat bastards, he'd rather not know it. But he had a mission, he had to check. He wouldn't be the soldier he was if he turned back because things got a little difficult. People eating people was perhaps more than a little difficult, but the reality was 10 creatures with teeth or 10 enemy soldiers with Kalashnikovs were both challenging propositions. The main gate was out of the question. That's where the mini death parade had emerged from. Half of that side of the field was a stone wall, only 4 to 5 feet tall. It wouldn't be a problem to get over. Kenneth eased his way to the wall, glancing regularly at the feeding beasts. Gently, he peeked over the decaying stone wall another two or three just standing, not doing too much. They were closer to the gate and facing the opposite direction. The fat bastard was slowly making its way towards the woods at the far end of the third field.

Blood-stained wool and animal carcasses littered the field. Any meat long since picked clean from the bones. The grass wasn't as long. The field a little narrower and a small barbed wire fence separated the field from the woods, but it had many gaps where it had collapsed. Kenneth waited for the big one to reach the woods and then climbed over the wall. He kept low and quickly made it over to the tree line. The fence was laying across the ground, small lumps of greying flesh attached to most of the barbs where they had pushed through. At the edge of the woods, he scouted as far as he could see in front of him; it appeared to be clear. The light was good and the trees not so thick as to likely shield a swarm of creatures. The only issue was that fatty was well out of sight, but there was little chance it'd be able to sneak up on Kenneth. He made his move into the woods, avoiding twigs, holes and stopping at the slightest sound of the wind blowing across his path. It was narrow and didn't take long even with the extra care he was taking. He neared the edge of the woods. The camp started to become visible. Kenneth brought the rifle up to his shoulder and looked through the sight. The camp was huge, unbelievably so. Multiple levels of huge fences, several towers on the perimeter and internally. Kenneth could see several structures and a lot of tents. He could also see people, hundreds and hundreds of people. Thank fuck.

The relief was short-lived. A gunshot rang out from one of the towers and a person close to that tower fell, then stood back up. They weren't people, they were infected, all of them. Only a few men in the towers survived, trapped high above a murderous mob of cannibalistic maniacs. Those unlucky few were beyond help. They would either succumb to starvation, fall prey to the creatures or most likely eat a bullet. From the camp up to the edge of the woods, a series of fresh bodies and monsters devouring them. The nurse must have been part of a group that tried to make a break for it. Maybe at Petworth, they would still be standing, they'd be able to spare some troops, perhaps even have a functioning Ajax or Warrior armoured fighting vehicle that could clear out the horde and rescue those trapped.

Kenneth had checked Chichester, and it had indeed fallen, the mission now was Petworth and then Southampton. He turned and was face to face with the big one, barely a foot away, its mouth opened revealing gore encrusted chipped teeth. Its breath was a mix of rotten meat and vomit. How the hell did it get so close without him noticing? There was no time to ponder, it was upon him. He grabbed his knife and plunged the blade into the creature's skull, the thin weak blade barely scraped the skull. He tried again, this time it successfully penetrated the skull but as the thing wretched backwards, the blade snapped, the handle having at most an inch of remaining blade. It staggered forward and Kenneth dodged out of the way as it tried in vain to grab him. Kenneth smashed this tiny broken blade repeatedly into its head until it was just a handle. It kept on coming and Kenneth stumbled back falling on to his arse. He shouldered his rifle and stopped himself from pulling the trigger, instead adjusting his grip to the barrel and swinging it at the beast, striking the protruding blade and slamming it into the brain. It slumped down next to Kenneth, a vile grey liquid running from its open mouth. Kenneth gasped for breath as he hurriedly got back to his feet avoiding the creature's fluids, wiping the butt of his rifle across the ground to clear any potential contamination. He looked around in case the scuffle had attracted any attention. It hadn't, but he wasn't about to linger. He abandoned the caution he had previously displayed and retraced his way back through the three fields. The monsters milled around still unaware of his presence. The nurse was still providing a meal to two of the infected, the others had moved on.

Back at the Land Rover, Kenneth examined his map and checked on his next route. He pondered for a moment if the diversion North was worthwhile and perhaps, he should just continue on to Southampton. He paused as he mentally weighed up the options. Of course, he was going to Petworth. He started the engine and popped the car into gear and pulled away.

64

Peter was relieved when he had nothing but empty fields in front of him and the husk of a town behind. He was sure he had got back on track but took every opportunity he could to confirm this. On the way out of town, he'd found a few small bottles of lemonade and a packet of mints, something at least but not exactly a meal. The town was far enough away that he felt safe to have a brief sit down. He began to attach the blade to the mop handle to create his second spear, ready to use the lessons of the first iteration to make sure it didn't suffer the same fate. Once complete, Peter allowed himself a moment to enjoy the view. It would have been beautiful had there not been the threat of a flesh-eating monster behind every tree or bush. The silence put him at ease until the inevitable sound of a scream or roar in the distance pulled him back to reality. He took a mouthful of lemonade, popped in a mint to suck, and decided it was time to crack on. He struggled to his feet, using his spear to steady himself and began to hobble in the direction he was sure was correct, trying to get a little closer to the main road where he might see a sign to confirm this.
Within an uneventful mile he saw a sign, he was heading in the right direction, albeit still with a long way to go. He checked his surroundings and then moved away from the road to follow it from a safe distance. So far to go, he'd happily sleep for a week already and it was only the second day. He'd

be far happier when the signs started showing less than 40 miles and he'd broken the back of his trek. Until then, he'd feel very much at the beginning of his journey. Maybe he'd get lucky and be able to hitch a lift from another survivor, not that he'd seen any. But why would he? He was being cautious. These things were everywhere, especially in the towns. He'd been lucky so far to only have a couple of close encounters, but he'd spent a great deal of time hiding in his own home. He knew it was possible to be invisible if you were willing to slowly starve to death. Who knows how many survivors he passed by as they quietly hid in the doomed security of their homes, praying for rescue? He thought he might pass an army patrol, see a helicopter or a group of survivors hardened by fighting. But nothing. Everything was either abandoned, appeared to be or had a few of these things sniffing around. His hope of stumbling upon help had faded after that first day. He feared he'd be on his own until he got to Southampton.

*

Gareth looked a shadow of his former self. He was wearing a pair of supermarket jeans, a hoodie, he hadn't shaved in over a week and smelled bad. He carried a double-barrelled shotgun on his back and a lump of wood in his hands; the grey blood of the monsters stained the business end. The last camp he'd been in was small and cramped. It wasn't run by the military and didn't have the supplies or defences they would have offered. It was almost a relief when the feeders overwhelmed the defences and the inhabitants either fought or ran. He wasn't ashamed of running. He was still alive, hungry, tired but alive. He hadn't seen a live human for a few days, but he had seen plenty of those things and evaded them. When he saw that man, he wasn't sure whether to hug him or rob him. It was a close call, but he decided there was safety in numbers and this guy wasn't in great shape. If they found trouble he'd at least serve as a distraction. He hadn't seen him, and Gareth wasn't sure how to approach. He didn't want to startle him.

He might have a gun. Best not tap him on the shoulder or get too close.

"Excuse me!" he shouted out in a terribly British way.

The man turned round so quickly he nearly fell over. Gareth waved and smiled, the man waved and smiled back. They both gingerly approached one another, neither dared to hold out their hand or get too close.

"Gareth."

"I'm Peter." They stood awkwardly for a moment not really knowing what to do next. "Where are you from?" Gareth got the exchange moving.

"Redhill," Peter quietly responded. Gareth shrugged his shoulders.

"West London, but I spent the last two weeks in this shitty little camp in Windsor, before that a large army camp. I guess the same thing happened at yours as always happens, those damn things outside and idiots inside."

"I wasn't in a camp. I stayed at home," Peter replied.

"Well, you didn't miss much. Food was tasteless and minimal, crime was rife and either the soldiers or whoever claimed authority acted like dicks. I was in an eight-man tent with 15 other people in the army camp. You'd think at a time like this people wouldn't masturbate at every opportunity but Jesus, this one guy. And the group I met up with, their camp, even worse. Anyway, you did well staying at home. Is it close?" The chance for a safe space was enticing. If this guy had survived there, it must be safe.

"A few days from here, I'm making my way to Southampton. They have a huge camp there, air support, tens of thousands of troops, tanks and ships." How had Gareth not heard of the big camp? "By my reckoning we head to Farnborough, just follow the path of the A31 and we'll be there in a few days if we're lucky." Peter was assuming Gareth would join him.

"I don't know where I'm heading. The camps aren't good. You really don't want that. But I'll come with you for a day or so. Do you have any food?" Gareth wasn't carrying anything besides his piece of wood and the shotgun, he'd spotted Peter's bag when deciding whether to greet or beat him, but it didn't look to contain a great deal of anything.

Peter rummaged in his pocket and pulled out a pack of mints that he offered to Gareth who took them gladly.

"This is it? Mints?" He tossed a couple in his mouth and pocketed the packet.

They walked a little and chatted casually. They covered their previous lives before the plague and Gareth expressed how impressive he was, how many beautiful women he had bedded, the millions he'd made, his cars and apartments. By the time he'd finished, Peter didn't feel like talking about his mundane life. Gareth liked Peter. He was a bit of a boring little man, but by being alive he'd proved he wasn't completely useless. What Gareth really liked was that he knew the type of person Peter was - one who'd be easy to manipulate; he was a follower.

Peter stopped dead and dropped slowly to one knee and pulled Gareth with him. Ahead two feeders swayed next to a car that had crashed into a short stonewall. Peter had got used to seeing this behaviour, with no food around, they would sometimes just wait for a sign of an animal or human before using energy to pursue them.

"We can take them." Gareth was confident, overconfident. They could see two, but there could be more.

"With your gun?" Peter was glad to finally have some firepower nearby.

Gareth shrugged, "Too noisy, my timber and your spear. It'll be a doddle."

"I'd rather not. We could cut across that field, bypass them and lose maybe only 10 minutes." Peter had become adept and evading these things. He was far more comfortable running than fighting.

"Look, there's only two of them and that car, there might be something there." Gareth would not take no for an answer. He knew you have to take risks to get rewards, hiding in fields wouldn't put food in their bellies.

"There might be more. There are always more." Peter didn't want to appear to be afraid, he was, but he didn't want his new friend to know he was a coward.

"Trust me Pete, we can do this," Gareth strode ahead, obliging Peter to follow him.

They were close to the two monsters, a third was on the floor trapped under the car, it wouldn't be an unreasonable burden to take care of. Gareth struck first from behind, felling the creature. Peter leapt forward with his spear and forced it into the second creature's head, but he had neither the power nor the aim. The blade slid across the back if its head, severing the ear clean off but performing no useful damage. It swung quickly around to face him, an angry snarl with a glint of delight that a meal was now close. Peter tried again finding its throat, but it wasn't to be put off by a small inconvenience such as this. Peter could smell its rotten breath as it was about to bite; he was frozen with fear. He heard wood hitting skull, and it fell to his side. Gareth stood before him, the grey blood dripping from his piece of lumber.

"Pete, have you not used that before?" Peter was still frozen as Gareth mopped up the three downed feeders caving each of their skulls in until they moved or murmured no more.

"Snap out of it," Gareth gave Peter a bit of shake as he eyed around making sure they were alone.

The car was his next priority. He could see the windscreen was damaged and the front passenger and side windows had been caved in; blood stained the remaining glass and paintwork. The passenger was still in her seat belt but all the flesh above her waist had been consumed, barely any meat remained on the bones, a small patch of hair remained matted with blood. The driver had fared no better. The back seats had several black bags, and suitcases stacked up, a potential treasure trove. Gareth didn't waste any time and started ripping them open, desperate to discover what he'd won. The first bag yielded nothing more than a few cheap suits, a pair of well-used dress shoes, a collection of double cuff shirts, and a handful of polyester ties. Utter crap the lot. Gareth discarded it on the road, the next bag was full of equally useless women's clothes. Frustration was creeping in. These people were running for their lives and they packed cheap formal wear. The next bags had family pictures, a few trinkets and a few articles of clothing that, if in a larger size, may have fit Peter or Gareth. There wasn't anything useful here. Gareth pulled out a laptop and tossed it to the floor to join the rest of the rubbish, but a picnic cooler caught his eye. He hauled it out and placed it on the floor.

"I hope you're hungry," Peter stood over the cooler, eager to see what it would provide them. Gareth excitedly popped the top, and they both recoiled back in disgust. The foul stench was worse than a well-fed feeder. Gareth was the first to look back inside. The contents of fruit, meat and sandwiches had fared badly. The cooler packs had lost their effectiveness some weeks prior.

"Were they fleeing the dead or going for a fucking picnic?" Gareth had a point. These people were running from the dead and packed nothing of use.

Peter started prodding through the cooler, removing the rotten produce and carefully picking out a few cans of Pepsi, two bars of chocolate and a few bags of crisps.

"These should be all right. They're all sealed so a quick rinse and they should be fine." It wasn't much, but it was something.

"I did the work. You carry and clean it and you can have a can and a bag of crisps," Gareth stated this as a fact to Peter, who couldn't tell if he was being serious or not. He decided to believe Gareth was joking.

65

It wasn't much of a modern home, but the old farmhouse was solid. The age of the tired building might actually help, a wood-fired stove, thick stone walls, small windows and plenty of space surrounding it. It was self-contained, defendable, had great visibility, and it was all they had.

"We can stay here a night, two if we manage to gather some supplies," Amy announced as they finished clearing the last room ensuring none of the feeders were present. Bo had already started searching for anything useful.

"I thought all these country bumpkins were tooled up; there's got to be at least a single sodding cartridge in this gaff," Bo carried on rummaging. A loud whistle emanated from downstairs.

"Good news. We have tea. Who'd like a cuppa?" Babs was making herself at home in the kitchen.

Amy beckoned the rest of the group in.

"Don't get too comfortable. We might not be staying long," she entered the kitchen and had a cup of tea shoved at her by Babs.

"Sorry there wasn't any milk, but I popped in an extra sugar," Amy took it gladly.

"What's the food looking like?"

"Lots in the fridge. It's all pretty rancid, but there may be some jars that are salvageable. A few random tins, some dried pasta and cereal. He liked his cornflakes. I've found three boxes." Babs was proud of her finds. It wasn't enough, but it was a start.

They hadn't investigated the surroundings. There were several cattle carcasses in one of the fields, but Amy had hopes of perhaps a few vegetables ready to harvest and maybe a free-range chicken or two that had evaded being eaten alive. It would be dark soon, and as much as Amy wanted to take the comfy seat in the livingroom, finish her tea and have a nap, it wasn't on the cards. Too much to do. The group was exhausted and hungry. She needed to scout the area, but this group needed attention.

"Babs, do you think you could put something together for everyone, leave something for tomorrow." Babs nodded and looked confused at her available options.

Amy wandered outside with the rifle firmly held in her arms. The farm was small, it looked like it had been a dairy farm but not of any size. The few mutilated cow carcasses she'd seen wouldn't fill a single milk float. A rabbit startled her as it ran across her path as she drew closer. Amy nearly blew its furry head off but steadied herself. Rabbits, at least there might be a meal or two. The outbuilding caught Amy's attention. It was in the far corner of the courtyard. Maybe some tools or fuel. Amy fantasised about finding a few bags of grain, not that she'd know what to do with them. It was so peaceful, not a car or a plane, no phones ringing, chatters of a crowd. Just the wind and the odd bird tweeting. Maybe before this plague it would have been equally idyllic, a far cry from the streets of Croydon, but now it was blissful. The ground outside the building was stained red. Amy shouldered the rifle and surveyed the area. Three badly decomposed bodies lay outside the entrance, they were in bad shape but generally whole. A single hand lay amongst the bodies, but not belonging to any of them. Their flesh was greying, but it was hard to know for sure if they were infected or just decomposing. Amy edged closer, the small door was open, another of the feeders lay across the threshold motionless, very much dead. Amy checked her rifle, suddenly unsure of herself and her ability to use this firearm. It felt heavy and cumbersome, despite its bull-pup design, long and unwieldy. Carefully she stepped over the body and peered inside. Dried blood stained the floor and surrounded two bodies, much of their flesh removed and bone showing. A double-barrelled shotgun placed between the two bodies; it was broken open and missing any shells, several empties lay on the floor uselessly spent buying the two poor souls a few extra minutes at best. The last stand of two desperate people with nowhere to go. Judging by the state of them, they probably fell victim early on. They probably didn't even know what was attacking them. The fear and confusion they must have felt, putting buckshot into a man who didn't stop coming. They had successfully dispatched four of the feeders, injured a few more, not bad having seen trained soldiers be far less effective. Not that it did them any good. The building wasn't as big as it had initially looked. A few tools hung on a wall, some would be useful, a hatchet or axe, but that was pretty much it. The shotgun would put a smile on Bo's face, but it would need a good clean and he'd have to share a few of his precious cartridges.

Amy left the building. It could all wait until morning. She allowed the rifle to hang from her shoulder as she walked back towards the farmhouse. She didn't see them, but they saw her. Their eyes watched from the safety of field, the grass had grown long with no cattle to feed on them. They sat back silently and waited. These are the first people they'd seen for a few days, they weren't about to rush in.

66

It never hurt to be too cautious. They watched the farmhouse and the activity in and around it. They were people, mainly old or lame but definitely people and not the dead.

"There's a policewoman, maybe it's an outpost?" Peter was squinting as he tried to identify the people ahead as they unknowingly went about their business.

"More likely bait than an outpost. Look at them, half are pensioners, the other half are hardly the best and the brightest. I've seen two guns, not enough to see off more than a handful of those bastards." Gareth was ready to give it a swerve. "They can't offer us anything. Maybe a few scraps of food, but they'll be a liability at best. At worst, they'll kill us for the gun," Gareth slowly moved backwards expecting Peter to follow him. "Look, big groups are bigger trouble, if you want to introduce yourself, by all means, but I'm not coming with you." Peter rose to his feet gingerly.

"I will." It was an uncharacteristic piece of bravery from Peter. He was sure it would pass soon, but not before he reached the new group.

They were only just over 100 metres away, but he was tired, the ground uneven and overgrown. He concentrated on not breaking his ankle but wary that he didn't want to sneak up on these people and startle them into thinking he was a threat. He'd never been mistaken for a threat before and today seemed like it would be a bad time to reverse that trend. As he got closer two people emerged from the main farmhouse, unaware of his approach. Peter froze to the spot before thrusting his hands hard and fast in the air.

Gareth watched from a safe distance, "Fucking moron."

"Excuse me, sorry." Politeness again seemed appropriate. The two people were weary-looking elderly men and he startled them. Without saying a word, they made their way back inside the farmhouse as quickly as their ageing bodies would allow them. Bo appeared brandishing his shotgun.

"Can I help you pal?"

This was a bad idea, what was he thinking? Peter pushed his hands even further in the air, hoping this old guy wouldn't shoot him.

"I don't know, I'm, I'm human?" Well, of course he was a fucking human. Bo could see this guy was on the verge of wetting himself and not about to mount a tactical assault, so he lowered his gun.

"Are you alone?"

Peter hesitated, he didn't want to risk Gareth if these people weren't friendly. "

Yes." He lied.

Bo sighed and lifted the shotgun again.

"How many? Don't lie, you ain't very good at it." Peter looked towards Gareth's location.

"For fuck's sake," Gareth ducked a little further down whilst maintaining a visual of the situation as Bo started looking in his direction.

"Just the one, I promise," Bo lowered his shotgun and tucked it under his arm before cupping his hands around his mouth

"Do you want to join us, or do you prefer to watch sweetheart?" He chuckled to himself as he moved a hand to his brow looking out for any movement.

"Damn it," Gareth stood up and held the shotgun above his head with both hands, he was strong but the weight was still uncomfortable.

Bo signalled for him to approach and Gareth begrudgingly obliged. As he walked across the crooked ground, he cursed his misfortune of meeting Peter. Even if this group was friendly, they were useless. He would have to feed himself and them and they would offer nothing in return besides grumbles and stories he didn't care to listen too. Maybe he'd get lucky and this old boy with the shotgun would shoot him.

"Place the shooter on the floor, don't be clever. I'm old but I've pulled this trigger a 1,000 times and I swear I'm faster than you'll be," Gareth carefully placed the shotgun on the floor. "Where are you from, where are you going?"

Amy emerged, "Bo, lower it. A little." Bo obliged. "Names?" Peter and Gareth answered honestly.

"Were you in the Chipstead camp?" It was possible, the camp was big, and many escaped, it was more likely than these two wandering the countryside unmolested by the dead.

"We just met. I was in London and evacuated by two of yours to a rescue camp, before ending up in a smaller camp. They fell. They always do." Amy turned to Peter.

"I was in my house until a few days ago. Now I'm heading to the big camp in Southampton." He said it as if everyone knew about the Southampton university camp and naturally heading there.

"Sit down over there." Gareth and Peter plopped down onto the grass as instructed.

"Southampton?" Amy had heard of other camps and knew Southampton was important but not much more.

"It's the last stand, well, the big one. Half the fucking queen's army is sat there shining their tanks and choppers. So was the rumour anyway."

"Is it worth heading there?"

"Bollocks no. Those fucking hungry bastards didn't do for us, it was those with the guns and the tanks. Imagine that 10 or 20 times bigger. We're better off here with the bloody odd squad."

Amy approached the captives. "What do you want?"

"This daft one wants to get beaten up by a bunch of scared

squaddies by the coast. I'm just surviving." Amy looked them both up and down. They didn't seem like a threat, especially the shorter overweight one. The good-looking one she wasn't so sure about, but she could handle him, he was cocky and seemed to hold a high opinion of himself. He'd prove useful; another able-bodied adult under the age of 70 to carry some of the weight this group represented.

"I can't say we're not in a bad shape, we have elderly, injured and we've been used to the safety of a big fence and big guns. Bo and myself aside, we're soft. We could use all the able-bodied adults we can find to help us, and we can help you."

No wonder she was a cop. This was a negotiation and straight away she laid out why she needed them and what was wrong with their group.

"If we don't join you, you'll shoot us?" How far would she try to push them?

"God no, you can fuck off for all I care. I'm not into killing anyone who didn't make me do it. You can go, or you can stay. If you stay, you must pull your weight."

"And that of a few others," Gareth interrupted to show he knew they'd add value.

"It's true, but ultimately, we'll be stronger together."

"With all due respect officer, but this group doesn't look like it'll provide me much more than several decoys I can outrun. I have him for that." Gareth was only half-joking.

"We could stay a few days, rest up and lend a hand." Peter was tired, but more than that he hoped he could persuade this group to travel with him to Southampton. He was getting used to having company and didn't want to give it up. Gareth let out a deep and exaggerated sigh.

"We'll stay a night. We'll help you out and then we're off."

67

It had been a productive few days. The farm had been easy to fortify. The old stone walls that around the farmhouse and the surrounding land were thick and sturdy, any gaps were easy enough to fill with debris or makeshift defences. Gareth despite his protests, was a hard and able worker, Peter was enthusiastic, but his talents really weren't well suited to manual labour. The food in the cupboards was sparse, any cattle long since devoured, but there was a vegetable patch of a decent size that had some edible produce. The elderly may have not been able to batter a feeder to death, but those vegetables had never been treated so well. Bo had created a few rabbit snares but so far, they hadn't supplied a single bunny for the pot. They were all losing weight and energy levels dipped as tempers rose.

Gareth and Amy walked the field towards the farmhouse returning from their first supply run to a neighbouring farm.

"We got lucky, but they'll be busts now, you know that, right? There are more of those things and less food. We can't feed everyone for long." Gareth's patience had all but run out, Peter had tried to persuade him to stay and if it was just down to those feeble arguments, he'd have gone after that first night. He wanted to have a crack at Amy. She was beautiful, physically in great shape and best of all, she didn't want to eat him. It had been several weeks before the outbreak since he'd gotten laid, and Amy was his best bet outside of one of the pensioners. He stuck around, worked hard and been useful. He'd given her the full charm offensive but so far she had resisted it. He thought he had seen her eyeing him up and sure she wasn't a dyke so had hoped it was only a matter of time. His patience was wearing thin, and he'd already decided he'd spend one more night then leave. He'd take some supplies, the rifle if he could or some extra shotgun shells if that was easier. Peter could stay, there wasn't any point in asking him as all he'd do was fuck things up.

"I know it will get harder, but that was a good trip, it should keep us going for a week if we're careful. We can head in the other direction tomorrow and see what we find." Their options were limited, Amy knew they had to play the hand they had.

"If the group was smaller, we might make it. Just two or three less mouths to feed might make the food go far enough for a few weeks until some of those crops the pensioners love so much start to really contribute." Gareth wasn't wrong, but he wasn't in the right. Despite his charm, Amy knew this was the real Gareth, a self-centred prick who would sell his own grandmother.

"I'm not abandoning anyone."

"Three to save the rest, four to be certain." Gareth had thought through the maths, but Amy had heard enough and stormed ahead back towards the farmhouse. Any last inkling Gareth had of staying was put down. He was going, and he wasn't about to be kind over what he would take. Hell, he'd scavenged more than anyone else. He deserved it.

Peter approached Amy wearing an awkward and gormless smile. She was in no mood for pleasantries and burst past him, Peter was confused and looked to Gareth for an explanation who was happy to deliver one.

"You've got a real way with women Petey. She says she knows you've been watching her bathe."

"I've not. I wouldn't."

"It's fine, Pete. She's an attractive woman."

"But I wouldn't."

Gareth smiled "She's fine. I think she's on her monthlies, it's fine. You need to come out on one of these trips, hanging around with those old people is not good for you."

"They're not all old, anyway. I hate it out there. I'm not cut out for fighting monsters."

Gareth knew Peter wasn't lying, but there was something he liked about Peter showing his vulnerabilities, admitting to them and laying them out for all to see. It was refreshing, something he rarely saw in business and even less after the feeders started appearing. It also tickled his ego. He was better than this man, and it was there for all to see.

"Pete, if you want to make it in this frightening new world, get involved, you can't just lock yourself in a house and wait for it to all blow over. This isn't going to get better. This is it now and I won't always be there to watch out for you."

68

It was pitch black in the farmhouse. People slept wherever there was space in the bedrooms, livingroom and hallways. Bo rudely awoke Gareth shaking his shoulder as he slept in an armchair.

"Come on pretty boy, it's your shift."

It was nearly 5am and the faint glimmer of light from the earliest signs of dawn were beginning to show. He'd asked for this shift, having previously insisted on doing the first sentry duty. It normally entailed little more than staying awake and checking if any feeders came too close. Amy would often perform a perimeter check inside of the thick stone walls, but when you had an assault rifle, it was a little easier being a little braver. Gareth normally sat watching people, never leaving the house just watching those sleep. Hearing them breathe and snore he felt more connected to other human beings than he had ever done, and still he was about to abandon them all.

Gareth slowly rose to his feet and saw Bo leave to one of the bedrooms to join Babs. He would have a coffee, a stretch then gather supplies before leaving just before the sun fully rose. He'd have maybe an hours head start before his departure would be noticed. They'd be foolish to follow him. The supplies in the kitchen weren't much, but he helped himself all the same. A few tins and packets, bottled water and chocolate. He'd never been one for chocolate but wanted the calories. He had seven shotgun shells left but decided it wasn't worth the risk getting any of Bo's, and Amy was all but fucking that rifle as she held it so tight. So a hatchet would suffice at improving his defensive capabilities.

Slowly, he crept to the front door, eager not to wake any of the occupants.

"Gareth? What are you doing?" Fucking Peter. It had to be him.

"I thought I heard something, outside I'm just going to check. Go back to sleep." Peter looked at Gareth, squinting in the darkness, something wasn't right.

"What's in the bag?" Gareth positioned his backpack out of view.

"Peter, go to fucking bed," Gareth opened the door and stepped out as Peter grabbed his shoulder.

"Don't, we need you." Gareth shook him off and pushed him back inside.

"If you say anything I swear I'll kill you," he slowly closed the door and walked off as more sunlight crept over the horizon.

*

Peter stood in the hallway in front of a closed bedroom door. He had to say something but couldn't. He didn't really think he and Gareth were friends, but they could have been. He had little doubt that Gareth would follow through with his threat, but he had even less doubt that the group needed that whatever food Gareth had taken. He reached out, gently knocked and waited a moment. With no response, he knocked again, only harder and louder. Amy opened the door, naked and exhausted. The room had no bed and would have struggled to fit anything bigger than an infant's cot. This had become Amy's room only because it was too small for anyone else to want to sleep in it. Peter looked at Amy's perfect physique. Her small pert breasts caught the sunlight through a window.

"Get over them Peter, they're just tits." Peter stumbled back about a foot with a look of shame. "What's wrong?" Amy was too tired to beat around the bush, as she always was and didn't think she'd be disturbed for a couple of hours.

"He's gone, Gareth, he's left and taken some of the supplies," Amy huffed as she hurriedly dressed herself.

"Where did he go and when?"

Amy was only half-dressed as she entered Bo and Bab's room.

"Bo, Gareth has gone and taken food. I'm going for an early run. You're in charge." Bo mumbled something to himself as he sat up and tried to understand what was happening.

"All right, you get the prick."

She led Peter out of the farmhouse. He had his spear; she had the rifle.

"Peter, you will need to do the right thing. If we catch up to him. It might get nasty." Peter nodded, he was aware of what could happen but hoped it wouldn't go that way. He almost hoped they wouldn't find him, but he had to be seen to try.

The pace was a struggle for Peter, and the farmhouse wasn't even out of sight yet and he could feel himself struggling to keep his breathing under control. A small patch of woodland lay a little further ahead. The pace would have to slow there as they took greater care. The ground evened out as they moved closer. The woodland was dense but little more than a thick pocket of trees at the corner of four fields. As they entered, Peter could feel his heart beating like a jackhammer in his chest, the dark shadows and sound of a few song birds put him on edge. Amy looked back and waited for Peter to draw level. There was no point in getting frustrated. He was five times more able than most of the group, but the bar was depressingly low. Peter had stopped dead in his tracks and began to lower himself to a crouch, silently signalling with his head as he lowered. Amy followed suit and turned, afraid what she might see, what Peter was fixated on. It was Gareth. His backpack slung over both shoulders and shotgun firmly in hand. He was crouching behind a tree staring out to the other side of the woodland to an open field. He really hadn't got far, maybe he had changed his mind, remorse possibly coursed through him about what his act of selfishness meant to the lives of many more. He wasn't looking back. He was looking forward. His heart hadn't prevented him going further, his survival instinct had.

"What the fuck Gareth?" Amy was more exasperated than angry he turned slowly around as the 5.56mm muzzle pressed against the back of his neck.

"You need to get down, now." He was calm but forceful. Amy looked out into the field and moved down next to Gareth.

"What the fuck?" She couldn't believe what she saw. She signalled Peter to move up and join them. He awkwardly scrambled over and stared open-mouthed ahead.

There were hundreds of the feeders in the field, slowly wandering in circles or standing still and waiting. There were several of the big ones, waddling through the regular ones. Some were older, infected early, bags of skin and bone. Others were new, maybe just a few days old, their flesh not yet robbed of all of its colour or shape. Nothing seemed to keep them in the field apart from a weak wire fence bordering the woodland and the gate that was still half-open, any effort would have seen them breakthrough. It was unclear how they got here or why they stayed after they had devoured the livestock, but there they were, waiting for a meal to present itself.

Gareth knew he was in trouble. He had thought he wouldn't have been followed, he didn't take too much and hoped it wouldn't be worth the calories. Obviously he didn't count on a former police officers' strong natural instinct for justice.

"You shouldn't have come after me."

"Well we did, and now we have this situation. Why didn't you just go round?" He'd asked himself the same question, he couldn't think of a good answer.

"We should go back." Peter had long breached his comfort

level and was doing everything he could to not run in the opposite direction. Amy shook her head.

"We can't go back. We need to lead these things away. We're less than half a mile from the house. If these things got loose, we don't have enough bullets or shells to take out half of them. We'd be wiped out."

Dread began to fill Peter as he realised what Amy would suggest. It would be suicide, for him at least, if not his two fitter companions.

"We need to lead them away. Make a lot of noise, ping a few of them then have them chase us for a few miles before we break away." Gareth crossed his head.

"The three youngest sacrificing themselves for the elderly and infirm. Where's the fucking sense in that?"

Amy paused for a moment. These two would never budge. Through fear or selfishness, they were not about to put the needs of the group above their own. She stood herself up, to the horror of her two male companions, shouldered the rifle and let out two single shots with the first striking the torso of one of the big feeders, the second a kneecap of a regular one. The big one stumbled back and let out a loud roar in disapproval, the regular crumbled to the floor, its thin and wiry leg missing flesh and the muscle snapped as it hit the ground.

"Run!" Amy screamed as she set off in the opposite direction of the house.

Peter and Gareth gave chase as the monsters began to mass at the small fence pushing against it. It creaked and deformed until the sheer weight of the fiends collapsed several sections of it and those behind climbed over them in a hurry to catch up to their fresh meals. Gareth turned and let off two desperate blasts from his shotgun peppering several of the nearest group. He soon caught up with Amy.

"You're fucking crazy," she turned and let two three-round bursts out felling a single pursuer and aggravating several more.

"This way you hungry fucks!" she screamed at the top of

her lungs.

Peter was nearly crying. So many. So close. It was all right for Amy and Gareth, they had guns and they were fit. Maybe they were banking on him falling first and succumbing to the hands and mouths of those greedy things to buy themselves more time. He became angry. Those arseholes weren't sacrificing themselves, they were sacrificing him. He gained a yard of pace and punched through the pain. He'd show those fuckers. He wouldn't be their offering to the feeders. He would not die today.

Amy and Gareth sporadically stopped, putting a few more ineffectual shots into the following herd. Peter wondered if they'd be tempted to put one in his leg to slow him down, but he couldn't do much if they did. Amy was firing aware that it wasn't having a real effect on stopping the pursuers, but more noise would maintain their interest and make sure they continued following. Gareth wasn't in on the plan and very much just wasting his ammo.

"You need to stop shooting. I've got more rounds than you. Save them if they get close."

Peter had nearly caught up with his fitter comrades and cursed them under his breath as they began to put more space between themselves and the feeders.

"Okay, slow down a little get your breath back. We can't push too far ahead and risk them losing interest." Amy had barely broken a sweat and Peter was in the middle of coughing up a lung.

"Fuck you. I'll keep on going. You can dangle your arse in front of them if you want, but I'll keep on jogging if it's just the same to you," Gareth continued leaving a panting Peter and Amy taking aim to let another burst of fire into the crowd.

"You okay, Peter?" Peter looked up at Amy with hate in his eyes.

"You, you left me to die. I can't keep up with you two, look at me." Amy fired another single round felling a single feeder.

"You are capable of this. You're here aren't you. Now let's go," she patted Peter on the shoulder and encouraged him to get moving to keep their lead intact.

69

The Range Rover Discovery was caked in blood and body parts. All uselessly tinged with grey, not a scrap of edible meat amongst its gory mess. Natasha had finished the last of her fresh meat that morning. It wasn't enough to satisfy but it settled her. Since society fell, good meals had become few and far between. The lesson she had learned was that turning up covered in blood was a bad idea. Her prey were suspicious of strangers, one soaked in blood wouldn't get too close. When she had been desperate, she had approached a couple, she hadn't even thought of how she looked, she was just too hungry. She hadn't noticed the man had a knife until he slashed out at her, he nipped her shoulder, but she had been too quick. His wife could only look on in horror as Natasha ripped out his throat and gorged herself on his flesh. Natasha used his knife to butcher the woman, packing away for a takeaway meal what she couldn't force down. The wound to her shoulder was mild, it didn't bleed much, her greying blood clotting quickly, scarring over within a day. But next time she might not be so lucky. Look like the living, feed like the dead. She scavenged cloths with nearly the same reverence as meat. Running out of her normal human disguise would only make food harder to come by. The government camps were not a safe place for her. There was plenty of food but plenty of guns and scientists prodding the voluntarily incarcerated for answers to this plague. She had spent time right at the beginning in a tiny camp where she witnessed this firsthand. Fortunately for her, but not the rest of those seeking sanctuary within the fences, they had built it in haste, with little thought given about what would happen next. Unlike the camps established even days later, it was constructed far too close to a major built-up area. It was easy to get people to, but hard to stop the feeders from getting close. When dozens, became hundreds and then thousands, the soldiers couldn't stop them. The sheer mass of feeders collapsed the fence and within an hour, Natasha was eating with her own kind, fighting the dead not for survival but for food. She ate well that day.

She had been driving for an hour, hunting. She was looking for survivors, people she could befriend then eat. She'd been doing that for a few weeks with success, but people were a declining resource. Her breakfast was a day old, She wanted something fresh to satisfy her hunger, and there he was, an attractive man running towards her from over the brow of the hill, dinner but first a date, perhaps. Gareth waved his arms, his shotgun above his head desperate to get her attention. Natasha stopped the car and awaited this desperate man to come to her. He made up the ground quickly and she wound the window down.

"Are you going my way?" Natasha couldn't contain her excitement. Gareth smiled back

"There are hundreds of them coming this way. We need to go." As much as he was happy to see an attractive woman willing to flirt, he knew what was coming.

"Get in then." Gareth didn't need asking twice and made his way to the front passenger seat. The state of the outside of the car didn't faze him, the car was immaculate inside. Gareth signalled to get moving, bashing the dashboard with his fists.

"Come on!" Natasha smirked as she followed his orders, purposefully at a slower pace to make Gareth uncomfortable.

Peter was the first to emerge and catch sight of the car, Amy was close behind facing their pursuers. Peter tried to scream at Amy that there was a car, but his lungs were on fire and his breath blocking any words. Amy fired into the feeders as they continued to close unhindered by tiredness or lack of breath, the rifle clicked as she pulled on the trigger and noticed the bolt had held open. The empty magazine dropped to the floor and pinged as it bounced off the hard ground. Amy fumbled for a fresh magazine as she turned and saw what Peter had tried to tell her about.

The car moved off slowly. Amy regained focus and loaded the rifle and fired twice at the feeders behind and turned back towards the vehicle. The car stopped dead, then reversed at speed. Peter started to jog towards it, safety was so close, but his energy was nearly spent. Amy caught up and grabbed him by the arm and dragged him forward. The car was yards away, the driver's window wound down and a slim, attractive girl smiled at them.

"I'm Natasha and I'll be your Uber driver." Gareth took a step out of the car.

"Hurry the fuck up," Amy helped Peter into the back before climbing in herself just as the first of the beasts reached the car.

A full 100 of them had already emerged from the woods, following them, the food. More continued to spill out eager to catch sight of their meal.

"We need them to follow us for a few miles, don't lose them." Amy was still on mission, if this mob lost interest they could head in any direction with the farmhouse providing an easy meal if they stumbled across it.

"I was joking about being your Uber driver. My car. I choose the music where we go and what we do," Natasha's smile had gone as Amy changed tact and pleaded.

"Please, we need to lead them away." Amy wasn't above threatening their new friend, but she hoped it wouldn't come to that.

"Okay, but I have little petrol so if they get too close, I'm putting my foot down and we're putting some distance on them," Natasha looked around for landmarks, obviously further meals were nearby and once she had finished with these three, she would make sure she found her way back.

Peter continued to get his breath back, Gareth looked far from comfortable and Amy gave herself a moment to calm down and checked her rifle and depleted ammo supply.

"Where were you heading, are you with a group?" Amy suddenly gained a curiosity of their saviour.

"There is nowhere to go, I'm just driving looking for food, trying to be safe." Natasha was so matter-of-fact, so confident and calm it was as if she was talking about her plans for the weekend.

"And you're alone?" Gareth chipped in, as interested in her relationship status as he was of other survivors.

"Just little old me." The slow and steady speed kept their pursuers close, but not too close.

"If you take it a few miles, then we'll arc around and head back to the farm. You'd be welcome to stay with us." Amy saw this girl had the ingenuity and a survival instinct to make it this far on her own.

"By us, she means the apocalypse retirement home. If pensioners are your thing, you'll love it." Gareth chipped in.

The elderly - they were tough to eat but easy to kill so Natasha was game on visiting the old people when needed.

*

The foursome stood beside the bloodied car on a small country road.

"I told you I was low on petrol."

The following herd was way off in the distance, maybe a mile or slightly more, on foot they would easily increase that distance in a few hours until the pursuers would completely lose them. It might take a day to get back to the farm unless they could source another vehicle. Amy's main concern was getting the hungry mob as far away from the farm as possible, but she wasn't about to pass up the opportunity for scouting this new area.

"We should quick time it another half a mile then we'll arc round. Anything interesting we should take a look."

Gareth entered the day fed up taking orders from this bossy cow; he wasn't any happier with doing so now.

"I'm not fucking going back. You find another slave to look after your nostalgia and whimsey brigade." Peter was tired, scared, and angry.

"Will you just shut up, Gareth! There are two types of people left, those who are alive and those who are dead. There's no longer any damn room for people to be arseholes!"

Natasha knew there was a third type. One was neither dead nor alive, but somewhere in between.

"Lord only knows how many people are left, and you want to abandon them to look after your damn self? Give me strength. We'll probably all be dead before the year is out so why are you so damn eager to live your last miserable days alone?" A newly forthright Peter took aback Gareth and Amy. Natasha just smiled.

Gareth saw his out. He didn't have to be alone or a servant to the elderly.

"Maybe I'll go with Natasha. What do you say?" Natasha stood back.

"Look, I can see you guys have your issues, and these days who hasn't, I know I've got my own problems. But this isn't the time or place for a domestic."

"Can we at least move away from them. We can sort this shit out later," Amy was already walking away as she spoke and Peter followed like a puppy.

Natasha began to trot off in line when Gareth grabbed her arm pulling her to a stop.

"You need to listen. She's trying to save the world. She'll put you to work serving those old fucks and I know she'd trade your young beautiful life for one of theirs. Think about it, death will follow her." Gareth begrudgingly followed and Natasha's smile widened. *This was too easy.*

70

It was getting late, and they were further away from the farm than ever. Every corner seemed to hide smaller groups of the feeders. Every time they tried to start their long arc back towards the farm, they were faced with a mob of teeth and claws with no other thought than to devour them. Throughout the day, they had unwittingly been moving towards a small town and the groups had grown in numbers and viciousness. Gareth's shotgun, out of shells had become little more than a heavy bat, Amy's rifle was down to its last few rounds. Peter was a bag of nerves, but Natasha remained unfazed. Her biggest concern was to make sure that one of those dumb hungry fucks didn't mess with her food.

Amy led them down the narrow country road and signalled for the others to stop as they reached another junction, a series of low growls emanated from beyond the corner. These country lanes and roads were killers, easy to evade, but with no visibility it was all too easy to bump into a threat. There were at least two of them lurking, maybe a few more but there were over a dozen less than half a mile away following them.

"Everyone ready?" Gareth and Natasha nodded.

Gareth raised his hatchet up ready to bring it down on a beast, Natasha had a large carving knife that she readied into position, Peter held his spear close as if it were a loved one.

"Go!"

Amy rounded the corner first firing two shots, Gareth followed and took a run at the nearest creature striking it hard in the face with the hatchet connecting beautifully, knocking it and several teeth flying. Natasha calmly walked up to another, it didn't acknowledge her as she stuck her blade into its eye socket. Peter followed up the rear, not eager to get involved but not wanting to be completely useless. A loud groan stopped them all in their tracks.

A fat bastard let itself be seen from where it had been standing close to the hedgerow. Even for the big ones, this was huge. Its facial features hidden behind the large boils, nose enveloped and just two dots for eyes but the angry gnashing mouth remained prominent.

"Fuck me, they are a sight, Petey. I thought you were bullshitting me."

Gareth gestured at Amy and her rifle. She obliged firing a single shot into the monster. A flap of scalp and bone flipped off of the top of its skull, forcing it to take half a step back before proceeding on towards them. A louder, angrier groan came from its mouth. Amy went to fire again, but the rifle clicked.

"I'm out," she looked to Gareth.

"Hell no."

Peter faded back hoping to go unnoticed but he needn't have bothered. No one was looking to him to take this thing on.

"Let me." Natasha confidently strode forward, her blade dripping with grey blood.

She hadn't come close to one of these before but assumed like the little ones, it wouldn't pay her any attention. She lifted the large carving knife as she closed the distance. The big one was having none of it. It swatted her to the floor before she had the chance to strike down into its skull. It didn't pay her any more attention as she slowly crawled backwards out of its way, hurt and in shock.

Amy grabbed Peter's spear and moved next to Gareth. "Age before beauty."

Gareth smirked, "Ladies first, I insist."

Amy examined her weapon briefly, and it didn't impress her. The creature let out another loud groan inviting them to try. The spear entered under its chin with a pop, thick grey blood oozed from the wound as it swung at the spear snapping it in half. Amy quickly stepped back as it angrily threw its head side to side desperate to remove the remaining segment of the spear as Gareth swung at it with the hatchet, missing by an inch and getting knocked on his arse for his trouble. Natasha was back on her feet. She'd be damned if she would lose all this fresh meat to an unthinking beast, no matter how big it was. It had already passed her so she took the opportunity to approach from behind, stabbing down into its upper back repeatedly, it writhed in pain and screamed with anger as it swung once more at her putting her onto the floor with the knife still embedded firmly between its shoulder blades. Gareth looked to Amy for direction, but she had none. They couldn't go back, and this giant of a feeder had slowed little for the abuse it had taken. Gareth handed the hatchet to Amy and took the shotgun from his back and held it like an overweight and oversized bat, ready to take a swing.

"Peter, we have to get around it." The fight had failed, they now had to run, it was big and was strong, but it didn't seem to be fast. Gareth took his opportunity whilst Amy was shouting and taking its attention, he darted around it and joined up with Natasha, helping her to her feet. At least she'd have one meal.

"Peter, come on!" Amy pleaded but Peter was frozen, this was it for him. He hoped it would be quick, but at least it'd be over. Amy gave up and manoeuvred around it as quickly as she could, but it didn't care. It wanted him. Peter was all it cared for now. Natasha looked on helplessly. Two meals were better than nothing. Shame about Peter; he had as much meat as the other two combined but she wouldn't go hungry. He closed his eyes as he stood shaking, waiting for it to take him. It was 6 feet away, then 5, then 4, his three companions could only look on in horror, unable to assist. Its head fell apart like a cracked watermelon, a fine spray of grey blood, brain and bone fizzed narrowly to Peter's side before it collapsed to the ground. Peter ran around the bloated corpse to join the others who shared in his confusion and relief.

"You lot make enough noise. Lord knows how you made it this far. You need to be careful with the big ones, they don't fuck about."

A tall handsome black man with a Welsh twang, dressed in army fatigues, emerged from further down the road. He walked up to the group, his rifle lowered but ready to be put into action if needed.

"Lance Corporal Kenneth Addo, pleased to meet you." His beaming smile was reassuring even if no one had any reason to trust the military. "It will get dark soon. I've got a secure house about 200 meters down the road. Or you can stay here."

"I'm done. I can't carry on." Peter sat himself on the floor and crossed his legs, seemingly deciding to stay put for the short remainder of his life. Amy stood over him.

"We'll bed down for the night. It'll be better in the morning." They were all hungry, none more so that Natasha. All day she'd been walking with her food as it burned calories, but her dinner was close. They'd sleep, and she'd make her move. Amy, Gareth and this big chunk of uniformed dark meat would be her first. She'd slit their throats as they slept and bathe in their blood. She'd keep Peter around as a fresh meal. He'd be easy to subdue and after a day or two she'd have gorged herself on the others, and she'd be ready to make use of him.

71

The house was small and run down. It would have been derelict long before the outbreak. The windows boarded up years before, hope of a clean bed and running water didn't last long, what it had in its favour was the distance from the road and a distinct lack of neighbours. Kenneth had at least attempted to clean out one bedroom so that the pigeon shit and mouldy furniture didn't assault all the senses. A single sleeping bag, a small stash of scavenged tinned food and several bladed tools, cleavers, knives and a splitting maul. Peter had popped himself down in the far corner, his back firmly implanted against the wall. Gareth had picked himself out the cleanest spot in the room. He didn't ask, he just laid down and closed his eyes trying to get some rest. Amy, Natasha, and Kenneth stood in the middle of the room.

"I don't mind taking the first shift. You guys look nearly as dead as those things," Kenneth held his rifle close to his chest ready for his guard duty. He wasn't sure he completely trusted his guests, but the feeling was mutual.

"I'll take the first watch," Natasha was eager to eat and reached for the Kenneth's rifle.

"I don't think so princess. Have this," Kenneth produced a small folded blade and handed it to Natasha.

"You hear anything, wake me," Amy smiled at her new friends. At last, some doers to back her up.

"A word ma'am," Kenneth hadn't spoken to anyone for over a week, and he was more than a little rusty.

"Amy, please."

They both left the bedroom to the privacy of the landing.

"Amy, I've been away from my men for too long, I've been to several camps, each supposedly well-armed and prepared, all I've seen is those things. You're the first friendly faces I've seen since I left Wellworth."

Amy interrupted, "I've heard of Wellworth."

"It's a research facility, I came out looking for help."

"And you found it in this derelict?"

Kenneth dropped his smile, "There's nothing out there. The towns and cities are infested or have been levelled. As you've seen, you get within half a mile of civilisation and it becomes much less civilised. I've seen signs of life, but it's small, it's hiding, it will not bounce back and it's not going to put these things down. We're fucked."

"We have a farm, it's not too far from here. We'll be heading back in the morning. We have people, not a lot, but people. You're welcome to join us. Fuck, you're more than welcome, I insist."

Kenneth smiled back at the inviting offer, "If I can't find a way to Southampton, I need to get back to Wellworth I've already been away for too long. You should join us."

"I've been in a camp run by the military. I'm not going into another one. I think you'd be hard pushed to find anyone who'd do that. At least with the dead you know where you stand."

Kenneth understood, every camp he'd come across had fallen and knowing the pressures the military would face could only imagine the potential abuses.

"Sleep on it. We're a dwindling race us human beings. We should stick together."

They both walked back into the bedroom. Gareth was snoring and Peter had his eyes closed, still propped up in the corner as Natasha played with the knife she'd been given.

"You kids should get some sleep. In four hours I'm waking

up big Kenny."

*

Moonlight broke into the room through one of the decaying boards covering a window. Gareth still snored as the others breathed heavily in their sleep. Outside was silent, not a bird fox or vole stirred, either they'd already become prey or had the sense to be quiet. Natasha could feel her stomach tearing into itself. She was starving, it'd been too long, and she felt she could lose control. Now she'd have to make her move whilst there was the slither of an opportunity. Gareth stirred, that wouldn't help, but she knew just what to do. Silently, she crept over to him, he was close to waking. Carefully she unbuckled his belt and opened his fly before reaching in. Not bad, a good-looking guy with a meaty cock. Gently, she massaged it with her hand, careful not to be too rough, as it swelled and enlarged. She moved down and started going down on him. He stirred becoming slowly aware but enjoying the experience. Coming up for air she examined his erection, rock hard and maybe 8 inches. Such a shame, such a waste.

"Don't stop," Gareth whispered.

Natasha looked up and smiled as she adjusted herself over him and started gently riding him. He started to sit up and Natasha shook her head as she guided him back down. Gareth held her hips and tried to control her pace, trying to make her go faster. As much as he was enjoying himself, time wasn't with them. The last thing he wanted was for one of the others to wake and ruin his fun. Natasha adjusted her position and leaned down, her nose grazing Gareth's before they locked mouths. It was a messy passionate kiss, as the knife entered Gareth's ear canal and pierced his brain he couldn't have cried out even if he had wanted. He went limp almost immediately, she could feel his last breath escaping into her mouth. Natasha carried on riding him for a moment or two longer before she couldn't help herself anymore and licked the blood as it began to pool on the floor. She knew she had to act quickly and strike before they discovered her, but the hunger was taking control. Just a bite, just to settle her stomach before the noise of it rumbling woke the others. The neck was soft and easy to rip into. It always was. Just one bite. It was intoxicating, fresh meat that was still so warm. Maybe another. Natasha bit down harder for her second bite, a small pop followed by a crunch as the cartilage gave way. She didn't even pause to see if the others stirred. Just one more bite then she'd start getting to work on the others.

"Will you two pack it in?" A pissed off Welshman didn't want to waste his downtime listening to a couple having a quickie. "You're supposed to be on watch."

Natasha swallowed a chunk of flesh before she could answer, "I'm nearly done."

Two quick pelvic thrusts, a wipe of her mouth and she rolled off, careful to shield the knife from view. Kenneth rolled back over and closed his eyes. One down, three to go. She thought of her plan to keep Peter alive for a few days, it would be difficult but fresh meat was so much tastier and satisfying than rotting flesh. If she could, he'd survive the night. He wouldn't be a threat even if he knew what was coming. Amy would be last. Kenneth was a giant and would have to be next.

Slowly, she got to her feet and walked as quietly as she could across the room to Kenneth, knife ready to find its way into his brain. One foot in front of the other, slow but methodical so as not to disturb any debris and give her actions away. She lifted the blade, eager to get the job done quickly so she could quickly move to Amy. The floorboards creaked beneath her just as she was about to strike. Kenneth quickly turned and caught sight of the blade, catching Natasha's hand as she brought it down. Natasha struck Kenneth in the face with her left hand as they wrestled for the blade. He used his strength and size to roll on top of Natasha securing her by both wrists as she writhed beneath him desperate to get the knife and escape his clutches, Kenneth could finally see her face. Blood smeared around her mouth and chin, as she snapped her teeth at him, he edged back.

"What the fuck?"

Natasha took her chance and pulled his left hand towards her and bit down hard, Kenneth punched her in the face with his right hand before throwing himself backwards clutching the gaping wound. Amy sat up and stared at the fuss. Natasha was dazed. She'd never taken a hit to the face before and she didn't much care for it. The minor injuries she's received so far may have stung or pinched, but a full-on punch to the face, this stunned her and for a moment she didn't have control. Something inside her made her jump to her feet, an instinct that felt like it wasn't her own,. It wanted to survive. It wanted to get out of there. She wasn't sure where she was but something inside told her to run,. She'd be dead if she stayed. Leave the food, run. Natasha picked up the knife and disappeared out of the door just as Amy stood trying to assess the situation.

"She fucking bit me!" Kenneth held his hand up as if proof was required, a large chunk of flesh missing below his thumb.

Amy was quick to notice Gareth's body with more than just the single chunk missing. Peter was perfectly still, Amy felt the need to walk over and give him a good kick to see if he was alive, his jolt into life confirmed he was.

"We need to get it off. I'm sorry," Amy told him.

Kenneth looked at the wound again, "But she wasn't infected, she was normal."

Amy grabbed Kenneth's hand and could just about make out a grey residue caking around the wound. Amy flung Kenneth's hand down.

"It has to go, you know it does."

Kenneth winced with pain. He knew she was right. He wished he'd never helped them, never taken them back and allowed himself to be attacked. It was a mess. He was facing become one of the dead or losing a hand.

"For fuck's sake, in my pack, there's clean dressings. Don't take too much off and make it clean."

Amy retrieved the dressing and grabbed the maul.

"Fuck off. You'll take my hand off and break every bone in

my wrist, grab a cleaver, a sharp one."

Amy checked a couple of cleavers before quickly deciding.

Peter was getting the gist of what had occurred but kept back, trying to stay out of the way.

"Find something he can bite down on."

He hadn't noticed Gareth yet. The little light there was in the room didn't illuminate his body enough to notice the pool of blood surrounding his lifeless body.

"Gareth is..." he began to splutter out but was interrupted by Kenneth.

"We fucking know. Get me something to bite down on."

Peter looked around and picked up a dirty rag and a small piece of wood and sheepishly offered them up to Kenneth who snatched the wood and tried it on for size, squeezing it between his teeth. He looked up at Peter and nodded in approval as Amy returned, clutching the cleaver and bandages, breaking open an alcohol wipe and cleaning the area on Kenneth's wrist near the wounded hand. Kenneth was trying to work himself up to what was about to happen. He breathed fast and heavy, pounding his own chest as he psyched himself up.

"Okay, okay. Do it!" Kenneth laid down on the ground holding his hand along the floorboards stretched out and closed his eyes.

"Ready?" Amy wasn't looking forward to this task either.

Kenneth nodded and screwed up his face, bracing himself for the unpleasantness that would follow. Amy held the cleaver over Kenneth's wrist lifted it high above her head and brought it down as hard as she could. A sickening crack and Kenneth gasped for air.

*

It was dark outside and silent. The house was behind her as she stood at the property boundary, but still she felt the need to run. She stumbled across the rough ground and only stopped when she tripped over a mound of earth in the field.

She sat up and looked behind her to check if she was being followed, but there were no pursuers. Damn it, four good meals lost, and she'd only managed an appetiser. Gareth was going to waste. She'd caused a fatal blow to Kenneth, but that might take time to show. Peter wasn't a threat, but Amy would be a problem. She didn't want to walk away from perhaps the only fresh meat within 10 miles, but she didn't fancy taking a bullet to the face either. She cursed herself for blowing her element of surprise.

She had interacted with the dead a few times, except for the big one, she had been able to apply some influence on them. They didn't attack her, and they would follow her until something distracted them. There were enough milling around that she could herd them up and take them to the house. She'd have to be careful, but it was worth a try, even if she'd have to share her meal.

72

The sun was trying to find its way over the horizon and the few songbirds around made their presence known. Natasha knew it was time to strike. They'd surely move out when it was light and whilst they'd be easy prey in an open field; her friends would struggle to keep up. Finding a few friendly teeth hadn't been difficult. She'd got nearly 40 of these basic feeders to follow her, all in various states of decay, all starving for flesh. She'd have to share, but she'd get her fill and that was better than nothing. She ambled up the road leading her entourage to the path of the house. A face at an upstairs window peaked around a broken board. They knew she was here. It wouldn't make a difference. They couldn't run and fighting would be futile. She just had to stay close enough to the action to make sure she got her fair share of the spoils, but not so close that she risked becoming a target.

"Go in there!" she shouted at the confused beasts. They looked at her unsure of what she was. She didn't smell like food, but she sounded like it. Their base minds weren't able to process the information, so they just ignored it, a few from the back started to wander off.

"No! Food! Meat! People! They're in there!"

They didn't move. Natasha strode forward to the head of the pack and tried to open the door, but it wouldn't budge. She cursed her luck and then started banging on it.

"You can't stay there forever!"

Kenneth was sat in the room's corner holding his rifle, Amy carefully peeked outside looking at the large number of feeders surrounding them. Peter was Peter, he paced nervously in the room, careful to keep away from any windows.

"There's too many, even if we made every round a perfect headshot I think we'd be short and you two will not be much use in a fistfight."

Kenneth signalled over to his bag, and Peter rummaged around inside and produced an L109A1 high explosive fragmentation grenade. Peter's face turned white.

"Careful with that Peter. It's my only one, and it makes a big bang."

Natasha was having no more luck rallying her troops, but the more noise and fuss she made, the longer they kept an interest if only to add menace to her malice.

"I don't feel right." Kenneth just about stood up and steadied himself. "I think I'm changing."

Amy offered him a glance before continuing to observe the dead outside.

"Bullshit, you've lost a lot of blood, but you'll be fine."

Kenneth looked at the bandaged stump, blood showing through.

"This isn't my first major wound, but this is different." He sounded quieter, sad. He believed what he said. It didn't matter what Amy had to say.

"Unless you've lost a hand before, this is different." Kenneth awkwardly checked his rifle, propping it between his body and the wall as he released the magazine before inserting it back in.

"You need to go before she figures out how to get in and you're trapped with me."

"You're coming with us. You're not dead yet." Amy was angry at the suggestion of leaving Kenneth behind.

"You will need to run, and I can't. I can shoot, just, and I can give them something to think about. How's the back looking?"

Peter sneaked a look, "There are six, maybe seven but they're pretty spread out."

Kenneth forced a pained smile, "Good. You can drop safely down from that window. Peter, I will throw that grenade out front. Once it goes off, that's your cue to climb out of the window and drop to the ground."

Kenneth handed him the bloody cleaver, "You'll need this. Amy, I'll start shooting out of the front and see if I can nail that bitch." Kenneth fumbled for a magazine out of his pouch, "Sorry, there's only a dozen or so rounds. Clear a path for the big man then join him, don't forget my backpack, fill it with what you can. I won't be needing it."

"We can fight them off here. We don't need to leave you." Amy hoped he'd listen but knew he wouldn't.

Kenneth held out the grenade, "It's hard to get the pin out with just one hand."

Amy obliged and Kenneth threw the grenade in the middle of the feeders, close to Natasha.

It landed a few feet from her and she looked down.

"Fuck!" Natasha ran a few feet then threw herself to the ground. The explosion rocked her eardrums, a piece of shrapnel tore into her stomach, the pain was sharp and burned. The closest feeders were all thrown to the floor sporting wounds throughout their bodies, the greying blood clotting nearly as quickly as it appeared. One flapped and floundered on the floor, its legs unable to stand, another lay motionless with half of its skull missing and dark grey brain on display. The rest raised back to their feet, confused and angry they all began snarling and groaning at their unseen attacker. Natasha stood up clutching her wound, her more basic companions may have been pissed off, but they didn't feel the pain in the same way. She screamed at the top of her voice and her followers fell silent. Natasha took a deep breath and screamed even louder running at the door and this time they joined her in her attack.

Kenneth began shooting out of the window, careful to make his shots count but he wasn't on top form and it showed in his marksmanship. Three shots and he scored a solitary hit to one attacker's torso doing little to slow it down. Peter sat on the window ledge, his feet hanging outside, Amy fired next to him taking down two of the creatures.

"Go, go now!"

Peter twisted around and lowered himself to the ground as Amy downed another monster.

"Come with us, please!"

Kenneth offered one of his beaming smiles before firing again, this time connecting with a face sending the body tumbling to the floor.

Amy lowered herself from the window to catch sight of Peter smashing a creature in the face with the cleaver. Finally, she was impressed, but she didn't expect it to last long. They jogged through the small number feeders that remained in their path until they were clear. Gunshots continued to ring out.

The front door was nearly open. Natasha held herself back as her followers did the hard work. She flinched with every gunshot, wary that one may find its way to her. The door finally gave, and the hungry beasts fought each other to get through first, to be the one to get that first taste.

The house was well behind them before Amy and Peter turned around, a few stragglers followed, not many and not fast. Five gunshots rang out in quick succession and then silence. A brief pause and then Amy put her hand on Peter's shoulder before they carried on.

73

The middle of the field gave them plenty of visibility but did little to shelter them from hungry eyes. At least if they were to be set upon, they'd have time to react. Amy was rummaging through the backpack Kenneth had told her to take. After the seven tins of miscellaneous meat and vegetables, she'd hoped for weapons or ammunition but those hopes soon dispersed. A few articles of clothing, but Kenneth was almost a giant; they'd be little use. A picture of Kenneth with a group of soldiers and another with his family. A couple of protein bars and a sealed food packet from a ration pack rounded out the food. At least it would be something to take back to the farm. Peter sat in silence, staring out into the distance. Amy tapped him on the shoulder with a protein bar that he gratefully accepted and immediately unwrapped and devoured. Amy tucked into the other bar as she continued looking through the bag. A bar of soap, more clothes and a map. Amy unfolded and examined it. Kenneth's path was documented with the camps, masses of feeders, potential supplies, and useful structures all marked off. Each cross or marking a display of how fucked the world was. It was hard to follow a timeline, but it mapped a path out to Southampton. Of course it did. Peter would be happy if she told him. They needed to get back to the farm, but what if Natasha was following them? She knew about the farm, they'd talked about it, maybe she'd follow them. Maybe she'd track back and try to find it on her own, anyway. Maybe they were already dead, and it didn't fucking matter. Maybe none of it fucking mattered. Life had boiled down to sitting in the middle of a field, eating a protein bar, considering how a packet of cold biryani would taste whilst hoping a dead person wouldn't eat you.

Southampton, the rumours were of the single largest military presence in the United Kingdom after the outbreak. Tanks, soldiers and air support. It either stood and would have the same issues as any of the other camps. Or it had fallen and would house thousands of the feeders. There was another option. Kenneth's map had a path back to Wellworth. It showed where to avoid, where they might find supplies and it led back to a small secure location that may not yet have succumb to the same degradation in morality as any other camp. It was closer and offered some hope, enough to get Peter moving.

"Peter, have you ever been to Lewes?"

They were just sitting in the middle of a field, without a care in the world. They were nearly a kilometer away, but Natasha imagined they were laughing and joking. Those arseholes, why couldn't they have just let her eat them? The house hadn't gone so well. Her faithful minions had charged the good meat before she got a chance, she imagined they'd nailed Kenneth straight away and then started on Gareth. She didn't hang around to find out. She caught sight of Amy and Peter fleeing and took the snap decision to follow them. They'd lead her back to their group and she'd have food for weeks. Or if that took too long, she'd kill them in their sleep. Following them had been tiring. Her energy levels were down and anxiety up. She had to keep her distance but couldn't risk losing them. If they found a functional car, she would be in trouble. But if her travels had taught her anything, the pool of usable cars and clear roads were forever diminishing.

Her prey got themselves up from the ground and slowly began to walk. Natasha eyed up her potential routes to follow. Cover was sparse, but at this distance she stood a good chance of either being missed or mistaken for a more simple monster. Their slow pace was a relief. Her stomach growled and her body gave a slight shudder as if she needed reminding that she was hungry. If only she'd taken a few more bites of Gareth. Such a waste that those brainless morons got a feed for all of her hard work. There was little point in dwelling on the feast that could have been. It only made her salivate.

74

The engine failed to turnover. It didn't matter how much she tried, Amy couldn't get it going. The beat-up Vauxhall Astra had been abandoned in the middle of the road, in the middle of nowhere for a reason, because it was a piece of shit. Either it had given up or run out of fuel. Either way this car wasn't going anywhere. Amy hopped out and slammed the door hard joining Peter who sat on the car's bonnet.

"Maybe the next one Pete."

Peter shrugged his shoulders. He really wasn't expecting the car to run; none of the others had. Amy had been easier going since their escape. Peter didn't appear so scared, and maybe she saw that he was trying. She didn't have to know every instinct he had was telling him to grab that rifle and put one of the two remaining rounds through his own eye socket.

Amy tore open the food pouch and scooped her hand in, the thick cold concoction was mainly rice and vegetables, she looked back inside before handing it to Peter.

"There you go, don't eat it all at once." Peter smiled and looked inside before gratefully wolfing down the contents.

"I've had better curries, but it has its charm. It just needs a bottle of Cobra to wash it down with."

Beer would have been a nice touch, but a few litres of water would have been even better. A few days without food was possible, even with their previous minimal calorie intake. But they hadn't had so much as a drop of muddy rainwater in hours, the easy option was to find one of the areas Kenneth had marked as having supplies. An easier option was to find a recently inhabited house and drinking a bathtub full of tap water. Better risk that now rather than later. Amy finished her handful of cold biryani and could feel it passing down her throat.

"We'll check out the next property to bed down for the night." Peter was pleased that he wasn't the one to suggest it.

Natasha was suffering far more than her prey through lack of sustenance. She had never allowed it to get too bad. She always saved a little something back, but now had nothing. She began to worry. What if she became like the others, a base unthinking beast? She was still Natasha at the moment, fitter, more beautiful and with more interesting dietary requirements than before, but she was still herself, barely. She sat behind a van that had slid onto its side. She could smell them from their briefest of contact when they walked through the area. Her skin was sweaty, the viscous grey liquid had a meaty aroma, it smelled nearly good enough to eat. But when she had given it a lick, it had tasted the same as the dead. Further down the road a handful of feeders shuffled closer. They weren't a concern for her, maybe they too could smell the fresh meat. She didn't need the competition but if there were only a few of them they'd prove easy enough to dispatch. Natasha peeked around the corner of the van. Amy and Peter were standing in silence as Amy was examining their map. Natasha felt something close, breathing on her ankle, its warm breath was wet. Natasha froze, not sure what it was. It couldn't be more dangerous than her. She was of no interest to the dead and a human wouldn't likely to be licking her calf. It tickled. Slowly she turned her head, an Alsatian sheepishly licked away enjoying her tasty sweat.

"Come here fella, are you all alone?" Natasha beckoned it over and it gingerly approached.

A social beast, it hadn't seen a friendly face for a long time. It wanted a friend nearly as much as it wanted a belly full of food. Gently, she offered her hand, it accepted and licked it. They locked eyes as her hand moved first under its chin then behind its ear. That was the spot. They both relaxed and the good boy began to pant as Natasha really went to work giving him the contact he so desired. He was getting the only thing he truly wanted. She was about to get what she truly wanted too.

Peter hopped off of the car's bonnet first, eager to find somewhere safe to sleep with the possibility of some fresh water. Amy joined him as they began to walk on down the road. The sudden yelp and whimper of a dog stopped them in their tracks. They looked around but could only see feeders at a fair distance behind them, nothing as close as the horrible sound the dog made suggested. They looked at each other, not needing to say anything as they started at a faster pace.

It was good to get something in her belly. The meat tasted bitter, the dog was malnourished but it took the edge off. Picking the fur out of her mouth reminded her of Renton. Not the love or the guilt, the disappointment. People tasted so much better than animals. Peter would be delicious.

75

The sunlight was beating its way through the curtains, finding its way onto the king-size bed where both Amy and Peter slept soundly. Peter was hugging the edge of the mattress, desperate to not encroach on Amy's personal space. The bedroom was tidy, except for the mess the current inhabitants had created. A chest of draws moved across the room to block the only door, cups and bottles of water littered most surfaces with tins of consumed baked beans and spaghetti hoops. Amy watched Peter. This funny little chubby man. Sweet, but an absolute pussy. He'd done well to make it this far, when it came to fight or flight, there was a lot to be said for running or hiding for that matter. Amy had been doing everything by the book and seen the worst of humanity - you didn't need to eat human flesh to be a monster. She had seen the best and the bravest die, mostly horribly. Yet Peter lived. He needed a lot of help along the way, but here he was. Maybe there would be others, like Bo and Babs, small groups looking after each other. It could be how they survive. With a few weeks, some weapons and manpower, the farm could have been a safe haven. Time, guns and people, none of which were in abundant supply. Natasha... how many more like her were there? Passing as human only to make their move when those they have befriended feel safe. Nowhere would be safe.

"Time to get up," she gave him a nudge and Peter stirred

and sat up. They packed light. Raiding the draws, they found some suitable clean clothes to replace their dirty ones. A few water bottles were refilled, but not too many to weigh them down. Both Amy and Peter attempted to drink as much water as they could before they left.

Natasha felt less and less need to sleep as the days passed. Her body and mind didn't cry out for it. With a full belly, she'd found no need to sleep. Only when she grew weaker did her eyelids feel heavy. The dog had done its job, and she hadn't needed to sleep. She hadn't wasted her time. She led several feeders to positions around the house, some had strayed, but not too far. She hoped they'd prove enough of a deterrent that her food would take the front exit and she wouldn't miss them. The front door slowly opened, Amy poked out her head before fully emerging with Peter following close behind. Natasha let them get a bit of a head start. She could smell them, it was faint. But the longer she followed, the more obvious it became to her even if she didn't fully trust it yet. They spotted a few lurking feeders and hurried off down the street. It was a small housing estate on the edge of a small village. Natasha didn't know it or care to. The feeders were sparse, but there were obvious signs of conflict, burnt-out cars, shell cases and minor explosive damage to buildings. When the government had ordered the evacuations, they had returned with firepower to halt the dead. Some places it had been more effective than others. Natasha had seen villages that had been completely levelled and towns all burned to the ground. Others had little sign of a major internal conflict. This place seemed fairly average. There had been a fight, a decent one, but they stopped short of dumping tons of ordinance on to the town. A few gunshots here, a small explosion there. Probably all from the initial evacuations.

Amy and Peter had opened up a sufficient lead as Natasha began to follow, shuffling along pretending she was less of a threat in case they saw her. They were little more than a mile out of town when they came across a very small camp, abandoned and damaged. A few feeders lurked within the torn down fences, their attention taken by a crow berating them from the safety of the single abandoned watchtower. Amongst them the devoured remains, bones, scraps of clothes and blood smears. It was impossible to imagine that every camp, big or small had fallen. When they got to Wellworth, they would hopefully have an answer. They carefully gave the camp a wide berth, wary of what may have escaped and could lurk in the surrounding area. Slowly and quietly, they moved, listening for any sign of trouble.

With the camp behind them, they began to ease up as Amy tried her luck with another car. The Volvo estate looked in immaculate condition except for the dried blood clinging to the outside of the open driver's door and window. Cautiously she circled the car. It seemed clear, the open rear passenger door helping give a complete view inside. The keys were still in the ignition, a bonus but not necessarily a good sign. If the driver left in the hurry, as the bloodstains supported, they could have left the engine ticking over and battery now long since dead. Peter took the opportunity to open up the map on the car's bonnet and check their agonisingly slow progress. Amy tried the key, the engine struggled but didn't start. She gave it another desperate go. Peter placed his bottle of water on the map to keep it in place as he looked up to Amy. She was beautiful, strong, and clever. If you're going to survive the apocalypse, it would be hard to choose a better companion. He noticed the estate's large boot. Several boxes had been packed in, the car may be another bust, but maybe there would be something useful.

Natasha could smell them in the wind and could hear the engine being forced to kick into life and resisting every attempt. Every time she saw them get into a vehicle, she felt a twang of panic. Every time it failed to move, she nearly laughed. Again, she could feel the tension rising. She hadn't been alone in hearing the engine being forced to kick into life and the bitter battle it was a part of to remain at rest.

Peter swung open the boot, a suitcase fell out and startled him, Amy looked back to see what the noise was before continuing on the car. Peter picked up the case, and it opened up. Just clothes, he kicked them to the side and reached further in.

Feet slowly shuffled, a weak murmur from hungry mouths.

"God damn it." Amy struggled, she stopped and took a deep breath to compose herself, the car was so close to starting, it just refused to cooperate. Peter looked to his companion before continuing to rummage. He never tired of seeing the pointless junk people took with them. As amusing as it was, a machine gun, water and a year's supply of food would have been better. He pulled out another box of tat and dug further in.

The smell of the prey grew stronger. They picked up their pace, desperate to taste the flesh and fill their bellies.

Natasha spotted the mob approaching and watched as they began cascading past her. Maybe 20, young and old, all hungry. She was helpless to stop or dissuade them. All she could do was watch as they carried on towards her food.

The first couple were 20 feet away, still unnoticed by either Peter or Amy. She again tried the engine, and it kicked into life. Peter looked up with a big smile.

"Fuck yeah!" Amy's delight lasted as long as it took to turnaround and beam proudly at Peter. Her face dropped and Peter froze for a second before he turned round and saw barely 10 feet away the nearest feeder.

"Get in!" Amy slammed the car into gear and Peter jumped into the estate's large boot. It grabbed Peter's ankle as the car started to move.

Natasha watched helplessly as perhaps the last fresh meal in the county started to drive off. She screamed in anger and frustration. The foul monster turned as if Natasha were addressing it directly. Peter kicked out as he held on for dear life and the car picked up speed sending the map and water off of the bonnet as the car hit a pothole. Despite its distraction, it didn't loosen its grip. Peter desperately felt around with one hand for something to use as a weapon, a lamp produced an answer. He flung it at the creature now being dragged along behind the car, its grip on his ankle the only thing stopping it from bouncing off the tarmac. The lamp made only a glancing blow, opening up a small gash on its temple, but the creature didn't care. Peter kicked out again and again until finally, he could feel its hold loosening.

Natasha walked with purpose towards the mob as it slowly gave pursuit. She could just make out the car as the feeder holding on lost its grip and skidded along the road to a grey pulpy stop. They were gone, but all was not lost. It blew along the floor and through the legs of the mob. As it reached Natasha, she placed her foot down on it firmly. The map. She allowed herself to smile once again.

"So, that's where we're going."

76

They must have driven around in circles for nearly an hour. Without the map, they only had a rough direction in which to head. They knew the town it neighboured, but secret military research bases were rarely signposted. Every country track, road, or bridleway had fresh tyre marks from a fruitless drive.

"Well, I don't know. What do you want to do? Carry on driving until the tank is dry or try to head back to the farm?" Amy was frustrated but not angry. She didn't blame Peter for losing the map, but they were so damn close.

Peter noticed them first. Two feeders excitedly approached from the main road heading out of town, both wearing army fatigues. It had to be. Amy clocked them and her question was answered. They were close, no point in stopping now. They drove past the two former squaddies who couldn't keep up.

They approached a junction, a bus was lying on its side and small blue car had smashed into it, entering through the roof. It could have been easy to miss the small side road. Before the outbreak, many would have passed it daily without even noticing a local secret. A sign gave further hope: "Private Property: Strictly No Trespassing". Amy pulled the car onto the side road and edged down forward. Mounds of earth flanked the road; it felt almost like driving through a tunnel. It took a little over 100 metres to open up as the road started up a small hill. As the car reached its peak they could see the other side, Wellworth. The compound wasn't huge, a few small outbuildings, a large single storey one and then the main building, three or four storeys in height. A tall fence surrounded the site, and they surrounded the fence.

Hundreds of the dead. They weren't attacking, they weren't walking around. They were mainly still, just swaying as the wind caught them.

"Well, that's fucked it." Amy was ready to turn back there and then. Was there nowhere safe on this stinking fucking planet anymore?

Surely, it was impossible to get inside, or even close. Two rounds of ammunition, a cleaver and a few blades would not get them too far.

"When they see us, they'll help. They have to." Peter was still optimistic.

There must be people still there, otherwise, why would the dead be? More soldiers like Kenneth, determined and well-armed. They drove closer to the site, a few feeders turned as the car's engine alerted them to its presence. Slowly, they moved forward as more feeders noticed their arrival before Amy slammed on the brakes.

"I can't see anything in there. If there is no one left, all we're doing is ringing the dinner bell for all these bastards."

They were being watched, but not from eyes from the Wellworth compound. It was good they were here, it was bad that so many of the creatures were so close. They'd had a good head start, and Natasha feared they'd beaten her here and either already safely inside or abandoned the idea. Her ability to walk amongst the other feeders gave her luxuries that a healthy person couldn't enjoy. She didn't have to rush for fear of being eaten, within half an hour of Amy and Peter driving off, she'd found a working vehicle. Soon, she was on her way and with the map, she found her way to Wellworth with ease. She felt it prudent to keep her distance. Walking up to the front gate was just as likely to be welcomed by a bullet to the face as a smile. Far better to hang back and watch.

"We should go, there's nobody home." Amy put the car in

reverse and began her retreat. Peter looked desperately for a sign that their journey wasn't a waste.

"Wait!" Peter pointed to a window at the top floor of the main building, the light was on and there appeared to be movement. Amy stopped the car and looked to the building.

"So, maybe there's one person there. We're not getting through that mob and even if we could. We'd just be trapping ourselves."

Peter looked at her, "We should try."

Amy's slow retreat had brought their car within 100 metres of Natasha. She salivated as she observed them, willing the car to continue its slow crawl to her. But nothing. It was now or never. They might drive off and she'd never find them or even be foolhardy enough to get past those damn dumb feeders. Either way, she had an opportunity, and she would take it. Natasha kept low as she moved to the car. The light was fading, she hoped it'd be enough to remain unseen. With 80 metres left, her stomach grumbled in anticipation. Then 50 metres and she wiped the saliva from her mouth. Now, 20 metres and she could see them talking.

"Christ knows how I made it this far. Please, let's at least try. If no one's home we can drive off." Peter was winning Amy over.

His hope replaced quickly by confusion. He didn't know what was happening. The door swung open so fast and he found himself on his back looking up at the sky. His shoulder screaming with pain. He expected another attack, a blow to come raining down onto his face or teeth to rip out his throat. Instead, he saw Natasha stride past him and into the car. Amy had already grabbed the cleaver and lashed out catching Natasha's outstretched hand, barely a scratch but an effective warning. Natasha pulled back and turned her attention towards Peter. She grabbed him by the scruff off the neck and dragged him further away, far easier prey. Amy reached back into the rear passenger seat, grabbing desperately until she felt it, the rifle. She wrenched the rifle around the seats awkwardly and brought it to her shoulder.

"You can't understand how hungry I am," Natasha stood over Peter as he cowered on the floor. "If you don't have this fucking hunger, this craving, you could never know. I'm not a bad person." Natasha could barely speak through her salivating.

"You're a monster!" Peter closed his eyes. He knew what would come, no need to watch.

Amy looked through the sight and snatched at the trigger, the round slammed into Natasha's back sending her tumbling forward, blood spraying over Peter. The pain was intense, it burned then ached all in an instant, the air punched out of her as the round passed clean through her back and out of her chest. Natasha struggled to her knees clutching her chest, the thick grey sticky blood was already starting to seal the wound.

"Back off him now!" Amy still had the rifle pointed at Natasha.

An evil grin spread across Natasha's face, "You're not in charge here."

She looked towards Wellworth, the dinner bell had been rung, all the hungry ears could hear its pitch. Amy looked over as the whole damn herd started to shuffle towards them.

"Peter, get back in the car, now!"

Peter tried to stand but Natasha lashed out and grabbed him by the throat and smashed his head on the ground. His eyes rolled back in his head as he lost consciousness and his body went limp.

"If I squeeze hard enough and pierce his skin, he's got enough of my blood on him to turn him. If I try a little harder, I might even be able to choke the life out of him."

The mob continued to move across the field to the trio. Amy looked at them then back at Natasha and Peter.

"You can't save him and yourself, can you?"

Amy could take the shot, but even if she killed Natasha, she wouldn't have time to get to him and drag him into the car. The closest feeders were maybe 30 metres away and making good progress.

"Fuck!" Amy screamed. Natasha smiled.

She squeezed the trigger, and the round hit low into Natasha's gut and she fell on top of Peter. Her body covered Peter, the wound oozing more of the greying blood onto him. Amy looked on for a sign of Peter moving, nothing. She dropped the rifle in the passenger footwell and drove the car towards the downed pair. Several of the creatures were close, and the first bounced off the car bonnet as a growing number moved to intercept her. She stopped a foot away and looked at Peter, he could already be dead. Several creatures began clawing at the windows until they obscured her view. He was gone. She had to go. The wheels spun desperate for traction before the car moved, feeders knocked left and right. It was slower going over the ground and the monsters didn't drop too far back, all eager to follow for a chance of a taste.

77

Peter began to stir. His head was fuzzy. His eyes didn't want to open, but he forced them to. Night had fallen and besides the sound of a few feeders, it was quiet. He tried to sit up but couldn't move. He looked down at Natasha laying across him. For a second, he panicked, but she was still, Peter rolled her off him and she flopped to the ground beside him. She looked dead. He was caked in her blood and her skin pale, he gave her a soft nudge and nothing. Peter decided to believe she was dead. He held his head as he focused on his surroundings, a field, several of the dead and Wellworth.

It was lit up like a Christmas tree, floodlights illuminated the site and area around it. No wonder so many of the dead had found their way to it. There were a few feeders at the fence, but not many, maybe a dozen he could see compared to the hundreds that were there when he arrived. Where was Amy? The car was nowhere in sight. She wouldn't have left him, would she? Of course she would. She was smart. He looked down on himself, he was covered in Natasha's grey sticky blood. She either thought he was dead or led hundreds of the dead away to save him. He didn't and wouldn't blame her, but once again he was alone. He looked down at Wellworth, lights were on, maybe somebody was home. He wobbled as he stood, he felt woozy, maybe he was infected? He smiled to himself, that would solve several problems and the ones it led to wouldn't be his own. He staggered as he walked towards the gates. It was a short walk, but he wasn't being bothered by any feeders. They barely looked at him, either Natasha's blood masked his humanity, or he really was turning into one of them, time would tell.

The gates weren't locked, some secure government research site this was. Peter swung open the latch and slid the door open just wide enough from him to squeeze through before closing it quickly. It wouldn't take much for one or two to take an interest, get inside and make the whole site uninhabitable. The bright lights did little for Peter's sore head, but he could see the layout. It looked bigger now he was inside. Shell cases were scattered around but no blood, no signs of them having breached the fence.

"Hello, I'm not dead. I'm human!" Peter screamed as loud as he could, hoping for a response. "I'm a normal boring human," he whispered to himself.

He walked to the front of the main building. The doors opened automatically, and he stepped in. The lights began to illuminate as he approached them revealing a plain building, one that was more likely to house an accountancy firm than a secret government research centre. Peter couldn't help but feel a twang of disappointment, lack of people was one thing, but this was just an office building. It appeared little different from where he had worked. Where was all the bleeding edge technology, the elite soldiers, the scientists? He wandered down the hallway and noticed the security office. He knocked gently, then again harder after no answer. He tried the handle and slowly pushed the door open.

The office had two large banks of monitors showing live feeds from cameras dotted around the site. Peter started searching the desks and cupboards. There must be guns or at the very least a chocolate bar or packet of cheese and onion crisps. Besides an array of pens, paper clips, and a novelty stapler, there was nothing. Peter turned his attention to the monitors, most showed either empty rooms or the floodlit outside areas, but two were a little more interesting. The first marked as 'Director's office', a lone figure sat at a desk, the second labelled 'Research Lab 1' several people appeared to be working away. Peter moved closer with a smile, the relief swept over him. *Thank fuck.* He rushed to the corridor; the lab was on the first floor, the office on the second. He jogged to the stairs eager to see his new companions, he bound up the steps with a vigor he hadn't felt in a long time. He got to the lab and his face dropped.

The double doors were barricaded with several large pieces of furniture rammed against them, two military webbed belts helped to fasten them shut. As he approached, he could see through the reinforced glass, maybe 20 feeders in white coats and army fatigues, some stood still, others shuffled aimlessly. Wellworth hadn't escaped the carnage that had afflicted everywhere else. There was still the figure in the office, but Peter had lost the skip in his step. He exited the stairwell on the second floor and he could hear the radio. It was muffled but became clearer as he approached.

"God bless. This is an official government announcement. It is with great regret that we have had to abandon these Great British Isles. All military forces have been withdrawn, civilians evacuated, and an interim government formed. If you remain on the mainland, survive, we will return, and we will take back our land from the dead. We are not alone. You are not alone. Our thoughts and prayers are with you, God bless. This is an official government announcement..."

Peter arrived at the office, the door was open and there in the chair sat a man in an officer's uniform. The life was drained from his face, pale and distressed. A small wound under his chin and a large splash of blood and brain matter had evacuated through a large hole at the top of his head spreading a crimson mess against the wall and ceiling. Peter approached, in front of the Major, a journal, two Glock magazines and a note with a simple message. "We tried, but you failed us. Sorry. Fuck you." The repeated radio message began to irk him and he switched it off before he picked up the pistol from the floor. It was surprisingly free of gore. Not so long ago, the scene would have horrified him. It was a sign of the times that a corpse that didn't move didn't freak him out. It was better that than the alternative. He pocketed the journal, and with the bravery a 9mm pistol can offer, he carried on searching the facility.

78

Dawn was breaking, a lone songbird was brave enough to sing on its own. Natasha was on her back in the middle of the field looking up towards the sky. She had been conscious for 10 minutes, any movement resulted in a dull pain throbbing through her body. They continued to shuffle past her, the feeders that had followed Amy and gave up made their way back to Wellworth to resume their haunting. She had to move, she couldn't stay there forever. If she would die, it wouldn't be in some shitty field in East Sussex. The two exit wounds had developed a new rubbery skin. It was still thin and tender, but it was better than a gaping hole. She threw herself onto her knees and climbed to her feet wincing with pain. She hadn't felt this bad since she changed. Where to go? She looked across at Wellworth. She was in no shape to fight and there could be 100 armed squaddies in there. Her car wasn't too far away, she could drive and find somewhere to rest. Food was unlikely but not an impossibility. The car was still there. The engine started at the first attempt to her relief. Natasha was alone, tired, hungry, and injured. The car pulled away slowly, no need to rush. She followed the road and began to feel dizzy.

The country road required more concentration than she could spare as the car drifted all over the tarmac. Natasha gave it everything she had to focus but within half an hour, she couldn't do it anymore. The car was barely going 15 miles per hour when it left the road and hit a tree. The airbag deployed sparing Natasha from further damage. She flung the door open and rolled out of the car. The engine was visible from under the crumpled bonnet, smoke escaped displaying it was now a useless chunk of metal. She crawled on her hands and knees. *Surely this was it,* she thought and perhaps even wished. Her vision was failing, she felt exceptionally weak, but the pain had nearly gone. Just a little further.

"Are you okay there, miss?" A friendly male voice enquired.

Natasha rolled onto her back and tried to focus on this potential meal. "Jeez, you look in a bad way. Are you human, feeder or other?" Natasha couldn't make out his face, no point in lying now she'd be dead soon.

"Other." She couldn't see him smile but he did.

"And there was me thinking I was the only one. You look like you could do with a meal." He gently picked her up.

"My place isn't too far. You'll feel better with some fresh meat in your belly and we'll get you sorted." He was kind. Natasha was relieved and so grateful, she may have been a monster, but she didn't want to die and appreciated this act of kindness.

"Thank you, I'm Natasha."

"You're welcome Natasha, my name is William Johnson."

*

The house was a small cottage, isolated but quite idyllic. Inside it was much bigger than it appeared. Natasha was gently placed on a sofa as William rushed out to emerge moments later with a bowl of flesh.

"That will get you some strength back. Take it easy. There's plenty more where that came from."

Natasha reached in and grabbed a handful of meat shovelling it into her mouth with strength that had been absent since she had been shot.

"Easy, I have a whole cellar full of the good stuff." She

could feel her body getting stronger, her eyesight sharpened, and the mind regained a degree of clarity.

"There you go. It's a good thing you ran into me. I don't think you had much longer, but you're safe now, here with me." Finally she could get a good look at her saviour. William was athletic, in his late thirties and reasonably good looking.

"Thank you. I don't know how to repay you." Natasha was genuinely thankful and intrigued.

"The fact you exist is all I need. I'm not alone. I'm not the only one of my kind. We are the next step. Stronger than the ordinary people, we're extraordinary. Smarter than those moronic drones." William was going full stride.

"What about the big ones?"

"I'd say we're smarter, we're definitely more mobile. However, I've only seen one. Interesting, I wonder how many more subspecies have emerged." William drifted off into thought at the prospect.

"So, you're set up here?"

William let out a boastful smile, "Plenty of fresh food, a generator with enough fuel to see through several winters in comfort and none of the mindless feeders can get in to ruin any of it."

"Fresh food?"

William led Natasha through to the kitchen, she was steadier but still not 100 percent. He opened an unassuming door in the corner and turned on a light, a narrow staircase led down to the cellar. It was dark, a single fluorescent tube struggled to illuminate the space and there they were. At least 15 people of all ages chained to the wall; they cowered in fear as William came into view.

"Impressive," Natasha spoke softly, and it was.

"I've helped rescue these poor souls from the uncertainty of the new world. I feed them." William motioned to a large supply of military rations and tinned food. "Protect them from being ripped apart by the mindless monsters and they feed me." This time he motioned to a girl in her late twenties with her right leg amputated below the knee and her left arm below the elbow. He was insane but brilliant. He really did have it all worked out. She felt like a moron for driving around hoping to stumble across a survivor or two. This was how it was done, farm, don't hunt. Less energy expended and a much more reliable source of sustenance.

"This is a wonderful place, you're very lucky." It wasn't luck, it was hard work and planning. They both knew it.

"You can be lucky too. Stay for a little or a long time. This place could use the touch of a beautiful woman."

"Maybe I will." Natasha was falling in love with the idea of settling down.

79

Amy had been retracing her journey as best she could, but she knew she was getting close. The car finally gave up its last drop of fuel and glided to a halt. She didn't have much, an empty rifle, a cleaver and her remaining few scraps of supplies but it didn't matter. She just wanted to see the friendly faces back at the farm. If they weren't there or had been killed, that would probably be it for Amy, life would be a pointless struggle alone. Some local landmarks looked familiar and then she saw the woods, where Natasha had seemingly rescued them.

"Nearly there," Amy told herself.

The horde that had emerged had long since gone, at least they had managed to lead this murderous mob away from the farm. Just a few corpses indicated they had ever been there. Cautiously, she walked through the woods, not a sign of life or the feeders. As she broke through to the field, she could make out the house.

"A bit further," she repeated.

The field seemed so big. Each step appeared to make little difference to her progress and the farm seemed no closer. She pulled herself together, ready for the worst and hoping for the best.

"Come on, it's close." Amy tried again to keep herself going.

Finally, she was close enough to make out figures. She

pleaded in her head for them to be her people and not the dead.

"It's fine. It'll be fine."

As she approached the boundary, she could see the defences were being worked on by new faces, a handful of tents were pitched in the grounds. And she saw Bo. Waving with a big smile, Babs by his side as people worked busily around them. She couldn't stop herself from crying. They were all okay, she wasn't alone, and it wasn't all over. They had a community and others would come, good and bad. But together there would be a chance.

Printed in Great Britain
by Amazon